William J. Rolfe

Shakespeare's Tragedy of Julius Caesar

William J. Rolfe

Shakespeare's Tragedy of Julius Caesar

Reprint of the original, first published in 1875.

1st Edition 2024 | ISBN: 978-3-38525-115-1

Verlag (Publisher): Outlook Verlag GmbH, Zeilweg 44, 60439 Frankfurt, Deutschland
Vertretungsberechtigt (Authorized to represent): E. Roepke, Zeilweg 44, 60439 Frankfurt, Deutschland
Druck (Print): Books on Demand GmbH, In de Tarpen 42, 22848 Norderstedt, Deutschland

SHAKESPEARE'S

TRAGEDY OF

JULIUS CÆSAR.

EDITED, WITH NOTES,

BY

WILLIAM J. ROLFE, A.M.,

FORMERLY HEAD MASTER OF THE HIGH SCHOOL, CAMBRIDGE, MASS.

WITH ENGRAVINGS.

NEW YORK:

HARPER & BROTHERS, PUBLISHERS,

FRANKLIN SQUARE.

1875.

PREFACE.

THIS play has been edited on the same plan as its predecessors in the series, but, no "expurgation" being required, the text is given without abridgment.

In editing Professor Craik's "English of Shakespeare," which is mainly a "philological commentary" upon *Julius Cæsar*, I did not allow myself to forget that I was dealing with another man's book. I made no alterations in the text, except to correct a few misprints, and I retained the greater part of the notes without modification or criticism. My own notes were inclosed in brackets, and were prepared as nearly as possible on the same plan as those to which they were a supplement.

In the present edition of *Julius Cæsar*, on the other hand, I have worked on a plan of my own. The text is not that of Professor Craik's book, but is the result of a careful collation of the Folio of 1623 with the modern editions. In the notes I have drawn from Professor Craik as from other authorities, and have invariably given him due credit. I must leave it to the student and to the teacher to decide which of the two books is the better for his purposes. Whichever he may take, he will find the other more or less useful for collateral study and reference.

The references to Dyce in the notes are to his *second* edition (London, 1864–1867), while those in "The English of Shakespeare" are to the *first* edition. The readings of the two are different in many passages. The references to Hudson are to his *first* edition (Boston, 1851–1856), not to the revised edition just published. The readings of the first folio are taken from Staunton's photo-lithographic fac-simile (London, 1866).

Cambridge, Feb. 10, 1872.

THE TIBER.

CONTENTS.

[Act IV., Scene 3.]

CAIUS JULIUS CÆSAR.

INTRODUCTION

TO

JULIUS CÆSAR.

I. THE HISTORY OF THE PLAY.

"The Tragedie of Julius Cæsar"* was first published in the Folio of 1623, where it occupies pages 109–130 in the division of "Tragedies." It was printed with remarkable accuracy, and no play of Shakespeare's presents fewer textual difficulties.

The date at which the drama was written has been variously fixed by the critics. According to Malone, it "could not have appeared before 1607." Collier argues that it must

* This is the title at the beginning of the play and at the head of each page, but in the Table of Contents (or, as it is called, "A Catalogve of the seuerall Comedies, Histories, and Tragedies contained in this Volume") it is given as "The Life and Death of Julius Cæsar."

have been acted before 1603. Knight believes it to be "one of the latest works of Shakespeare." Craik* comes to the conclusion that it "can hardly be assigned to a later date than the year 1607, but there is nothing to prove that it may not be of considerably earlier date." White infers from the style that "it was probably brought out between 1605 and 1608." Gervinus (in his *Shakespeare Commentaries*) decides that it "was composed before 1603, about the same time as *Hamlet;*" and he adds that this is "confirmed not only by the frequent external references to Cæsar which we find in *Hamlet*, but still more by the inner relations of the two plays." More recently (in his *Introduction to Julius Cæsar*, 1865†), Halliwell has shown that it was written "in or before the year 1601." This appears "from the following lines in Weever's *Mirror of Martyrs*, printed in that year—lines which unquestionably are to be traced to a recollection of Shakespeare's drama, not to that of the history as given by Plutarch:

> " 'The many-headed multitude were drawne
>   By Brutus' speech, that Cæsar was ambitious;
>   When eloquent Mark Antonie had showne
>   His vertues, who but Brutus then was vicious?' "

II. THE HISTORICAL SOURCES OF THE PLAY.

It appears from Peck's "Collection of divers curious historical pieces, etc." (appended to his *Memoirs of Oliver Cromwell*), that a Latin play on this subject, entitled "Epilogus Cæsaris interfecti," had been written as early as 1582, by Dr. Richard Eedes, and acted at Christ Church College, Oxford. This was very likely the drama referred to in *Hamlet* (iii. 2):

> "*Hamlet.* My lord, you play'd once i' th' university, you say?
> *Polonius.* That did I, my lord; and was accounted a good actor.
> *Hamlet.* What did you enact?
> *Polonius.* I did enact Julius Cæsar: I was kill'd i' th' Capitol;
> Brutus kill'd me."

---

* *English of Shakespeare*, Rolfe's ed., pp. 44–49.
† Quoted by Dyce in his *second* edition (1866).

ROME.

Stephen Gosson also, in his *School of Abuse,* 1579, mentions a play entitled "The History of Cæsar and Pompey;" and there were doubtless other early English plays based on the story of Cæsar. But the only source from which Shakespeare appears to have derived his materials was Sir Thomas North's version of *Plutarch's Lives* (translated from the French of Amyot), first published in 1579. He has followed his authority closely, not only in the main incidents, but often in the minutest details of the action. This has been well stated

by Gervinus in his *Shakespeare Commentaries* .* " The com-
ponent parts of the drama are borrowed from the biographies
of Brutus and Cæsar in such a manner that not only the historical action in its ordinary course, but also the single characteristic traits in incidents and speeches, nay, even single
expressions and words, are taken from Plutarch ; even such
as are not anecdotal or of an epigrammatic nature, even such
as one unacquainted with Plutarch would consider in form
and manner to be quite Shakespearian, and which have not
unfrequently been quoted as his peculiar property, testifying
to the poet's deep knowledge of human nature. From the
triumph over Pompey (or rather over his sons), the silencing
of the two tribunes, and the crown offered at the Lupercalian
feast, until Cæsar's murder, and from thence to the battle of
Philippi and the closing words of Antony, which are in part
exactly as they were delivered, all in this play is essentially
Plutarch. The omens of Cæsar's death, the warnings of the
augur and of Artemidorus, the absence of the heart in the
animal sacrificed, Calphurnia's dream ; the peculiar traits of
Cæsar's character, his superstition regarding the touch of
barren women in the course, his remarks about thin people
like Cassius ; all the circumstances about the conspiracy
where no oath was taken, the character of Ligarius, the with-
drawal of Cicero ; the whole relation of Portia to Brutus, her
words, his reply, her subsequent anxiety and death ; the circumstances of Cæsar's death, the very arts and means of
Decius Brutus to induce him to leave home, all the minutest
particulars of his murder, the behaviour of Antony and its
result, the murder of the poet Cinna ; further on, the conten-
tion between the republican friends respecting Lucius Pella
and the refusal of the money, the dissension of the two concerning the decisive battle, their conversation about suicide,
the appearance of Brutus's evil genius, the mistakes in the

* Bunnett's Translation, London, 1863. This passage immediately precedes the one quoted in the " Critical Comments on the Play" below.

battle, its double issue, its repetition, the suicide of both friends, and Cassius's death by the same sword with which he killed Cæsar—all is taken from Plutarch's narrative, from which the poet had only to omit whatever destroyed the unity of the action."

The period of the action of the play extends from the feast of the *Lupercalia*, in February of the year 44 B.C., to the battle of Philippi, in the autumn of the year 42 B.C.

MARCUS JUNIUS BRUTUS.

III. CRITICAL COMMENTS ON THE PLAY.

[From Hazlitt's "Characters of Shakespeare's Plays."]

Shakespeare has in this play and elsewhere shown the same penetration into political character and the springs of public events as into those of every-day life. For instance, the whole design of the conspirators to liberate their country fails from the generous temper and overweening confidence of Brutus in the goodness of their cause and the assistance of others. Thus it has always been. Those who mean well themselves think well of others, and fall a prey to their security. That humanity and honesty which dispose men to resist injustice and tyranny render them unfit to cope with the cunning and power of those who are opposed to them. The friends of liberty trust to the professions of others because they are themselves sincere, and endeavour to reconcile the public good with the least possible hurt to its enemies, who have no regard to anything but their own unprincipled ends, and stick at nothing to accomplish them. Cassius was better cut out for a conspirator. His heart prompted his head. His watchful jealousy made him fear the worst that might happen, and his irritability of temper added to his inveteracy of purpose, and sharpened his patriotism. The mixed nature of his motives made him fitter to contend with bad men. The vices are never so well employed as in combating one another. Tyranny and servility are to be dealt with after their own fashion; otherwise they will triumph over those who spare them, and finally pronounce their funeral panegyric, as Antony did that of Brutus :—

> "All the conspirators, save only he,
> Did that they did in envy of great Cæsar;
> He only in a general honest thought,
> And common good to all, made one of them."

The quarrel between Brutus and Cassius is managed in a masterly way. The dramatic fluctuation of passion, the calmness of Brutus, the heat of Cassius, are admirably described; and the exclamation of Cassius on hearing of the death of Portia, which he does not learn till after their reconciliation, "How 'scap'd I killing when I cross'd you so?" gives double force to all that has gone before. The scene between Brutus and Portia, where she endeavours to extort the secret of the conspiracy from him, is conceived in the most heroical spirit, and the burst of tenderness in Brutus—

> "You are my true and honourable wife:
> As dear to me as are the ruddy drops
> That visit my sad heart"—

is justified by her whole behaviour. Portia's breathless impatience to learn the event of the conspiracy, in the dialogue

with Lucius, is full of passion.　The interest which Portia
takes in Brutus, and that which Calphurnia takes in the fate
of Cæsar, are discriminated with the nicest precision.　Mark
Antony's speech over the dead body of Cæsar has been justly
admired for the mixture of pathos and artifice in it: that of
Brutus certainly is not so good.

The entrance of the conspirators to the house of Brutus is
rendered very impressive.　In the midst of this scene we
meet with one of those careless and natural digressions which
occur so frequently and beautifully in Shakespeare.　After
Cassius has introduced his friends one by one, Brutus says,—

> "They are all welcome.
> What watchful cares do interpose themselves
> Betwixt your eyes and night?
>   *Cassius.* Shall I entreat a word?　[*Brutus and Cassius whisper.*
>   *Decius.* Here lies the east: doth not the day break here?
>   *Casca.* No.
>   *Cinna.* O pardon, sir, it doth; and yon gray lines,
> That fret the clouds, are messengers of day.
>   *Casca.* You shall confess that you are both deceiv'd:
> Here, as I point my sword, the sun arises;
> Which is a great way growing on the south,
> Weighing the youthful season of the year.
> Some two months hence, up higher toward the north
> He first presents his fire, and the high east
> Stands, as the Capitol, directly here."

We cannot help thinking this graceful familiarity better than
all the fustian in the world.

The truth of history in *Julius Cæsar* is very ably worked
up with dramatic effect.　The councils of generals, the doubtful turns of battles, are represented to the life.　The death
of Brutus is worthy of him : it has the dignity of the Roman
senator with the firmness of the Stoic philosopher.　But what
is perhaps better than either is the little incident of his boy
Lucius falling asleep over his instrument, as he is playing to
his master in his tent, the night before the battle.　Nature
had played him the same forgetful trick once before, on the

night of the conspiracy.　　The humanity of Brutus is the same on both occasions.

> " It is no matter :
> Enjoy the heavy honey-dew of slumber.
> Thou hast no figures nor no fantasies,
> Which busy care draws in the brains of men,
> Therefore thou sleep'st so sound."

[From Knight's Comments on the Play.]*

Nothing can be more interesting, we think, than to follow Shakespeare with Plutarch in hand.　The poet adheres to the facts of history with a remarkable fidelity.　A few hard figures are painted upon a canvas ; the outlines are distinct, the colours are strong ; but there is no art in the composition, no grouping, no light and shadow.　This is the historian's picture.　We turn to the poet.　We recognize the same figures, but they appear to live ; they are in harmony with the entire scene in which they move ; we have at once the reality of nature and the ideal of art, which is a higher nature.　Compare the dialogue in the first act between Cassius and Brutus, and the same dialogue as reported by Plutarch, for an example of the power by which the poet elevates all he touches, without destroying its identity.　When we arrive at the stirring scenes of the third act, this power is still more manifest.　The assassination scene is as literal as may be ; but it offers an example apt enough of Shakespeare's mode of dramatizing a fact.　When Metellus Cimber makes suit for his brother, and the conspirators appear as intercessors, the historian says, " Cæsar at the first simply refused their kindness and entreaties ; but afterwards, perceiving they still pressed on him, he violently thrust them from him."　The poet enters into the mind of Cæsar, and clothes this rejection of the suit in characteristic words.　Hazlitt, after noticing the profound knowledge of character displayed by Shakespeare in this play, says : " If there be any exception to this

* *Pictorial Edition of Shakespeare : Tragedies*, vol. ii. p. 349 foll.

remark, it is in the hero of the piece himself. We do not much admire the representation here given of Julius Cæsar, nor do we think it answers the portrait given of him in his *Commentaries.* He makes several vapouring and rather pedantic speeches, and does nothing. Indeed, he has nothing to do. So far the fault of the character is the fault of the plot." The echoes of this opinion are many, and smaller critics wax bold upon the occasion. Boswell says: "There cannot be a stronger proof of Shakespeare's deficiency in classical knowledge than the boastful language he has put in the mouth of the most accomplished man of all antiquity, who was not more admirable for his achievements than for the dignified simplicity with which he has recorded them." Courtenay had hazarded, in his notice of *Henry VIII.*, the somewhat bold assertion that "Shakespeare used very little artifice, and, in truth, had very little design, in the construction of the greater number of his historical characters." Upon the character of Julius Cæsar, he says that Plutarch's having been supposed to pass over this character somewhat slightly is "a corroboration of my remark upon the slight attention which Shakespeare paid to his historical characters. The conversation with Antony about fat men, and with Calphurnia about her dreams, came conveniently into his plan ; and some lofty expressions could hardly be avoided in portraying one who was known to the whole world as a great conqueror. Beyond this our poet gave himself no trouble." This is certainly an easy way of disposing of a complicated question. Did Shakespeare give himself no trouble about the characterization of Brutus and Cassius? In them did he indicate no points of character but what he found in Plutarch? Is not his characterization of Cæsar himself a considerable expansion of what he found set down by the historian? At *the exact period of the action of this drama,* Cæsar, possessing the reality of power, was haunted by the weakness of passionately desiring the title of king. Plutarch says :

"The chiefest cause that made him mortally hated was the covetous desire he had to be called king." This is the pivot upon which the whole action of Shakespeare's tragedy turns. There might have been another method of treating the subject. The death of Julius Cæsar might have been the catastrophe. The republican and monarchical principles might have been exhibited in conflict. The republican principle would have triumphed in the fall of Cæsar; and the poet would have previously held the balance between the two principles, or have claimed, indeed, our largest sympathies for the principles of Cæsar and his friends, by a true exhibition of Cæsar's greatness and Cæsar's virtues. The poet chose another course. And are we, then, to talk, with ready flippancy, of ignorance and carelessness—that he wanted classical knowledge — that he gave himself no trouble? "The fault of the character is the fault of the plot," says Hazlitt. It would have been nearer the truth had he said, the character is determined by the plot. While Cæsar is upon the scene, it was for the poet, largely interpreting the historian, to show the inward workings of "the covetous desire he had to be called king," and most admirably, according to our notions of characterization, has he shown them. Cæsar is "in all but name a king." He is surrounded by all the external attributes of power ; yet he is not satisfied :—

"The angry spot doth glow on Cæsar's brow."

He is suspicious—he fears. But he has acquired the policy of greatness—to seem what it is not. To his intimate friend he is an actor :—

"I rather tell thee what is to be fear'd
Than what I fear ; for always I am Cæsar."

When Calphurnia has recounted the terrible portents of the night—when the augurers would not that Cæsar should stir forth—he exclaims :—

> " The gods do this in shame of cowardice :
> Cæsar should be a beast without a heart
> If he should stay at home to-day for fear."

But to whom does he utter this, the "boastful language'
which so offends Boswell? To the servant who has brough·
the message from the augurers; before *him* he could show
no fear. But the very inflation of his language shows that he
did fear; and an instant after, when the servant no doubt is
intended to have left the scene, he says to his wife,—

> " Mark Antony shall say I am not well,
> And, for thy humour, I will stay at home."

Read Plutarch's account of the scene between Decius and
Cæsar, when Decius prevails against Calphurnia, and Cæsar
decides to go. In the historian we have not a hint of the
splendid characterization of Cæsar struggling between his
fear and his pride. Wherever Shakespeare found a minute
touch in the historian that could harmonize with his general
plan, he embodied it in his character of Cæsar. Who does
not remember the magnificent lines which the poet puts into
the mouth of Cæsar?—

> " Cowards die many times before their deaths;
> The valiant never taste of death but once.
> Of all the wonders that I yet have heard,
> It seems to me most strange that men should fear ;
> Seeing that death, a necessary end,
> Will come when it will come."

A very slight passage in Plutarch, with reference to other
events of Cæsar's life, suggested this : " When some of his
friends did counsel him to have a guard for the safety of his
person, and some also did offer themselves to serve him, he
would never consent to it, but said it was better to die once
than always to be afraid of death." . . . The tone of his last
speech is indeed boastful :—

> " I do know but one
> That unassailable holds on his rank,

B

> Unshak'd of motion ; and that I am he
> Let me a little show it."

That Cæsar knew his power, and made others know it, who can doubt? He was not one who, in his desire to be king, would put on the robe of humility. Altogether, then, we profess to receive Shakespeare's characterization of Cæsar with a perfect confidence that he produced that character upon fixed principles of art. It is true to the narrative upon which Shakespeare founded it ; but, what is of more importance, it is true to every natural conception of what Cæsar must have been at the exact moment of his fall.

[*From Ulrici's " Shakespeare's Dramatic Art."**]

The want of unity of interest is the common objection that has been most frequently brought against *Julius Cæsar.* And as long as this particular unity is confounded with the true ideal unity of art, defective composition, or a want of true organic unity, is the greatest censure that can be passed upon a work of art. Now if the unity of interest ought to centre entirely in one *personage* of the drama, then no doubt the objection is just, for it is divided between Cæsar, Brutus and Cassius, and Antony and Octavius. But we cannot for a moment concede that poetical interest is invariably personal ; we believe that it attaches as frequently to an idea. In the *historical* drama, the interest must indeed be one, but one *historically*, and then it will be one in a poetical sense also. But in a certain sense history does not at all trouble itself about persons ; its chief interest is in *facts*, and their effects and influences. Now in *Julius Cæsar* this interest is one throughout, and possesses a true and organic unity. One and the same thought is reflected in the fall of Cæsar, in the defeat and death of Brutus and Cassius, and also in the vic-

---

* English Translation, London, 1847, p. 534 foll. I have made a few verbal changes, and have corrected some palpable errors ; as "sworn friend" for "sworn enemy" (geschworenen Feinde).

tory of Antony and Octavius. No man, even though he be as great as Cæsar, or as noble as Brutus, is powerful enough to drag at will history in leading-strings; every one in his vocation may contribute his stone to building up the grand whole, but no one must presume to think that he may with impunity try experiments with it. The great Julius was but trying an experiment when he allowed the crown to be offered which he thrice rejected against his will. He could not tame his wild ambition—a fault which history perhaps might have pardoned; but he understood her not; he wished and attempted what she was not ready for: by this self-condemned error, by this arrogance, he precipitated his fate. But Brutus and Cassius erred no less in thinking that Rome could be saved by re-establishing the republic; as if the prosperity of a state depended on its form, and as if the individual could restore the lost morality of the nation by a magic word. As Cæsar thought life unendurable without the outward dignity of a crown, so they could not bear to live without the honour of external liberty, which they mistook for true intrinsic freedom of mind. They also were trying their own experiments with history. The avaricious and ambitious Cassius, as well as the noble-minded and disinterested Brutus, arrogantly thought themselves strong enough to control the course of events. Thus, in their case also, was error associated with presumption, and they doubly deserved the retribution that overtook them. Antony, on the other hand, with Octavius and Lepidus, the talented spendthrift with the clever actor and the good-hearted simpleton—neither half so able nor so noble-minded as their adversaries—nevertheless prevailed in the struggle, because they consented to follow the course of history and the spirit of their age, and understood how to use it. • In *Julius Cæsar*, therefore, we discern throughout the same ground-idea, and a well-distributed organic unity of historical interest in all the characters, whether leading or subordinate. It shines forth even in Portia's death, as well as in the fall of Cato, Cicero, and the other conspirators; Portia and Cato fell with Brutus, and the rest with Cassius, because they did not understand the progress of events, and thought to control it arbitrarily for themselves, or no less wantonly to put their hands into their bosoms, and "speak Greek." History, accordingly, here appears under one of its principal aspects—that of its despotic power and energy of development, by which, although worked out by individual minds, it yet rules the greatest of them, and reaches far beyond their widest calculations.

But what can justify apparitions and spirits in an *historical* drama? And in any case, why is it that the ghost of Cæsar appears to Brutus, whose designs, apparently at least, are pure and noble, rather than to Cassius, his sworn enemy? Because, though they appear to be such, they are not so in reality; the design is not really *pure* which has for its first step so arrogant a violation of right. Moreover, Cæsar had been more deeply wronged by Brutus than by Cassius. Brutus, like Coriolanus, had trampled under foot the tenderest and noblest affections of humanity for the sake of the phantom honour of free citizenship. Brutus, lastly, was the very soul of the conspiracy; if his mental energies should be paralyzed, and his strong courage unnerved, the whole enterprise must fail. And so, in truth, it went to pieces, because it was against the will of history—that is, against the eternal counsels of God. It was to signify this great lesson that Shakespeare introduced the ghost upon the stage. Only once, and with a few pregnant words, does the spirit appear; but he is constantly hovering in the background, like a dark thunder-cloud, and is, as it were, the offended and threatening spirit of history itself. It is with the same purpose that Shakespeare has introduced spectral apparitions into another of his historical pieces—*Richard III.* Both dramas belong to the same historical grade; they both represent important turning points in the history of the world—the close of an old, and the commencement of a new state of things—and in such times the guiding finger of God is more obviously apparent than at others.

●

[*From Gervinus's "Shakespeare Commentaries."**]

The fidelity of Shakespeare to his source [Plutarch] justifies us in saying that he has but copied the historical text. It is at the same time wonderful with what hidden and almost undiscernible power he has converted the text into a drama, and made one of the most effective plays possible. Nowhere else has Shakespeare executed his task with such simple skill, combining his dependence on history with the greatest freedom of a poetic plan, and making the truest history at once the freest drama. The parts seem to be only put together with the utmost ease, a few links taken out of the great chain of historical events, and the remainder united with a closer and more compact unity ; but let any one, following this model work, attempt to take any other subject out of Plutarch, and arrange only a dramatic sketch from it, and he will become fully aware of the difficulty of this apparently most easy task. He will become aware what it is to concentrate his mind on one theme strictly adhered to, as is here the case ; to refer persons and actions to one idea ; to seek this idea out of the most general truths laid down in history ; to employ, moreover, for the dramatic representation of this idea none but the actual historical personages ; and so at length to arrange this for the stage with that practised skill or innate ability, that with an apparently artless transcript of history, such an ingenious independent theatrical effect can be obtained as that which this play has at no time failed to produce. Indeed, Leonard Digges informs us with what applause *Julius Cæsar* was acted in Shakespeare's time, whilst

* Bunnett's Translation, London, 1863, vol. ii. p. 322 foll. As this translation was made "under the author's superintendence," I have quoted it *verbatim*, without collation with the original.

the tedious *Catiline* and *Sejanus*, which Ben Jonson had
worked at with such diligence and labour, were coldly received.   Immediately on its appearance the play roused the
emulation of all the theatres ; the renowned poets Munday,
Drayton, Webster, and Middleton wrote a rival piece, *Cæsar's
Fall*, in 1602, Lord Stirling a *Julius Cæsar* in 1604, and a
Cæsar and Pompey appeared in 1607.   At the period of the
Restoration, *Julius Cæsar* was one of the few works of Shakespeare that were sought out, represented, and criticised.   In
our own day, in Germany, we have seen it performed, seldom
well, but always with applause.   Separate scenes, like that
between Casca and Cassius during the storm, produce an
effect which can scarcely be imagined from merely reading
them ; the speech of Antony, heightened by the effect of external arrangement and the artifices of conversation, by proper pauses and interruptions, even with inferior acting, carries
away the spectator as well as the populace represented ; the
quarrel between Brutus and Cassius is a trial-piece for great
actors, which, according to Leonard Digges, created even in
his time the most rapturous applause ; and even the last act,
which has been often objected to, is capable of exciting the
liveliest emotion when well managed and acted with spirit.

*   *   *   *   *   *   *

The character of Cæsar in our play has been much blamed.
He is declared to be unlike the idea conceived of him from
his *Commentaries ;* it is said that he does nothing, and only
utters a few pompous, thrasonical, grandiloquent words, and
it has been asked whether this be the Cæsar that "did awe
the world?"   The poet, if he intended to make the attempt
of the republicans his main theme, could not have ventured
to create too great an interest in Cæsar ; it was necessary to
keep him in the background, and to present that view of him
which gave a reason for the conspiracy.   According even to
Plutarch, whose biography of Cæsar is acknowledged to be
very imperfect, Cæsar's character altered much for the worse

shortly before his death, and Shakespeare has represented him according to this suggestion. With what reverence Shakespeare viewed his character as a whole we learn from several passages of his works, and even in this play from the way in which he allows his memory to be respected as soon as he is dead. In the descriptions of Cassius we look back upon the time when the great man was natural, simple, un-dissembling, popular, and on an equal footing with others. Now he is spoiled by victory, success, power, and by the re-publican courtiers who surround him. He stands close on the borders between usurpation and discretion ; he is master in reality, and is on the point of assuming the name and the right ; he desires heirs to the throne ; he hesitates to accept the crown which he would gladly possess ; he is ambitious, and fears he may have betrayed this in his paroxysms of epi-lepsy ; he exclaims against flatterers and cringers, and yet both please him. All around him treat him as a master, his wife as a prince ; the senate allow themselves to be called *his* senate ; he assumes the appearance of a king even in his house ; even with his wife he uses the language of a man who knows himself secure of power ; and he maintains every-where the proud, strict bearing of a soldier, which is repre-sented even in his statues. If one of the changes at which Plutarch hints lay in this pride, this haughtiness, another lay in his superstition. In the suspicion and apprehension before the final step, he was seized, contrary to his usual nature and habit, with misgivings and superstitious fears, which affected likewise the hitherto free-minded Calphurnia. These con-flicting feelings divide him, his forebodings excite him, his pride and his defiance of danger struggle against them, and restore his former confidence, which was natural to him, and which causes his ruin ; just as a like confidence, springing from another source, ruined Brutus. The actor must make his high-sounding language appear as the result of this dis-cord of feeling. Sometimes they are only incidental words intended to characterize the hero in the shortest way. Generally they appear in the cases where Cæsar has to combat with his superstition, where he uses effort to take a higher stand in his words than at the moment he actually feels. He speaks so much of having no fear that by this very thing he betrays his fear. Even in the places where his words sound most boastful, where he compares himself with the north star, there is more arrogance and ill-concealed pride at work than real boastfulness. It is intended there with a few words to show him at that point when his behaviour could most excite those free spirits against him. It was fully intended that he should take but a small part in the action ; we must not, therefore, say with Scottowe that he was merely brought upon the stage to be killed. The poet has handled this historical piece like his English historical plays. He had in his eye the whole context of the Roman civil wars for this single drama, not as yet thinking of its continuation in *Antony and Cleopatra.*

[From Craik's "English of Shakespeare."*]

It is evident that the character and history of Julius Cæsar had taken a strong hold of Shakespeare's imagination. There is perhaps no other historical character who is so repeatedly alluded to throughout his plays.

"There was never anything so sudden," says the disguised Rosalind in *As You Like It* (v. 2) to Orlando, speaking of the manner in which his brother Oliver and her cousin (or sister, as she calls her) Celia had fallen in love with one another, "but the fight of two rams, and Cæsar's thrasonical brag of I came, saw, and overcame : for your brother and my sister no sooner met, but they look'd ; no sooner look'd, but they lov'd ; no sooner lov'd, but they sigh'd ;" etc.

"O ! such a day," exclaims Lord Bardolph in the *Second Part of King Henry the Fourth* (i. 1) to old Northumberland,

* Rolfe's edition, p. 49 foll.

in his misannouncement of the issue of the field of Shrewsbury,—

> "So fought, so follow'd, and so fairly won,
> Came not till now to dignify the times
> Since Cæsar's fortunes."

And afterwards (in iv. 3) we have Falstaff's magnificent gasconade: "I have speeded hither with the very extremest inch of possibility: I have founder'd nine score and odd posts; and here, travel-tainted as I am, have, in my pure and immaculate valour, taken Sir John Colevile of the Dale, a most furious knight, and valorous enemy. But what of that? He saw me, and yielded; that I may justly say, with the hook-nos'd fellow of Rome, I came, saw, and overcame."

"But now behold," says the Chorus in the Fifth Act of *King Henry the Fifth*, describing the triumphant return of the English monarch from the conquest of France,—

> "In the quick forge and working-house of thought,
> How London doth pour out her citizens.
> The mayor, and all his brethren, in best sort,
> Like to the senators of th' antique Rome,
> With the plebeians swarming at their heels,
> Go forth, and fetch their conquering Cæsar in."

In the three Parts of *King Henry the Sixth*, which are so thickly scattered with classical allusions of all kinds, there are several to the great Roman dictator. "Henry the Fifth! thy ghost I invocate;" the Duke of Bedford apostrophizes his deceased brother in the *First Part* (i. 1):—

> "Prosper this realm, keep it from civil broils!
> Combat with adverse planets in the heavens!
> A far more glorious star thy soul will make
> Than Julius Cæsar, or bright—"

In the next scene the Maid, setting out to raise the siege of Orleans, and deliver her king and country, compares herself to

> "that proud insulting ship
> Which Cæsar and his fortune bare at once."

In the *Second Part* (iv. 1) we have Suffolk, when hurried away to execution by the seamen who had captured him, consoling himself with—

> "Great men oft die by vile bezonians :
> A Roman sworder and banditto slave
> Murder'd sweet Tully ; Brutus' bastard hand
> Stabb'd Julius Cæsar ; savage islanders
> Pompey the Great ; and Suffolk dies by pirates."

And afterwards (iv. 7) we have Lord Say, in somewhat similar circumstances, thus appealing to Cade and his mob of men of Kent :—

> "Hear me but speak, and bear me where you will.
> Kent, in the Commentaries Cæsar writ,
> Is term'd the civil'st place of all this isle ;
> Sweet is the country, because full of riches ;
> The people liberal, valiant, active, wealthy ;
> Which makes me hope you are not void of pity."

"O traitors ! murderers !" Queen Margaret in the *Third Part* (v. 5) shrieks out in her agony and rage when the prince her son is butchered before her eyes :—

> "They that stabb'd Cæsar shed no blood at all,
> Did not offend, nor were not worthy blame,
> If this foul deed were by to equal it :
> He was a man ; this, in respect, a child ;
> And men ne'er spend their fury on a child."

In *King Richard the Third* (iii. 1) is a passage of great pregnancy. "Did Julius Cæsar build that place, my lord ?" the young prince asks Buckingham, when it is proposed that he shall retire for a day or two to the Tower before his coronation. And when informed in reply that the mighty Roman at least began the building, he further inquires,—

> "Is it upon record, or else reported
> Successively from age to age, he built it ?"

"Upon record, my gracious lord," answers Buckingham. On which the wise royal boy rejoins,—

> "But say, my lord, it were not register'd,
> Methinks the truth should live from age to age,
> As 'twere retail'd to all posterity,
> Even to the general all-ending day."

And then, after a "What say you, uncle?" he explains the great thought that was working in his mind in these striking words :—

> "That Julius Cæsar was a famous man :
> With what his valour did enrich his wit,
> His wit set down to make his valour live.
> Death makes no conquest of this conqueror,*
> For now he lives in fame, though not in life."

Far away from anything Roman as the fable and locality of *Hamlet* are, various passages testify how much Cæsar was in the mind of Shakespeare while writing that play. First, we have the famous passage (i. 1) so closely resembling one in the Second Scene of the Second Act of *Julius Cæsar :*—

> "In the most high and palmy state of Rome,
> A little ere the mightiest Julius fell,
> The graves stood tenantless, and the sheeted dead
> Did squeak and gibber in the Roman streets ;
> As † stars with trains of fire, and dews of blood,
> Disasters in the sun ; and the moist star,
> Upon whose influence Neptune's empire stands,
> Was sick almost to doomsday with eclipse."‡

Then there is (iii. 2) the conversation between Hamlet and Polonius, touching the histrionic exploits of the latter in his university days : "I did enact Julius Cæsar : I was killed i'

---

* "*His* conqueror" is the reading of all the folios. "*This*" was restored by Theobald from the quarto of 1597, and has been adopted by Malone and most modern editors.

† Something is evidently wrong here ; but even Mr. Collier's annotator gives us no help.

‡ This passage, however, is found only in the quartos, and is omitted in all the folios.

th' Capitol ; Brutus kill'd me." " It was a *brute* part of him
to kill so *capital* a calf there" (surely, by-the-by, to be spoken
aside, though not so marked). Lastly, there is the prince's
rhyming moralization (v. 1) :—

> "Imperial Cæsar, dead and turn'd to clay,
> Might stop a hole to keep the wind away.
> O, that that earth which kept the world in awe
> Should patch a wall t' expel the winter's flaw !"

Many notices of Cæsar occur, as might be expected, in
Cymbeline. Such are the boast of Posthumus to his friend
Philario (ii. 4) of the valour of the Britons :—

> "Our countrymen
> Are men more order'd than when Julius Cæsar
> Smil'd at their lack of skill, but found their courage
> Worthy his frowning at."

Various passages in the First Scene of the Third Act :—

> "When Julius Cæsar (whose remembrance yet
> Lives in men's eyes, and will to ears and tongues
> Be theme and hearing ever) was in this Britain,
> And conquer'd it, Cassibelan, thine uncle
> (Famous in Cæsar's praises no whit less
> Than in his feats deserving it)," etc.

> "There be many Cæsars,
> Ere such another Julius."

> "A kind of conquest
> Cæsar made here ; but made not here his brag
> Of *came,* and *saw,* and *overcame :* with shame
> (The first that-ever touch'd him) he was carried
> From off our coast twice beaten ; and his shipping
> (Poor ignorant baubles !) on our terrible seas,
> Like egg-shells mov'd upon their surges, crack'd
> As easily 'gainst our rocks. For joy whereof
> The fam'd Cassibelan, who was once at point
> (O giglot Fortune !) to master Cæsar's sword,
> Made Lud's town with rejoicing fires bright,
> And Britons strut with courage."

"Our kingdom is stronger than it was at that time ; and, as I said, there
is no more such Cæsars ; other of them may have crook'd noses ; but to
owe such straight arms, none."

> " Cæsar's ambition
> (Which swell'd so much that it did almost stretch
> The sides o' th' world) against all colour here
> Did put the yoke upon 's ; which to shake off
> Becomes a warlike people, whom we reckon
> Ourselves to be."

Lastly, we have a few references in *Antony and Cleopatra :—*

> " Broad-fronted Cæsar,
> When thou wast here above the ground, I was
> A morsel for a monarch" (i. 5).

> " Julius Cæsar,
> Who at Philippi the good Brutus ghosted" (ii. 6).

> " What was it
> That mov'd pale Cassius to conspire ?   And what
> Made the all-honour'd, honest, Roman Brutus,
> With the arm'd rest, courtiers of beauteous freedom,
> To drench the Capitol, but that they would
> Have one man but a man ?" (ii. 6.)

> " Your fine Egyptian cookery
> Shall have the fame.   I have heard that Julius Cæsar
> Grew fat with feasting there" (ii. 6).

> " When Antony found Julius Cæsar dead,
> He cried almost to roaring ; and he wept
> When at Philippi he found Brutus slain" (iii. 2).

> "*Thyreus.* Give me grace to lay
> My duty on your hand.
> *Cleopatra.*   Your Cæsar's father oft,
> When he hath mus'd of taking kingdoms in,
> Bestow'd his lips on that unworthy place,
> As it rain'd kisses" (iii. 11).

These passages, taken all together, and some of them more particularly, will probably be thought to afford a considerably more comprehensive representation of " the mighty Julius" than the Play which bears his name.   We cannot be sure that that Play was so entitled by Shakespeare.   " The Tragedy of Julius Cæsar," or " The Life and Death of Julius Cæsar," would describe no more than the half of it.   Cæsar's part terminates with the opening of the Third Act ; after that, on to the end, we have nothing more of him but his dead body, his ghost, and his memory. The Play might more fitly be called after Brutus than after Cæsar. And still more remarkable is the partial delineation that we have of the man. We have a distinct exhibition of little else beyond his vanity and arrogance, relieved and set off by his good nature or affability. He is brought before us only as "the spoilt child of victory." All the grandeur and predominance of his character is kept in the background, or in the shade—to be inferred, at most, from what is said by the other *dramatis personæ*—by Cassius on the one hand and by Antony on the other in the expression of their own diametrically opposite natures and aims, and in a very few words by the calmer, milder, and juster Brutus—nowhere manifested by himself. It might almost be suspected that the complete and fulllength Cæsar had been carefully reserved for another drama. Even Antony is only half delineated here, to be brought forward again on another scene : Cæsar needed such reproduction much more, and was as well entitled to a stage which he should tread without an equal. He is only a subordinate character in the present Play ; his death is but an incident in the progress of the plot. The first figures, standing conspicuously out from all the rest, are Brutus and Cassius.

Some of the passages that have been collected are further curious and interesting as being other renderings of conceptions that are also found in the present Play, and as consequently furnishing data both for the problem of the chronological arrangement of the Plays, and for the general history of the mind and artistic genius of the writer. After all the commentatorship and criticism of which the works of Shakespeare have been the subject, they still remain to be studied in their totality with a special reference to himself. The man Shakespeare, as read in his works—Shakespeare as there revealed, not only in his genius and intellectual powers, but in his character, disposition, temper, opinions, tastes, prejudices—is a book yet to be written.

[*From Mrs. Jameson's "Characteristics of Women."*]

Almost every one knows by heart Lady Percy's celebrated address to her husband, beginning,

"O, my good lord, why are you thus alone?"*

and that of Portia to Brutus, in Julius Cæsar,

. . . "You've ungently, Brutus,
Stol'n from my bed."

The situation is exactly similar, the topics of remonstrance are nearly the same; the sentiments and the style as opposite as are the characters of the two women. Lady Percy is evidently accustomed to win more from her fiery lord by caresses than by reason: he loves her in his rough way, "as Harry Percy's wife," but she has no real influence over him; he has no confidence in her.

"*Lady Percy.* . . . In faith,
I'll know your business, Harry, that I will.
I fear my brother Mortimer doth stir
About this title, and hath sent for you
To line his enterprise; but if you go—
Hotspur. So far afoot, I shall be weary, love!"

The whole scene is admirable, but unnecessary here, because it illustrates no point of character in her. Lady Percy has no *character*, properly so called, whereas that of Portia is very distinctly and faithfully drawn from the outline furnished by Plutarch. Lady Percy's fond upbraidings, and her half playful, half pouting entreaties, scarcely gain her husband's attention. Portia, with true matronly dignity and tenderness, pleads her right to share her husband's thoughts, and proves it too.

"I grant, I am a woman, but, withal,
A woman that Lord Brutus took to wife;
I grant, I am a woman, but, withal,
A woman well reputed, Cato's daughter.

* 1 *Henry IV.* ii. 3.

> Think you, I am no stronger than my sex,
> Being so father'd, and so husbanded?
>
> . . . . .
>
> *Brutus.* You are my true and honourable wife:
> As dear to me as are the ruddy drops
> That visit my sad heart!"

Portia, as Shakespeare has truly felt and represented the character, is but a softened reflection of that of her husband Brutus: in him we see an excess of natural sensibility, an almost womanish tenderness of heart, repressed by the tenets of his austere philosophy: a stoic by profession, and in reality the reverse—acting deeds against his nature by the strong force of principle and will. In Portia there is the same profound and passionate feeling, and all her sex's softness and timidity held in check by that self-discipline, that stately dignity, which she thought became a woman "so fathered and so husbanded." The fact of her inflicting on herself a voluntary wound to try her own fortitude is perhaps the strongest proof of this disposition. Plutarch relates that on the day on which Cæsar was assassinated, Portia appeared overcome with terror, and even swooned away, but did not in her emotion utter a word which could affect the conspirators. Shakespeare has rendered this circumstance literally.

> "*Portia.* I prithee, boy, run to the senate-house;
> Stay not to answer me, but get thee gone.
> Why dost thou stay?
> *Lucius.*   To know my errand, madam.
> *Portia.* I would have had thee there and here again,
> Ere I can tell thee what thou should'st do there.
> O constancy! be strong upon my side:
> Set a huge mountain 'tween my heart and tongue!
> I have a man's mind, but a woman's might.
> . . . . . Ay me! how weak a thing
> The heart of woman is! O, I grow faint," etc.

There is another beautiful incident related by Plutarch which could not well be dramatized. When Brutus and Portia parted for the last time in the island of Nisida, she re strained all expression of grief that she might not shake *his* fortitude ; but afterwards, in passing through a chamber in which there hung a picture of Hector and Andromache, she stopped, gazed upon it for a time with a settled sorrow, and at length burst into a passion of tears.*

If Portia had been a Christian, and lived in later times, she might have been another Lady Russel; but she made a poor stoic. No factitious or external control was sufficient to restrain such an exuberance of sensibility and fancy ; and those who praise the *philosophy* of Portia and the *heroism* of her death, certainly mistook the character altogether. It is evident, from the manner of her death, that it was not deliberate self-destruction, " after the high Roman fashion," but took place in a paroxysm of madness, caused by overwrought and suppressed feeling, grief, terror, and suspense. Shakespeare has thus represented it :—

> "*Brutus.* O Cassius, I am sick of many griefs !
> *Cassius.* Of your philosophy you make no use,
> If you give place to accidental evils.
> *Brutus.* No man bears sorrow better.—Portia is dead.
> *Cassius.* Ha !—Portia ?
> *Brutus.* She is dead.
> *Cassius.* How 'scap'd I killing, when I cross'd you so ?—
> O insupportable and touching loss !—
> Upon what sickness?
> *Brutus.* Impatient of my absence,
> And grief that young Octavius with Mark Antony
> Had made themselves so strong ;—for with her death
> These tidings came.—*With this she fell distract,*
> And, her attendants absent, swallow'd fire."

So much for woman's philosophy !

* When at Naples, I have often stood upon the rock at the extreme point of Posilippo, and looked down upon the little island of Nisida, and thought of this scene till I forgot the Lazaretto which now deforms it : deforms it, however, to the fancy only, for the building itself, as it rises from amid the vines, the cypresses, and fig-trees which embosom it, looks beautiful at a distance.

C

CAIUS JULIUS CÆSAR.

JULIUS CÆSAR.

DRAMATIS PERSONÆ.

JULIUS CÆSAR.

OCTAVIUS CÆSAR,
MARCUS ANTONIUS, } Triumvirs, after the death of
M. ÆMIL. LEPIDUS, } Julius Cæsar.

CICERO,
PUBLIUS, } Senators.
POPILIUS LENA, }

MARCUS BRUTUS,
CASSIUS,
CASCA,
TREBONIUS, } Conspirators against Julius Cæsar.
LIGARIUS,
DECIUS BRUTUS,
METELLUS CIMBER,
CINNA,

FLAVIUS, } Tribunes.
MARULLUS, }

ARTEMIDORUS, a Sophist of Cnidos.

A Soothsayer.

CINNA, a Poet.

Another Poet.

LUCILIUS,
TITINIUS,
MESSALA, } Friends to Brutus and Cassius.
Young CATO,
VOLUMNIUS, }

VARRO,
CLITUS,
CLAUDIUS, } Servants to Brutus.
STRATO,
LUCIUS,
DARDANIUS, }

PINDARUS, Servant to Cassius.

CALPHURNIA, Wife to Cæsar.
PORTIA, Wife to Brutus.

Senators, Citizens, Guards, Attendants, etc.

SCENE, *during a great part of the Play, at Rome; afterwards at Sardis, and near Philippi.*

ROMAN VICTORY.

ACT I.

Scene I. *Rome. A Street.*

Enter Flavius, Marullus, *and a rabble of* Citizens.

Flavius. Hence! home, you idle creatures, get you home.
Is this a holiday? What! know you not,
Being mechanical, you ought not walk,
Upon a labouring day, without the sign
Of your profession?—Speak, what trade art thou?

   1 *Citizen.* Why, sir, a carpenter.

   Marullus. Where is thy leather apron, and thy rule?
What dost thou with thy best apparel on?—
You, sir; what trade are you?

   2 *Citizen.* Truly, sir, in respect of a fine workman, I am
but, as you would say, a cobbler.

Marullus. But what trade art thou? Answer me directly.

2 Citizen. A trade, sir, that I hope I may use with a safe conscience; which is, indeed, sir, a mender of bad soles.

Marullus. What trade, thou knave? thou naughty knave, what trade?

2 Citizen. Nay, I beseech you, sir, be not out with me : yet if you be out, sir, I can mend you.

Marullus. What mean'st thou by that? Mend me, thou saucy fellow?

2 Citizen. Why, sir, cobble you.

Flavius. Thou art a cobbler, art thou?

2 Citizen. Truly, sir, all that I live by is with the awl. I meddle with no tradesman's matters, nor women's matters : but withal I am, indeed, sir, a surgeon to old shoes; when they are in great danger, I recover them. As proper men as ever trod upon neat's leather have gone upon my handiwork.

Flavius. But wherefore art not in thy shop to-day? Why dost thou lead these men about the streets?

2 Citizen. Truly, sir, to wear out their shoes, to get myself into more work. But, indeed, sir, we make holiday to see Cæsar, and to rejoice in his triumph.

Marullus. Wherefore rejoice? What conquest brings he home?
What tributaries follow him to Rome,
To grace in captive bonds his chariot wheels?
You blocks, you stones, you worse than senseless things !
O, you hard hearts, you cruel men of Rome,
Knew you not Pompey? Many a time and oft
Have you climb'd up to walls and battlements,
To towers and windows, yea, to chimney-tops,
Your infants in your arms, and there have sat
The live-long day, with patient expectation,
To see great Pompey pass the streets of Rome :
And, when you saw his chariot but appear,
Have you not made an universal shout,

That Tiber trembled underneath her banks,
To hear the replication of your sounds
Made in her concave shores?
And do you now put on your best attire?
And do you now cull out a holiday?
And do you now strew flowers in his way, .
That comes in triumph over Pompey's blood?
Be gone!
Run to your houses, fall upon your knees,
Pray to the gods to intermit the plague
That needs must light on this ingratitude.
    Flavius. Go, go, good countrymen, and, for this fault,
Assemble all the poor men of your sort;
Draw them to Tiber banks, and weep your tears
Into the channel, till the lowest stream
Do kiss the most exalted shores of all.   [*Exeunt Citizens.*
See, whe'r their basest metal be not mov'd!
They vanish tongue-tied in their guiltiness.
Go you down that way towards the Capitol;
This way will I. Disrobe the images,
If you do find them deck'd with ceremonies.
    Marullus. May we do so?
You know it is the feast of Lupercal.
    Flavius. It is no matter; let no images
Be hung with Cæsar's trophies. I'll about,
And drive away the vulgar from the streets;
So do you too, where you perceive them thick.
These growing feathers pluck'd from Cæsar's wing
Will make him fly an ordinary pitch;
Who else would soar above the view of men,
And keep us all in servile fearfulness.   [*Exeunt.*

SCENE II. *The same.   A Public Place.*

Enter, in procession with Music, CÆSAR ; ANTONY, *for the course ;* CALPHURNIA, PORTIA, DECIUS, CICERO, BRUTUS, CASSIUS, *and* CASCA, *a great crowd following, amonø them a* Soothsayer.

Cæsar. Calphurnia,—
Casca.   Peace, ho ! Cæsar speaks. [*Music ceases.*
Cæsar. Calphurnia,—
Calphurnia.   Here, my lord.
Cæsar. Stand you directly in Antonius' way,
When he doth run his course.—Antonius.
Antony. Cæsar, my lord.
Cæsar. Forget not, in your speed, Antonius,
To touch Calphurnia ; for our elders say,
The barren, touched in this holy chase,
Shake off their sterile curse.
Antony.   I shall remember :
When Cæsar says, " Do this," it is perform'd.
Cæsar. Set on ; and leave no ceremony out.   . [*Music.*
Soothsayer. Cæsar.
Cæsar.   Ha ! who calls ?
Casca. Bid every noise be still.—Peace yet again.
                                        [*Music ceases.*
Cæsar. Who is it in the press that calls on me ?
I hear a tongue, shriller than all the music,
Cry, Cæsar.   Speak ; Cæsar is turn'd to hear.
Soothsayer. Beware the ides of March.
Cæsar.   What man is that ?
Brutus. A soothsayer bids you beware the ides of March.
Cæsar. Set him before me ; let me see his face.
Cassius. Fellow, come from the throng : look upon Cæsar.
Cæsar. What say'st thou to me now ?   Speak once again.
Soothsayer. Beware the ides of March.

Cæsar. He is a dreamer ; let us leave him :—pass.
   [*Sennet. Exeunt all but Brutus and Cassius.*
Cassius. Will you go see the order of the course?
Brutus. Not I.
Cassius.   I pray you, do.
Brutus. I am not gamesome : I do lack some part
Of that quick spirit that is in Antony.
Let me not hinder, Cassius, your desires ;
I'll leave you.
Cassius. Brutus, I do observe you now of late :
I have not from your eyes that gentleness
And shew of love as I was wont to have :
You bear too stubborn and too strange a hand
Over your friend that loves you.
Brutus.   Cassius,
Be not deceiv'd : if I have veil'd my look,
I turn the trouble of my countenance
Merely upon myself. Vexed I am
Of late with passions of some difference,
Conceptions only proper to myself,
Which give some soil, perhaps, to my behaviours :
But let not therefore my good friends be griev'd
(Among which number, Cassius, be you one),
Nor construe any further my neglect,
Than that poor Brutus, with himself at war,
Forgets the shews of love to other men.
Cassius. Then, Brutus, I have much mistook your passion ;
By means whereof, this breast of mine hath buried
Thoughts of great value, worthy cogitations.
Tell me, good Brutus, can you see your face?
Brutus. No, Cassius ; for the eye sees not itself,
But by reflection by some other things.
Cassius.   'Tis just :
And it is very much lamented, Brutus,
That you have no such mirrors as will turn

Your hidden worthiness into your eye,
That you might see your shadow.   I have heard,
Where many of the best respect in Rome
(Except immortal Cæsar), speaking of Brutus,
And groaning underneath this age's yoke,
Have wish'd that noble Brutus had his eyes.

    Brutus. Into what dangers would you lead me, Cassius,
That you would have me seek into myself
For that which is not in me?

    Cassius. Therefore, good Brutus, be prepar'd to hear:
And, since you know you cannot see yourself
So well as by reflection, I, your glass,
Will modestly discover to yourself
That of yourself which you yet know not of.
And be not jealous on me, gentle Brutus:
Were I a common laugher, or did use
To stale with ordinary oaths my love
To every new protester; if you know
That I do fawn on men, and hug them hard,
And after scandal them ; or if you know
That I profess myself in banqueting
To all the rout, then hold me dangerous. [*Flourish and shout.*

    Brutus. What means this shouting?   I do fear, the people
Choose Cæsar for their king.

    Cassius.   Ay, do you fear it?
Then must I think you would not have it.so.

    Brutus. I would not, Cassius ; yet I love him well.—
But wherefore do you hold me here so long?
What is it that you would impart to me?
If it be aught toward the general good,
Set honour in one eye, and death i' th' other,
And I will look on both indifferently :
For, let the gods so speed me, as I love
The name of honour more than I fear death.

    Cassius. I know that virtue to be in you, Brutus,

As well as I do know your outward favour.
Well, honour is the subject of my story.—
I cannot tell what you and other men
Think of this life ; but, for my single self,
I had as lief not be, as live to be
In awe of such a thing as I myself.
I was born free as Cæsar, so were you ;
We both have fed as well ; and we can both
Endure the winter's cold as well as he.
For once, upon a raw and gusty day,
The troubled Tiber chafing with her shores,
Cæsar said to me, " Dar'st thou, Cassius, now
Leap in with me into this angry flood,
And swim to yonder point ?" Upon the word,
Accoutred as I was, I plunged in,
And bade him follow : so, indeed, he did.
The torrent roar'd ; and we did buffet it
With lusty sinews ; throwing it aside,
And stemming it with hearts of controversy.
But ere we could arrive the point propos'd,
Cæsar cried, " Help me, Cassius, or I sink."
I, as Æneas, our great ancestor,
Did from the flames of Troy upon his shoulder
The old Anchises bear, so from the waves of Tiber
Did I the tired Cæsar. And this man
Is now become a god ; and Cassius is   .
A wretched creature, and must bend his body
If Cæsar carelessly but nod on him.
He had a fever when he was in Spain,
And, when the fit was on him, I did mark
How he did shake : 'tis true, this god did shake :
His coward lips did from their colour fly ;
And that same eye, whose bend doth awe the world,
Did lose his lustre. I did hear him groan :
Ay, and that tongue of his, that bade the Romans

Mark him, and write his speeches in their books,
Alas! it cried, "Give me some drink, Titinius,"
As a sick girl.   Ye gods, it doth amaze me,
A man of such a feeble temper should
So get the start of the majestic world,
And bear the palm alone.   [*Shout. Flourish.*
·   *Brutus.*   Another general shout!
I do believe, that these applauses are
For some new honours that are heap'd on Cæsar.
      Cassius. Why, man, he doth bestride the narrow world
Like a Colossus; and we petty men
Walk under his huge legs, and peep about
To find ourselves dishonourable graves.
Men at some time are masters of their fates:
The fault, dear Brutus, is not in our stars,
But in ourselves, that we are underlings.
Brutus and Cæsar: what should be in that Cæsar?
Why should that name be sounded more than yours?
Write them together, yours is as fair a name;
Sound them, it doth become the mouth as well;
Weigh them, it is as heavy; conjure with 'em,
"Brutus" will start a spirit as soon as "Cæsar."   [*Shout.*
Now, in the names of all the gods at once,
Upon what meat doth this our Cæsar feed,
That he is grown so great?   Age, thou art sham'd!
Rome, thou hast lost the breed of noble bloods!
When went there by an age, since the great flood,
But it was fam'd with more than with one man?
When could they say, till now, that talk'd of Rome,
That her wide walls encompass'd but one man?
Now is it Rome indeed, and room enough,
When there is in it but one only man.
O! you and I have heard our fathers say,
There was a Brutus once, that would have brook'd
Th' eternal devil to keep his state in Rome
As easily as a king.

Brutus. That you do love me, I am nothing jealous ;
What you would work me tó, I have some aim ;
How I have thought of this, and of these times,
I shall recount hereafter ; for this present,
I would not, so with love I might entreat you,
Be any further mov'd.   What you have said,
I will consider ; what you have to say,
I will with patience hear : and find a time
Both meet to hear and answer such high things.
Till then, my noble friend, chew upon this :
Brutus had rather be a villager,
Than to repute himself a son of Rome
Under these hard conditions as this time
Is like to lay upon us.
   Cassius.   I am glad,
That my weak words have struck but thus much shew
Of fire from Brutus.

Enter CÆSAR and his train.

   Brutus. The games are done, and Cæsar is returning.
   Cassius. As they pass by, pluck Casca by the sleeve ;
And he will, after his sour fashion, tell you
What hath proceeded worthy note to-day.
   Brutus. I will do so.—But, look you, Cassius,
The angry spot doth glow on Cæsar's brow,
And all the rest look like a chidden train :
Calphurnia's cheek is pale ; and Cicero
Looks with such ferret and such fiery eyes,
As we have seen him in the Capitol
Being cross'd in conference by some senators.
   Cassius. Casca will tell us what the matter is.
   Cæsar. Antonius.
   Antony. Cæsar.
   Cæsar. Let me have men about me that are fat ;
Sleek-headed men, and such as sleep o' nights :

Yond Cassius has a lean and hungry look ;
He thinks too much : such men àre dangerous.

Antony. Fear him not, Cæsar ; he's not dangerous.

Cæsar. Would he were fatter.—But I fear him not.
Yet, if my name were liable to fear,
I do not know the man I should avoid
So soon as that spare Cassius.   He reads much ;
He is a great observer, and he looks
Quite through the deeds of men : he loves no plays,
As thou dost, Antony ; he hears no music :
Seldom he smiles ; and smiles in such a sort,
As if he mock'd himself, and scorn'd his spirit
That could be mov'd to smile at anything.
Such men as he be never at heart's ease
Whiles they behold a greater than themselves,
And therefore are they very dangerous.
I rather tell thee what is to be fear'd
Than what I fear ; for always I am Cæsar.
Come on my right hand, for this ear is deaf,
And tell me truly what thou think'st of him.

> [*Sennet. Exeunt Cæsar and his train. Casca stays
> behind.*

Casca. You pull'd me by the cloak : would you speak with
me ?

Brutus. Ay, Casca ; tell us what hath chanc'd to-day,
That Cæsar looks so sad.

Casca. Why, you were with him, were you not ?

Brutus. I should not then ask Casca what had chanc'd.

Casca. Why, there was a crown offer'd him : and, being offer'd him, he put it by with the back of his hand, thus ; and
then the people fell a shouting.

Brutus. What was the second noise for ?

Casca. Why, for that too.

Cassius. They shouted thrice : what was the last cry for ?

Casca. Why, for that too.

Brutus. Was the crown offer'd him thrice?

Casca. Ay, marry, was't, and he put it by thrice, every time gentler than other; and at every putting-by mine honest neighbours shouted.

Cassius. Who offer'd him the crown?

Casca. Why, Antony.

Brutus. Tell us the manner of it, gentle Casca.

Casca. I can as well be hang'd, as tell the manner of it: it was mere foolery, I did not mark it. I saw Mark Antony offer him a crown;—yet 'twas not a crown neither, 'twas one of these coronets;—and, as I told you, he put it by once; but, for all that, to my thinking, he would fain have had it. Then he offer'd it to him again; then he put it by again; but, to my thinking, he was very loath to lay his fingers off it. And then he offer'd it the third time; he put it the third time by: and still as he refus'd it, the rabblement shouted, and clapp'd their chopp'd hands, and threw up their sweaty nightcaps, and utter'd such a deal of stinking breath because Cæsar refus'd the crown, that it had almost chok'd Cæsar; for he swooned, and fell down at it. And, for mine own part, I durst not laugh, for fear of opening my lips, and receiving the bad air.

Cassius. But, soft, I pray you. What! did Cæsar swoon?

Casca. He fell down in the market-place, and foam'd at mouth, and was speechless.

Brutus. 'Tis very like: he hath the falling sickness.

Cassius. No, Cæsar hath it not; but you and I, And honest Casca, we have the falling sickness.

Casca. I know not what you mean by that; but I am sure Cæsar fell down. If the tag-rag people did not clap him, and hiss him, according as he pleas'd and displeas'd them, as they use to do the players in the theatre, I am no true man.

Brutus. What said he, when he came unto himself?

Casca. Marry, before he fell down, when he perceiv'd the common herd was glad he refus'd the crown, he pluck'd me ope his doublet, and offer'd them his throat to cut.—An I had

been a man of any occupation, if I would not have taken him
at a word, I would I might go to hell among the rogues. And
so he fell. When he came to himself again, he said, if he had
done or said anything amiss, he desir'd their worships to think
it was his infirmity. Three or four wenches, where I stood,
cried, "Alas, good soul!"—and forgave him with all their
hearts. But there's no heed to be taken of them: if Cæsar
had stabb'd their mothers, they would have done no less.

Brutus. And after that he came thus sad away?

Casca. Ay.

Cassius. Did Cicero say anything?

Casca. Ay, he spoke Greek.

Cassius. To what effect?

Casca. Nay, an I tell you that, I'll ne'er look you i' th' face
again. But those that understood him smil'd at one another,
and shook their heads; but, for my own part, it was Greek to
me. I could tell you more news too: Marullus and Flavius,
for pulling scarfs off Cæsar's images, are put to silence. Fare
you well. There was more foolery yet, if I could remember it.

Cassius. Will you sup with me to-night, Casca?

Casca. No, I am promis'd forth.

Cassius. Will you dine with me to-morrow?

Casca. Ay, if I be alive, and your mind hold, and your dinner worth the eating.

Cassius. Good; I will expect you.

Casca. Do so. Farewell, both. [*Exit Casca.*

Brutus. What a blunt fellow is this grown to be!
He was quick mettle when he went to school.

Cassius. So is he now, in execution
Of any bold or noble enterprise,
However he puts on this tardy form.
This rudeness is a sauce to his good wit,
Which gives men stomach to digest his words
With better appetite.

Brutus. And so'it is.   For this time I will leave you :
To-morrow if you please to speak with me,
I will come home to you ; or, if you will,
Come home to me, and I will wait for you.
   Cassius. I will do so :—till then, think of the world.
[*Exit Brutus.*

Well, Brutus, thou art noble ; yet, I see,
Thy honourable metal may be wrought
From that it is dispos'd : therefore it is meet
That noble minds keep ever with their likes ;
For who so firm, that cannot be seduc'd ?
Cæsar doth bear me hard, but he loves Brutus :
If I were Brutus now, and he were Cassius,
He should not humour me.   I'will this night, ,
In several hands, in at his windows throw,
As if they came from several citizens,
Writings, all tending to the great opinion
That Rome holds of his name ; wherein obscurely
Cæsar's ambition shall be glanced at :
And, after this, let Cæsar seat him sure ;
For we will shake him, or worse days endure.   [*Exit.*

SCENE III.   *The same.   A Street.*

Thunder and lightning.   Enter, from opposite sides, CASCA,
with his sword drawn, and CICERO.

Cicero. Good even, Casca.   Brought you Cæsar home ?
Why are you breathless ? and why stare you so ?
   Casca. Are not you mov'd, when all the sway of earth
Shakes, like a thing unfirm ?   O Cicero,
I have seen tempests, when the scolding winds
Have riv'd the knotty oaks ; and I have seen
Th' ambitious ocean swell, and rage, and foam,
To be exalted with the threatening clouds :
But never till to-night, never till now,

D

Did I go through a tempest dropping fire.
Either there is a civil strife in heaven,
Or else the world, too saucy with the gods,
Incenses them to send destruction.
    Cicero. Why, saw you anything more wonderful?
    Casca. A common slave (you know him well by sight)
Held up his left hand, which did flame and burn
Like twenty torches join'd ; and yet his hand,
Not sensible of fire, remain'd unscorch'd.
Besides (I have not since put up my sword),
Against the Capitol I met a lion,
Who glar'd upon me, and went surly by,
Without annoying me : and there were drawn
Upon a heap a hundred ghastly women,
Transformed with their fear ; who swore they saw
Men all in fire walk up and down the streets.
And yesterday the bird of night did sit,
Even at noonday, upon the market-place,
Hooting and shrieking. When these prodigies
Do so conjointly meet, let not men say,
These are their reasons,—they are natural ;
For, I believe, they are portentous things
Unto the climate that they point upon.
    Cicero. Indeed, it is a strange-disposed time :
But men may construe things after their fashion,
Clean from the purpose of the things themselves.
Comes Cæsar to the Capitol to-morrow?
    Casca. He doth ; for he did bid Antonius
Send word to you, he would be there to-morrow.
    Cicero. Good night, then, Casca : this disturbed sky
Is not to walk in.
    Casca.   Farewell, Cicero.   [*Exit Cicero.*

Enter CASSIUS.

Cassius. Who's there?

Casca.   A Roman.

Cassius.   Casca, by your voice.

Casca. Your ear is good. Cassius, what night is this?

Cassius. A very pleasing night to honest men.

Casca. Who ever knew the heavens menace so?

Cassius. Those that have known the earth so full of faults.
For my part, I have walk'd about the streets,
Submitting me unto the perilous night;
And, thus unbraced, Casca, as you see,
Have bar'd my bosom to the thunder-stone:
And, when the cross blue lightning seem'd to open
The breast of heaven, I did present myself
Even in the aim and very flash of it.

Casca. But wherefore did you so much tempt the heavens?
It is the part of men to fear and tremble,
When the most mighty gods by tokens send
Such dreadful heralds to astonish us.

Cassius. You are dull, Casca; and those sparks of life
That should be in a Roman you do want,
Or else you use not. You look pale, and gaze,
And put on fear, and case yourself in wonder,
To see the strange impatience of the heavens:
But if you would consider the true cause,
Why all these fires, why all these gliding ghosts,
Why birds, and beasts, from quality and kind;
Why old men fool, and children calculate;
Why all these things change from their ordinance,
Their natures, and pre-formed faculties,
To monstrous quality; why, you shall find,
That heaven hath infus'd them with these spirits,
To make them instruments of fear and warning
Unto some monstrous state. Now could I, Casca,

Name to thee a man most like this dreadful night;
That thunders, lightens, opens graves, and roars
As doth the lion in the Capitol:
A man no mightier than thyself or me,
In personal action; yet prodigious grown,
And fearful, as these strange eruptions are.

    Casca. 'Tis Cæsar that you mean: is it not, Cassius?

    Cassius. Let it be who it is: for Romans now
Have thews and limbs like to their ancestors,
But, woe the while! our fathers' minds are dead,
And we are govern'd with our mothers' spirits;
Our yoke and sufferance show us womanish.

    Casca. Indeed, they say, the senators to-morrow
Mean to establish Cæsar as a king:
And he shall wear his crown by sea and land,
In every place, save here in Italy.

    Cassius. I know where I will wear this dagger, then;
Cassius from bondage will deliver Cassius:
Therein, ye gods, you make the weak most strong;
Therein, ye gods, you tyrants do defeat.
Nor stony tower, nor walls of beaten brass,
Nor airless dungeon, nor strong links of iron,
Can be retentive to the strength of spirit;
But life, being weary of these worldly bars,
Never lacks power to dismiss itself.
If I know this, know all the world besides,
That part of tyranny that I do bear
I can shake off at pleasure.   [*Thunder still.*

    Casca.   So can I:
So every bondman in his own hand bears
The power to cancel his captivity.

    Cassius. And why should Cæsar be a tyrant, then?
Poor man! I know, he would not be a wolf,
But that he sees the Romans are but sheep:
He were no lion, were not Romans hinds.

Those that with haste will make a mighty fire
Begin it with weak straws : what trash is Rome,
What rubbish, and what offal, when it serves
For the base matter to illuminate
So vile a thing as Cæsar ! But, O, grief !
Where hast thou led me? I, perhaps, speak this
Before a willing bondman : then I know
My answer must be made. But I am arm'd,
And dangers are to me indifferent.

    Casca. You speak to Casca ; and to such a man
That is no fleering tell-tale. Hold, my hand :
Be factious for redress of all these griefs,
And I will set this foot of mine as far
As who goes farthest.

    Cassius.   There's a bargain made.
Now know you, Casca, I have mov'd already
Some certain of the noblest-minded Romans
To undergo with me an enterprise
Of honourable-dangerous consequence ;
And I do know by this they stay for me
In Pompey's porch: for now, this fearful night,
There is no stir or walking in the streets ;
And the complexion of the element
In favour 's like the work we have in hand,
Most bloody, fiery, and most terrible.

Enter CINNA.

    Casca. Stand close a while, for here comes one in haste.
    Cassius. 'Tis Cinna ; I do know him by his gait :
He is a friend.—Cinna, where haste you so?
    Cinna. To find out you. Who's that? Metellus Cimber?
    Cassius. No, it is Casca ; one incorporate
To our attempt. Am I not staid for, Cinna?
    Cinna. I am glad on't. What a fearful night is this !
There's two or three of us have seen strange sights.

Cassius. Am I not staid for? Tell me

Cinna.   Yes, you are.—
O Cassius, if you could
But win the noble Brutus to our party!

Cassius. Be you content. Good Cinna, take this paper,
And look you lay it in the prætor's chair,
Where Brutus may but find it; and throw this
In at his window; set this up with wax
Upon old Brutus' statue: all this done,
Repair to Pompey's porch, where you shall find us.
Is Decius Brutus and Trebonius there?

Cinna. All but Metellus Cimber; and he's gone
To seek you at your house. Well, I will hie,
And so bestow these papers as you bade me.

Cassius. That done, repair to Pompey's theatre.

[*Exit Cinna.*

Come, Casca, you and I will yet, ere day,
See Brutus at his house: three parts of him
Is ours already; and the man entire,
Upon the next encounter, yields him ours.

Casca. O, he sits high in all the people's hearts;
And that which would appear offence in us,
His countenance, like richest alchemy,
Will change to virtue, and to worthiness.

Cassius. Him, and his worth, and our great need of him,
You have right well conceited. Let us go,
For it is after midnight; and, ere day,
We will awake him, and be sure of him.   [*Exeunt.*

COIN OF CÆSAR.

ACT II.

SCENE I. *The same. Brutus's Orchard.*

Enter BRUTUS.

Brutus. What, Lucius! ho!
I cannot, by the progress of the stars,
Give guess how near to day.—Lucius, I say :—
I would it were my fault to sleep so soundly.—
When, Lucius, when? Awake, I say! What, Lucius!

Enter LUCIUS.

Lucius. Call'd you, my lord?
Brutus. Get me a taper in my study, Lucius :
When it is lighted, come and call me here.
Lucius. I will, my lord. [*Exit.*
Brutus. It must be by his death : and, for my part,

I know no personal cause to spurn at him,
But for the general.   He would be crown'd :—
How that might change his nature, there's the question.
It is the bright day that brings forth the adder,
And that craves wary walking.   Crown him ?—that ;—
And then, I grant, we put a sting in him,
That at his will he may do danger with.
The abuse of greatness is, when it disjoins
Remorse from power ; and, to speak truth of Cæsar,
I have not known when his affections sway'd
More than his reason.   But 'tis a common proof,
That lowliness is young ambition's ladder,
Whereto the climber-upward turns his face ;
But when he once attains the upmost round,
He then unto the ladder turns his back,
Looks in the clouds, scorning the base degrees
By which he did ascend.   So Cæsar may.
Then, lest he may, prevent.   And, since the quarrel
Will bear no colour for the thing he is,
Fashion it thus : that what he is, augmented,
Would run to these and these extremities ;
And therefore think him as a serpent's egg,
Which, hatch'd, would, as his kind, grow mischievous,
And kill him in the shell.

Enter LUCIUS.

Lucius. The taper burneth in your closet, sir.
Searching the window for a flint, I found
This paper, thus seal'd up ; and, I am sure,
It did not lie there when I went to bed. [*Gives him the letter.*
    Brutus. Get you to bed again ; it is not day.
Is not to-morrow, boy, the ides of March ?
    Lucius. I know not, sir.
    Brutus. Look in the calendar, and bring me word.
    Lucius. I will, sir.   [*Exit.*

Brutus. The exhalations, whizzing in the air,
Give so much light, that I may read by them.
                . [*Opens the letter, and reads.*
"Brutus, thou sleep'st; awake, and see thyself.
Shall Rome, etc. Speak, strike, redress!"—
"Brutus, thou sleep'st; awake!"
Such instigations have been often dropp'd
Where I have took them up.
"Shall Rome, etc." Thus must I piece it out :—
Shall Rome stand under one man's awe? What! Rome?
My ancestors did from the streets of Rome
The Tarquin drive, when he was call'd a king.
"Speak, strike, redress!" Am I entreated
To speak, and strike? O Rome! I make thee promise,
If the redress will follow, thou receivest
Thy full petition at the hand of Brutus.

Enter LUCIUS.

Lucius. Sir, March is wasted fifteen days.
                  [*Knocking within.*
Brutus. 'Tis good. Go to the gate; somebody knocks.
                  [*Exit Lucius.*
Since Cassius first did whet me against Cæsar,
I have not slept.
Between the acting of a dreadful thing
And the first motion, all the interim is
Like a phantasma, or a hideous dream :
The genius and the mortal instruments
Are then in council; and the state of man,
Like to a little kingdom, suffers then
The nature of an insurrection.

Enter LUCIUS.

Lucius. Sir, 'tis your brother Cassius at the door,
Who doth desire to see you.

Brutus. Is he alone?

Lucius. No, sir; there are more with him.

Brutus. Do you know them?

Lucius. No, sir; their hats are pluck'd about their ears,
And half their faces buried in their cloaks,
That by no means I may discover them
By any mark of favour.

   Brutus.   Let 'em enter.   [*Exit Lucius.*
They are the faction.   O Conspiracy!
Sham'st thou to shew thy dangerous brow by night,
When evils are most free?   O, then, by day
Where wilt thou find a cavern dark enough
To mask thy monstrous visage?   Seek none, Conspiracy;
Hide it in smiles and affability:
For, if thou path, thy native semblance on,
Not Erebus itself were dim enough
To hide thee from prevention.

Enter CASSIUS, CASCA, DECIUS, CINNA, METELLUS CIMBER,
                 and TREBONIUS.

Cassius. I think we are too bold upon your rest:
Good morrow, Brutus; do we trouble you?

Brutus. I have been up this hour; awake, all night.
Know I these men that come along with you?

Cassius. Yes, every man of them; and no man here
But honours you; and every one doth wish
You had but that opinion of yourself
Which every noble Roman bears of you.
This is Trebonius.

   Brutus.   He is welcome hither.

Cassius. This, Decius Brutus.

   Brutus.   He is welcome too.

Cassius. This, Casca; this, Cinna; and this, Metellus Cimber.

Brutus. They are all welcome.

What watchful cares do interpose themselves
Betwixt your eyes and night?
   Cassius. Shall I entreat a word.   [*They whisper.*
   Decius. Here lies the east: doth not the day break here?
   Casca. No.
   Cinna. O, pardon, sir, it doth; and yon grey lines,
That fret the clouds, are messengers of day.
   Casca. You shall confess that you are both deceiv'd.
Here, as I point my sword, the sun arises;
Which is a great way growing on the south,
Weighing the youthful season of the year.
Some two months hence, up higher toward the north
He first presents his fire; and the high east
Stands, as the Capitol, directly here.
   Brutus. Give me your hands all over, one by one.
   Cassius. And let us swear our resolution.
   Brutus. No, not an oath: if not the face of men
The sufferance of our souls, the time's abuse,—
If these be motives weak, break off betimes,
And every man hence to his idle bed;
So let high-sighted tyranny range on,
Till each man drop by lottery. But if these,
As I am sure they do, bear fire enough
To kindle cowards, and to steel with valour
The melting spirits of women; then, countrymen,
What need we any spur, but our own cause,
To prick us to redress? what other bond,
Than secret Romans, that have spoke the word,
And will not palter? and what other oath,
Than honesty to honesty engag'd,
That this shall be, or we will fall for it;
Swear priests, and cowards, and men cautelous,
Old feeble carrions, and such suffering souls
That welcome wrongs; unto bad causes swear
Such creatures as men doubt; but do not stain

The even virtue of our enterprise,
Nor th' insuppressive metal of our spirits,
To think that or our cause or. our performance
Did need an oath ; when every drop of blood,
That every Roman bears, and nobly bears,
Is guilty of a several bastardy,
If he do break the smallest particle
Of any promise that hath pass'd from him.

Cassius. But what of Cicero ? Shall we sound him?
I think he will stand very strong with us.

Casca. Let us not leave him out.

Cinna.   No, by no means.

Metellus. O, let us have him ; for his silver hairs
Will purchase us a good opinion,
And buy men's voices to commend our deeds :
It shall be said, his judgment rul'd our hands ;
Our youths and wildness shall no whit appear,
But all be buried in his gravity.

Brutus. O, name him not: let us not break with him ;
For he will never follow anything
That other men begin.

Cassius.   Then leave him out.

Casca. Indeed, he is not fit.

Decius. Shall no man else be touch'd but only Cæsar?

Cassius. Decius, well urg'd.—I think it is not meet,
Mark Antony, so well belov'd of Cæsar,
Should outlive Cæsar. We shall find of him
A shrewd contriver ; and, you know, his means,
If he improve them, may well stretch so far
As to annoy us all ; which to prevent,
Let Antony and Cæsar fall together.

Brutus. Our course will seem too bloody, Caius Cassius,
To cut the head off, and then hack the limbs,
Like wrath in death, and envy afterwards ;
For Antony is but a limb of Cæsar.

Let us be sacrificers, but not butchers, Caius.
We all stand up against the spirit of Cæsar,
And in the spirit of men there is no blood :
O, that we then could come by Cæsar's spirit,
And not dismember Cæsar ! But, alas,
Cæsar must bleed for it ! And, gentle friends,
Let's kill him boldly, but not wrathfully ;
Let's carve him as a dish fit for the gods,
Not hew him as a carcass fit for hounds :
And let our hearts, as subtle masters do,
Stir up their servants to an act of rage,
And after seem to chide 'em. This shall make
Our purpose necessary, and not envious :
Which so appearing to the common eyes,
We shall be call'd purgers, not murderers.
And for Mark Antony, think not of him ;
For he can do no more than Cæsar's arm,
When Cæsar's head is off.
 Cassius.   Yet I fear him :
For in the ingrafted love he bears to Cæsar—
 Brutus. Alas, good Cassius, do not think of him :
If he love Cæsar, all that he can do
Is to himself,—take thought, and die for Cæsar :
And that were much he should ; for he is given
To sports, to wildness, and much company.
 Trebonius. There is no fear in him ; let him not die ;
For he will live, and laugh at this hereafter. [*Clock strikes.*
 Brutus. Peace ! count the clock.
 Cassius.   The clock hath stricken three.
 Trebonius. 'Tis time to part.
 Cassius.   But it is doubtful yet
Whether Cæsar will come forth to-day, or no :
For he is superstitious grown of late ;
Quite from the main opinion he held once
Of fantasy, of dreams, and ceremonies.

It may be, these apparent prodigies,
The unaccustom'd terror of this night,
And the persuasion of his augurers,
May hold him from the Capitol to-day.

Decius. Never fear that. If he be so resolv'd,
I can o'ersway him : for he loves to hear
That unicorns may be betray'd with trees,
And bears with glasses, elephants with holes,
Lions with toils, and men with flatterers ;
But, when I tell him he hates flatterers,
He says he does, being then most flattered.
Let me work ;
For I can give his humour the true bent,
And I will bring him to the Capitol.

Cassius. Nay, we will all of us be there to fetch him.

Brutus. By the eighth hour : is that the uttermost?

Cinna. Be that the uttermost, and fail not then.

Metellus. Caius Ligarius doth bear Cæsar hard,
Who rated him for speaking well of Pompey ;
I wonder none of you have thought of him.

Brutus. Now, good Metellus, go along by him :
He loves me well, and I have given him reasons ;
Send him but hither, and I'll fashion him.

Cassius. The morning comes upon's : we'll leave you, Bru-
          tus :—
And, friends, disperse yourselves ; but all remember
What you have said, and show yourselves true Romans.

Brutus. Good gentlemen, look fresh and merrily.
Let not our looks put on our purposes ;
But bear it as our Roman actors do,
With untir'd spirits, and formal constancy :
And so, good morrow to you every one.

                              [*Exeunt all but Brutus.*

Boy! Lucius !—Fast asleep? It is no matter ;
Enjoy the honey-heavy dew of slumber :

Thou hast no figures, nor no fantasies,
Which busy care draws in the brains of men ;
Therefore thou sleep'st so sound.

Enter PORTIA.

Portia. Brutus, my lord !
Brutus. Portia, what mean you ? Wherefore rise you now ?
It is not for your health, thus to commit
Your weak condition to the raw cold morning.
Portia. Nor for yours neither. You've ungently, Brutus,
Stole from my bed : and yesternight, at supper,
You suddenly arose, and walk'd about,
Musing, and sighing, with your arms across :
And, when I ask'd you what the matter was,
You star'd upon me with ungentle looks.
I urg'd you further ; then you scratch'd your head,
And too impatiently stamp'd with your foot :
Yet I insisted, yet you answer'd not ;
But, with an angry wafture of your hand,
Gave sign for me to leave you. So I did ;
Fearing to strengthen that impatience,
Which seemed too much enkindled ; and, withal,
Hoping it was but an effect of humour,
Which sometime hath his hour with every man.
It will not let you eat, nor talk, nor sleep ;
And, could it work so much upon your shape,
As it hath much prevail'd on your condition,
I should not know you, Brutus. Dear my lord,
Make me acquainted with your cause of grief.
Brutus. I am not well in health, and that is all.
Portia. Brutus is wise, and, were he not in health,
He would embrace the means to come by it.
Brutus. Why, so I do.—Good Portia, go to bed.
Portia. Is Brutus sick ? and is it physical
To walk unbraced, and suck up the humours

Of the dank morning?   What! is Brutus sick,
And will he steal out of his wholesome bed,
To dare the vile contagion of the night,
And tempt the rheumy and unpurged air
To add unto his sickness?   No, my Brutus ;
You have some sick offence within your mind,
Which, by the right and virtue of my place,
I ought to know of: and, upon my knees,
I charm you, by my once commended beauty,
By all your vows of love, and that great vow,
Which did incorporate and make us one,
That you unfold to me, yourself, your half,
Why you are heavy ; and what men to-night
Have had resort to you : for here have been
Some six or seven, who did hide their faces
Even from darkness.

Brutus.   Kneel not, gentle Portia.

Portia. I should not need, if you were gentle Brutus.
Within the bond of marriage, tell me, Brutus,
Is it excepted, I should know no secrets
That appertain to you?   Am I yourself
But, as it were, in sort, or limitation ;
To keep with you at meals, comfort your bed,
And talk to you sometimes?   Dwell I but in the suburbs
Of your good pleasure?   If it be no more,
Portia is Brutus' harlot, not his wife.

Brutus. You are my true and honourable wife ;
As dear to me as are the ruddy drops
That visit my sad heart.

Portia. If this were true, then should I know this secret.
I grant, I am a woman ; but, withal,
A woman that Lord Brutus took to wife :
I grant, I am a woman ; but, withal,
A woman well reputed, Cato's daughter.
Think you, I am no stronger than my sex,

Being so father'd, and so husbanded?
Tell me your counsels, I will not disclose 'em:
I have made strong proof of my constancy,
Giving myself a voluntary wound
Here, in the thigh: can I bear that with patience,
And not my husband's secrets?
    Brutus.   O ye gods,
Render me worthy of this noble wife!   [*Knocking within.*
Hark, hark! one knocks. Portia, go in a while;
And by and by thy bosom shall partake
The secrets of my heart.
All my engagements I will construe to thee,
All the charactery of my sad brows.
Leave me with haste.—   [*Exit Portia.*

   Enter LUCIUS *and* LIGARIUS.

           Lucius, who's that knocks?
Lucius. Here is a sick man that would speak with you.
Brutus. Caius Ligarius, that Metellus spake of.—
Boy, stand aside.—Caius Ligarius! how?
Ligarius. Vouchsafe good morrow from a feeble tongue.
Brutus. O, what a time have you chose out, brave Caius,
To wear a kerchief! Would you were not sick!
Ligarius. I am not sick, if Brutus have in hand
Any exploit worthy the name of honour.
Brutus. Such an exploit have I in hand, Ligarius,
Had you a healthful ear to hear of it.
Ligarius. By all the gods that Romans bow before,
I here discard my sickness. Soul of Rome!
Brave son, deriv'd from honourable loins!
Thou, like an exorcist, hast conjur'd up
My mortified spirit. Now bid me run,
And I will strive with things impossible,
Yea, get the better of them. What's to do?
   Brutus. A piece of work that will make sick men whole.
           E

Ligarius. But are not some whole that we must make sick?
Brutus. That must we also.   What it is, my Caius,
I shall unfold to thee, as we are going
To whom it must be done.
        Ligarius.   Set on your foot,
And with a heart new-fir'd I follow you,
To do I know not what ; but it sufficeth
That Brutus leads me on.
        Brutus.   Follow me, then.   [*Exeunt.*

        SCENE II.   *The same.   A Room in Cæsar's Palace.*

Thunder and lightning.   Enter CÆSAR *in his night-gown.*

  Cæsar. Nor heaven, nor earth, have been at peace to-night:
Thrice hath Calphurnia in her sleep cried out,
"Help, ho! they murder Cæsar!"—Who's within?

                Enter a Servant.

Servant. My lord?
Cæsar. Go bid the priests do present sacrifice,
And bring me their opinions of success.
Servant. I will, my lord.   [*Exit.*

                Enter CALPHURNIA.

Calphurnia. What mean you, Cæsar?   Think you to walk
        forth?
You shall not stir out of your house to-day.
Cæsar. Cæsar shall forth.   The things that threaten'd me
Ne'er look'd but on my back ; when they shall see
The face of Cæsar, they are vanished.
Calphurnia. Cæsar, I never stood on ceremonies,
Yet now they fright me.   There is one within,
Besides the things that we have heard and seen,
Recounts most horrid sights seen by the watch.
A lioness hath whelped in the streets ;

And graves have yawn'd, and yielded up their dead :
Fierce fiery warriors fought upon the clouds,
In ranks and squadrons, and right form of war,
Which drizzled blood upon the Capitol :
The noise of battle hurtled in the air,
Horses did neigh, and dying men did groan ;
And ghosts did shriek and squeal about the streets.
O Cæsar ! these things are beyond all use,
And I do fear them.

    Cæsar.   What can be avoided,
Whose end .s purpos'd by the mighty gods?
Yet Cæsar shall go forth ; for these predictions
Are to the world in general, as to Cæsar.

    Calphurnia. When beggars die, there are no comets seen ;
The heavens themselves blaze forth the death of princes.

    Cæsar. Cowards die many times before their deaths ;
The valiant never taste of death but once.
Of all the wonders that I yet have heard,
It seems to me most strange that men should fear ;
Seeing that death, a necessary end,
Will come when it will come.

Enter a Servant.

                What say the augurers?
    Servant. They would not have you to stir forth to-day.
Plucking the entrails of an offering forth,
They could not find a heart within the beast.

    Cæsar. The gods do this in shame of cowardice :
Cæsar should be a beast without a heart,
If he should stay at home to-day for fear.
No, Cæsar shall not. Danger knows full well
That Cæsar is more dangerous than he.
We are two lions litter'd in one day,
And I the elder and more terrible ;
And Cæsar shall go forth.

Calphurnia.			Alas ! my lord,
Your wisdom is consum'd in confidence.
Do not go forth to-day.   Call it my fear,
That keeps you in the house, and not your own.
We'll send Mark Antony to the senate-house ;
And he shall say you are not well to-day :
Let me, upon my knee, prevail in this.
	Cæsar. Mark Antony shall say I am not well ;
And, for thy humour, I will stay at home.

Enter DECIUS.

Here's Decius Brutus, he shall tell them so.
	Decius. Cæsar, all hail ! Good morrow, worthy Cæsar :
I come to fetch you to the senate-house.
	Cæsar. And you are come in very happy time
To bear my greeting to the senators,
And tell them that I will not come to-day.
Cannot, is false ; and that I dare not, falser :
I will not come to-day.   Tell them so, Decius.
	Calphurnia. Say, he is sick.
	Cæsar.				Shall Cæsar send a lie ?
Have I in conquest stretch'd mine arm so far,
To be afeard to tell grey-beards the truth ?
Decius, go tell them Cæsar will not come.
	Decius. Most mighty Cæsar, let me know some cause,
Lest I be laugh'd at when I tell them so.
	Cæsar. The cause is in my will ; I will not come :
That is enough to satisfy the senate.
But, for your private satisfaction,
Because I love you, I will let you know.
Calphurnia here, my wife, stays me at home :
She dream'd to-night she saw my statua,
Which, like a fountain with an hundred spouts,
Did run pure blood ; and many lusty Romans
Came smiling, and did bathe their hands in it.

And these does she apply for warnings and portents,
And evils imminent; and on her knee
Hath begg'd that I will stay at home to-day.

Decius. This dream is all amiss interpreted:
It was a vision fair and fortunate.
Your statue spouting blood in many pipes,
In which so many smiling Romans bath'd,
Signifies that from you great Rome shall suck
Reviving blood; and that great men shall press
For tinctures, stains, relics, and cognizance.
This by Calphurnia's dream is signified.

Cæsar. And this way have you well expounded it.

Decius. I have, when you have heard what I can say:
And know it now. The senate have concluded
To give this day a crown to mighty Cæsar.
If you shall send them word you will not come,
Their minds may change. Besides, it were a mock
Apt to be render'd, for some one to say,
"Break up the senate till another time,
When Cæsar's wife shall meet with better dreams."
If Cæsar hide himself, shall they not whisper,
"Lo, Cæsar is afraid?"
Pardon me, Cæsar; for my dear, dear love
To your proceeding bids me tell you this;
And reason to my love is liable.

Cæsar. How foolish do your fears seem now, Calphurnia!
I am ashamed I did yield to them.—
Give me my robe, for I will go:—

Enter PUBLIUS, BRUTUS, LIGARIUS, METELLUS, CASCA, TREBONIUS, *and* CINNA.

And look where Publius is come to fetch me.

Publius. Good morrow, Cæsar.

Cæsar.   Welcome, Publius.—
What, Brutus, are you stirr'd so early too?—

Good morrow, Casca.—Caius Ligarius,
Cæsar was ne'er so much your enemy,
As that same ague which hath made you lean.—
What is't o'clock?
   Brutus.   Cæsar, 'tis strucken eight.
   Cæsar. I thank you for your pains and courtesy.

Enter ANTONY.

See! Antony, that revels long o' nights,
Is notwithstanding up.—Good morrow, Antony.
   Antony. So to most noble Cæsar.
   Cæsar.   Bid them prepare within :—
I am to blame to be thus waited for.—
Now, Cinna.—Now, Metellus.—What, Trebonius!
I have an hour's talk in store for you.
Remember that you call on me to-day :
Be near me, that I may remember you.
   Trebonius. Cæsar, I will :—[*Aside*] and so near will I be,
That your best friends shall wish I had been further.
   Cæsar. Good friends, go in, and taste some wine with me ;
And we, like friends, will straightway go together.
   Brutus [*Aside*]. That every like is not the same, O Cæsar,
The heart of Brutus yearns to think upon !   [*Exeunt.*

SCENE III. *The same. A Street near the Capitol.*

●   *Enter* ARTEMIDORUS, *reading a Paper.*

Artemidorus. *Cæsar, beware of Brutus ; take heed of Cassius ; come not near Casca ; have an eye to Cinna ; trust not Trebonius ; mark well Metellus Cimber ; Decius Brutus loves thee not; thou hast wrong'd Caius Ligarius. There is but one mind in all these men, and it is bent against Cæsar. If thou beest not immortal, look about you : security gives way to conspiracy. The mighty gods defend thee ! Thy lover,*
                                 ARTEMIDORUS.

Here will I stand till Cæsar pass along,
And as a suitor will I give him this.
My heart laments, that virtue cannot live
Out of the teeth of emulation.
If thou read this, O Cæsar, thou mayst live ;
If not, the fates with traitors do contrive.   [*Exit.*

SCENE IV* *The same. Another part of the same Street,*
before the house of Brutus.

Enter PORTIA *and* LUCIUS.

Portia. I prithee, boy, run to the senate-house ;
Stay not to answer me, but get thee gone.
Why dost thou stay?
Lucius.   To know my errand, madam.
Portia. I would have had thee there, and here again,
Ere I can tell thee what thou shouldst do there.—
O constancy, be strong upon my side!
Set a huge mountain 'tween my heart and tongue!
I have a man's mind, but a woman's might.
How hard it is for women to keep counsel!—
Art thou here yet?   •
Lucius.   Madam, what should I do?
Run to the Capitol, and nothing else?
And so return to you, and nothing else?
Portia. Yes, bring me word, boy, if thy lord look well,
For he went sickly forth : and take good note
What Cæsar doth, what suitors press to him.
Hark, boy! what noise is that?
Lucius. I hear none, madam.
Portia.   Prithee, listen well ;
I heard a bustling rumour, like a fray,
And the wind brings it from the Capitol.
Lucius. Sooth, madam, I hear nothing.

Enter the Soothsayer.

Portia. Come hither, fellow. Which way hast thou been ?
Soothsayer. At mine own house, good lady.
Portia.   What is't o'clock ?
Soothsayer. About the ninth hour, lady.
Portia. Is Cæsar yet gone to the Capitol ?
Soothsayer. Madam, not yet : I go to take my stand,
To see him pass on to the Capitol.
    Portia. Thou hast some suit to Cæsar, hast thou not :
    Soothsayer. That I have, lady : if it will please Cæsar
To be so good to Cæsar as to hear me,
I shall beseech him to befriend himself.
    Portia. Why, know'st thou any harm's intended towards
      him ?
    Soothsayer. None that I know will be, much that I fear
      may chance.
Good morrow to you.   Here the street is narrow :
The throng that follows Cæsar at the heels,
Of senators, of prætors, common suitors,
Will crowd a feeble man almost to death :
I'll get me to a pláce more void, and there
Speak to great Cæsar as he comes along.
    Portia. I must go in.—Ay me ! how weak a thing
The heart of woman is !   O Brutus !
The heavens speed thee in thine enterprise !—
Sure, the boy heard me :—Brutus hath a suit,
That Cæsar will not grant.—O, I grow faint :—
Run, Lucius, and commend me to my lord ;
Say, I am merry : come to me again,
And bring me word what he doth say to thee.   [*Exeunt.*

ACT III.

SCENE I. *The same. The Capitol; the Senate sitting.*

A crowd of People in the Street leading to the Capitol; among them ARTEMIDORUS *and the* Soothsayer. *Flourish. Enter* CÆSAR, BRUTUS, CASSIUS, CASCA, DECIUS, METELLUS, TRE-· BONIUS, CINNA, ANTONY, LEPIDUS, POPILIUS, PUBLIUS, *and others.*

Cæsar. The ides of March are come.

Soothsayer. Ay, Cæsar ; but not gone.

Artemidorus. Hail, Cæsar ! Read this schedule.

Decius. Trebonius doth desire you to o'er-read,
At your best leisure, this his humble suit.

Artemidorus. O, Cæsar, read mine first ; for mine's a suit
That touches Cæsar nearer. Read it, great Cæsar.

Cæsar. What touches us ourself shall be last serv'd.

Artemidorus. Delay not, Cæsar ; read it instantly.

Cæsar. What ! is the fellow mad ?

Publius. Sirrah, give place.

Cassius. What ! urge you your petitions in the street ?
Come to the Capitol.

*Cæsar enters the Capitol, the rest following. All the
Senators rise.*

Popilius. I wish your enterprise to-day may thrive.

Cassius. What enterprise, Popilius ?

Popilius. Fare you well. [*Advances to Cæsar.*

Brutus. What said Popilius Lena ?

Cassius. He wish'd to-day our enterprise might thrive.
fear our purpose is discovered.

Brutus. Look, how he makes to Cæsar : mark him.

Cassius. Casca, be sudden, for we fear prevention.—
Brutus, what shall be done ? If this be known,
Cassius or Cæsar never shall turn back,
For I will slay myself.

Brutus. Cassius, be constant :
Popilius Lena speaks not of our purposes ;
For, look, he smiles, and Cæsar doth not change.

Cassius. Trebonius knows his time ; for, look you, Brutus,
He draws Mark Antony out of the way.

[*Exeunt Antony and Trebonius. Cæsar and the Senators take their seats.*

Decius. Where is Metellus Cimber ? Let him go,
And presently prefer his suit to Cæsar.

Brutus. He is address'd : press near and second him.
Cinna. Casca, you are the first that rears your hand.
Casca. Are we all ready?
Cæsar.   What is now amiss,
That Cæsar, and his senate, must redress?
Metellus. Most high, most mighty, and most puissant Cæsar,
Metellus Cimber throws before thy seat
An humble heart :—.   [*Kneeling.*
Cæsar.   I must prevent thee, Cimber.
These couchings, and these lowly courtesies,
Might fire the blood of ordinary men,
And turn pre-ordinance and first decree
Into the law of children. Be not fond,
To think that Cæsar bears such rebel blood,
That will be thaw'd from the true quality
With that which melteth fools ; I mean sweet words,
Low-crooked curtsies, and base spaniel fawning.
Thy brother by decree is banished ;
If thou dost bend, and pray, and fawn for him,
I spurn thee like a cur out of my way.
Know, Cæsar doth not wrong ; nor without cause
Will he be satisfied.
     Metellus. Is there no voice more worthy than my own,
To sound more sweetly in great Cæsar's ear
For the repealing of my banish'd brother?
     Brutus. I kiss thy hand, but not in flattery, Cæsar ;
Desiring thee that Publius Cimber may
Have an immediate freedom of repeal.
     Cæsar. What, Brutus !
     Cassius.   Pardon, Cæsar : Cæsar, pardon :
As low as to thy foot doth Cassius fall,
To beg enfranchisement for Publius Cimber.
     Cæsar. I could be well mov'd, if I were as you ;
If I could pray to move, prayers would move me :
But I am constant as the northern star,

Of whose true-fix'd and resting quality
There is no fellow in the firmament.
The skies are painted with unnumber'd sparks ;
They are all fire, and every one doth shine ;
But there's but one in all doth hold his place :
So, in the world ; 'tis furnish'd well with men,
And men are flesh and blood, and apprehensive ;
Yet, in the number, I do know but one .
That unassailable holds on his rank,   ·
Unshak'd of motion : and, that I am he,
Let me a little show it, even in this ;
That I was constant Cimber should be banish'd,
And constant do remain to keep him so.

    Cinna. O Cæsar !—

    Cæsar.   ·   Hence ! wilt thou lift up Olympus?

    Decius. Great Cæsar,—

    Cæsar.   Doth not Brutus bootless kneel?

    Casca. Speak, hands, for me.   ·

      [*Casca stabs Cæsar in the neck. Cæsar catches hold of
         his arm. He is then stabbed by several other Con-
         spirators, and at last by Marcus Brutus.*

    Cæsar. *Et tu, Brute.*—Then, fall, Cæsar. ·

      [*Dies. The Senators and People retire in confusion.*

    Cinna. Liberty ! Freedom ! Tyranny is dead !—
Run hence, proclaim, cry it about the streets.

    Cassius. Some to the common pulpits, and cry out,
" Liberty, freedom, and enfranchisement !"

    Brutus. People, and senators ! be not affrighted ;
Fly not ; stand still :—ambition's debt is paid.

    Casca. Go to the pulpit, Brutus.

    Decius.   And Cassius too.

    Brutus. Where's Publius?

    Cinna. Here, quite confounded with this mutiny.

    Metellus.. Stand fast together, lest some friend of Cæsar's
Should chance—

Brutus. ˙Talk not of standing.—Publius, good cheer;
There is no harm intended to ẙour person,
Nor to no Roman else: so tell them, Publius.
    Cassius. And leave us, Publius; lest that the people,
Rushing on us, should do your age some mischief.
    Brutus. Do so;—and let no man abide this deed,
But we the doers.

Enter TREBONIUS.

    Cassius. Where is Antony?
    Trebonius.   Fled to his house amaz'd.
Men, wives, and children stare, cry out, and run,
As it were doomsday.
    Brutus.   Fates! we will know your pleasures:
That we shall die, we know; 'tis but the time,
And drawing days out, that men stand upon.
    Casca. Why, he that cuts off twenty years of life
Cuts off so many years of fearing death.
    Brutus. Grant that, and then is death a benefit:
So are we Cæsar's friends, that have abridg'd
His time of fearing death.—Stoop, Romans, stoop,
And let us bathe our hands in Cæsar's blood
Up to the elbows, and besmear our swords;
Then walk we forth, even to the market-place,
And, waving our red weapons o'er our heads,
Let's all cry, Peace! Freedom! and Liberty!
    Cassius. Stoop, then, and wash.—How many ages hence,
Shall this our lofty scene be acted over
In states unborn, and accents yet unknown!
    Brutus. How many times shall Cæsar bleed in sport,
That now on Pompey's basis lies along,
No worthier than the dust!
    Cassius.   So oft as that shall be,
So often shall the knot of us be call'd
The men that gave their country liberty.

Decius. What! shall we forth?

Cassius.   Ay, every man away:
Brutus shall lead; and we will grace his heels
With the most boldest and best hearts of Rome.

Enter a Servant.

Brutus. Soft, who comes here? A friend of Antony's.

Servant. Thus, Brutus, did my master bid me kneel;
Thus did Mark Antony bid me fall down:
And, being prostrate, thus he bade me say.
Brutus is noble, wise, valiant, and honest;
Cæsar was mighty, bold, royal, and loving:
Say, I love Brutus, and I honour him;
Say, I fear'd Cæsar, honour'd him, and lov'd him.
If Brutus will vouchsafe that Antony
May safely come to him, and be resolv'd
How Cæsar hath deserv'd to lie in death,
Mark Antony shall not love Cæsar dead
So well as Brutus living; but will follow
The fortunes and affairs of noble Brutus,
Thorough the hazards of this untrod state,
With all true faith. So says my master Antony.

Brutus. Thy master is a wise and valiant Roman;
I never thought him worse.
Tell him, so please him come unto this place,
He shall be satisfied; and, by my honour,
Depart untouch'd.

Servant.   I'll fetch him presently. [*Exit Servant.*

Brutus. I know that we shall have him well to friend.

Cassius. I wish we may: but yet have I a mind
That fears him much; and my misgiving still
Falls shrewdly to the purpose.

Enter ANTONY.

Brutus. But here comes Antony.—Welcome, Mark Antony.

Antony. O mighty Cæsar! Dost thou lie so low?
Are all thy conquests, glories, triumphs, spoils,
Shrunk to this little measure? Fare thee well.—
I know not, gentlemen, what you intend,
Who else must be let blood, who else is rank:
If I myself, there is no hour so fit
As Cæsar's death's hour; nor no instrument
Of half that worth as those your swords, made rich
With the most noble blood of all this world.
I do beseech ye, if you bear me hard,
Now, whilst your purpled hands do reek and smoke,
Fulfil your pleasure. Live a thousand years,
I shall not find myself so apt to die:
No place will please me so, no mean of death,
As here, by Cæsar and by you, cut off,
The choice and master spirits of this age.

Brutus. O Antony! beg not your death of us.
Though now we must appear bloody and cruel,
As, by our hands, and this our present act,
You see we do, yet see you but our hands,
And this the bleeding business they have done.
Our hearts you see not: they are pitiful;
And pity to the general wrong of Rome
(As fire drives out fire, so pity, pity)
Hath done this deed on Cæsar. For your part,
To you our swords have leaden points, Mark Antony:
Our arms, in strength of malice, and our hearts,
Of brothers' temper, do receive you in,
With all kind love, good thoughts, and reverence.

Cassius. Your voice shall be as strong as any man's,
In the disposing of new dignities.

 Brutus. Only be patient, till we have appeas'd
The multitude, beside themselves with fear,
And then we will deliver you the cause
Why I, that did love Cæsar when I struck him,
Have thus proceeded.
  Antony.   I doubt not of your wisdom.
Let each man render me his bloody hand :
First, Marcus Brutus, will I shake with you ;—
Next, Caius Cassius, do I take your hand ;—
Now, Decius Brutus, yours ;—now yours, Metellus ;—
Yours, Cinna ;—and, my valiant Casca, yours ;—
Though last, not least in love, yours, good Trebonius.
Gentlemen all,—alas ! what shall I say ?
My credit now stands on such slippery ground,
That one of two bad ways you must conceit me
Either a coward or a flatterer.—
That I did love thee, Cæsar, O, 'tis true !
If then thy spirit look upon us now,
Shall it not grieve thee, dearer than thy death,
To see thy Antony making his peace,
Shaking the bloody fingers of thy foes,
Most noble ! in the presence of thy corse ?
Had I as many eyes as thou hast wounds,
Weeping as fast as they stream forth thy blood,
It would become me better, than to close
In terms of friendship with thine enemies.
Pardon me, Julius !—Here wast thou bay'd, brave hart ;
Here didst thou fall ; and here thy hunters stand,
Sign'd in thy spoil, and crimson'd in thy lethe.
O world ! thou wast the forest to this hart ;
And this, indeed, O world, the heart of thee.—
How like a deer, strucken by many princes,
Dost thou here lie !
  Cassius.   Mark Antony,—
  Antony. Pardon me, Caius Cassius :

The enemies of Cæsar shall say this ;
Then, in a friend, it is cold modesty.
   Cassius. I blame you not for praising Cæsar so ;
But what compact mean you to have with us?
Will you be prick'd in number of our friends ;
Or shall we on, and not depend on you?
   Antony. Therefore I took your hands ; but was, indeed,
Sway'd from the point, by looking down on Cæsar.
Friends am I with you all, and love you all ;
Upon this hope, that you shall give me reasons
Why, and wherein, Cæsar was dangerous.
   Brutus. Or else were this a savage spectacle.
Our reasons are so full of good regard,
That, were you, Antony, the son of Cæsar,
You should be satisfied.
   Antony.   That's all I seek :
And am moreover suitor that I may
Produce his body to the market-place ;
And in the pulpit, as becomes a friend,
Speak in the order of his funeral.
   Brutus. You shall, Mark Antony.
   Cassius.   Brutus, a word with you.—
[*Aside*] You know not what you do. Do not consent
That Antony speak in his funeral.
Know you how much the people may be mov'd
By that which he will utter?
   Brutus.   By your pardon ;—
I will myself into the pulpit first,
And show the reason of our Cæsar's death :
What Antony shall speak, I will protest
He speaks by leave and by permission ;
And that we are contented Cæsar shall
Have all true rites and lawful ceremonies.
It shall advantage more than do us wrong.
   Cassius. I know not what may fall ; I like it not.

Brutus. Mark Antony, here, take you Cæsar's body.
You shall not in your funeral speech blame us,
But speak all good you can devise of Cæsar ;
And say, you do't by our permission ;
Else shall you not have any hand at all
About his funeral.   And you shall speak
In the same pulpit whereto I am going,
After my speech is ended.
    Antony.   Be it so ;
I do desire no more.
    Brutus. Prepare the body, then, and follow us.

[Exeunt all but Antony.

    Antony. O, pardon me, thou bleeding piece of earth,
That I am meek and gentle with these butchers !
Thou art the ruins of the noblest man
That ever lived in the tide of times.
Woe to the hands that shed this costly blood !
Over thy wounds now do I prophesy
(Which, like dumb mouths, do ope their ruby lips
To beg the voice and utterance of my tongue) :—
A curse shall light upon the limbs of men ;
Domestic fury, and fierce civil strife,
Shall cumber all the parts of Italy :
Blood and destruction shall be so in use,
And dreadful objects so familiar,
That mothers shall but smile when they behold
Their infants quarter'd with the hands of war,
All pity chok'd with custom of fell deeds ;
And Cæsar's spirit ranging for revenge,
With Ate by his side, come hot from hell,
Shall in these confines, with a monarch's voice,
Cry "Havoc !" and let slip the dogs of war ;
That this foul deed shall smell above the earth
With carrion men groaning for burial.

Enter a Servant.

You serve Octavius Cæsar, do you not?

Servant. I do, Mark Antony.

Antony. Cæsar did write for him to come to Rome.

Servant. He did receive his letters, and is coming;
And bid me say to you, by word of mouth—
O Cæsar!—   [*Seeing the body.*

Antony. Thy heart is big; get thee apart and weep.
Passion, I see, is catching; for mine eyes,
Seeing those beads of sorrow stand in thine,
Began to water. Is thy master coming?

Servant. He lies to-night within seven leagues of Rome.

Antony. Post back with speed, and tell him what hath
    chanc'd.
Here is a mourning Rome, a dangerous Rome,
No Rome of safety for Octavius yet;
Hie hence, and tell him so. Yet, stay a while;
Thou shalt not back, till I have borne this corse
Into the market-place: there shall I try,
In my oration, how the people take
The cruel issue of these bloody men;
According to the which thou shalt discourse
To young Octavius of the state of things.
Lend me your hand.   [*Exeunt with Cæsar's body.*

SCENE II. *The same. The Forum.*

Enter BRUTUS *and* CASSIUS, *and a throng of* Citizens.

Citizens. We will be satisfied; let us be satisfied.

Brutus. Then follow me, and give me audience, friends.—
Cassius, go you into the other street,
And part the numbers.—
Those that will hear me speak, let 'em stay here;
Those that will follow Cassius, go with him;

And public reasons shall be rendered
Of Cæsar's death.

 1 *Citizen.*   I will hear Brutus speak.

 2 *Citizen.* I will hear Cassius ; and compare their reasons,
When severally we hear them rendered.

  [*Exit Cassius, with some of the Citizens.*   *Brutus goes
  into the Rostrum.*

 3 *Citizen.* The noble Brutus is ascended.   Silence !

 Brutus. Be patient till the last.

Romans, countrymen, and lovers ! hear me for my cause, and
be silent, that you may hear ; believe me for mine honour,
and have respect to mine honour, that you may believe ; censure me in your wisdom, and awake your senses, that you
may the better judge.   If there be any in this assembly, any
dear friend of Cæsar's, to him I say, that Brutus' love to Cæsar was no less than his.   If, then, that friend demand, why
Brutus rose against Cæsar, this is my answer,—Not that I
lov'd Cæsar less, but that I lov'd Rome more.   Had you
rather Cæsar were living, and die all slaves, than that Cæsar
were dead, to live all freemen ?   As Cæsar lov'd me, I weep
for him ; as he was fortunate, I rejoice at it ; as he was valiant, I honour him ; but, as he was ambitious, I slew him.
There is tears for his love ; joy for his fortune ; honour for
his valour ; and death for his ambition.   Who is here so base,
that would be a bondman ?   If any, speak ; for him have I
offended.   Who is here so rude, that would not be a Roman ?
If any, speak ; for him have I offended.   Who is here so vile,
that will not love his country ?   If any, speak ; for him have
I offended.   I pause for a reply.

 All. None, Brutus, none.

 Brutus. Then none have I offended.   I have done no more
to Cæsar than you shall do to Brutus.   The question of his
death is enroll'd in the Capitol ; his glory not extenuated,
wherein he was worthy, nor his offences enforc'd, for which
he suffer'd death.

Enter ANTONY *and others, with Cæsar's body.*

Here comes his body, mourn'd by Mark Antony : who, though
he had no hand in his death, shall receive the benefit of his
dying, a place in the commonwealth ; as which of you shall
not? With this I depart ; that, as I slew my best lover for
the good of Rome, I have the same dagger for myself, when
it shall please my country to'need my death.

All. Live, Brutus, live ! live !

1 *Citizen.* Bring him with triumph home unto his house.

2 *Citizen.* Give him a statue with his ancestors.

3 *Citizen.* Let him be Cæsar.

4 *Citizen.*   Cæsar's better parts
Shall now be crown'd in Brutus.

1 *Citizen.* We'll bring him to his house with shouts and
    clamours.

Brutus. My countrymen,—

2 *Citizen.*   Peace ! silence ! Brutus speaks.

1 *Citizen.* Peace, ho !

Brutus. Good countrymen, let me depart alone,
And, for my sake, stay here with Antony :
Do grace to Cæsar's corpse, and grace his speech
Tending to Cæsar's glories, which Mark Antony,
By our permission, is allow'd to make.
I do entreat you, not a man depart,
Save I alone, till Antony have spoke.   [*Exit.*

1 *Citizen.* Stay, ho ! and let us hear Mark Antony.

3 *Citizen.* Let him go up into the public chair ;
We'll hear him.—Noble Antony, go up.

Antony. For Brutus' sake, I am beholding to you.

4 *Citizen.* What does he say of Brutus?

3 *Citizen.*   He says, for Brutus' sake,
He finds himself beholding to us all.

4 *Citizen.* 'Twere best he speak no harm of Brutus here.

1 *Citizen.* This Cæsar was a tyrant.

3 *Citizen.*   Nay, that's certain ;
We are bless'd that Rome is rid of him.
  2 *Citizen.* Peace, let us hear what Antony can say.
  Antony. You gentle Romans,—
  All.   Peace, ho ! let us hear him.
  Antony. Friends, Romans, countrymen, lend me your ears ;
I come to bury Cæsar, not to praise him.
The evil that men do lives after them,
The good is oft interred with their bones ;
So let it be with Cæsar.   The noble Brutus
Hath told you, Cæsar was ambitious :
If it were so, it was a grievous fault,
And grievously hath Cæsar answer'd it.
Here, under leave of Brutus and the rest
(For Brutus is an honourable man,
So are they all, all honourable men),
Come I to speak in Cæsar's funeral.
He was my friend, faithful and just to me :
But Brutus says, he was ambitious ;
And Brutus is an honourable man.
He hath brought many captives home to Rome,
Whose ransom did the general coffers fill :
Did this in Cæsar seem ambitious ?
When that the poor have cried, Cæsar hath wept :
Ambition should be made of sterner stuff.
Yet Brutus says, he was ambitious ;
And Brutus is an honourable man.
You all did see, that on the Lupercal
I thrice presented him a kingly crown,
Which he did thrice refuse.   Was this ambition ?
Yet Brutus says, he was ambitious ;
And, sure, he is an honourable man.
I speak not to disprove what Brutus spoke,
But here I am to speak what I do know.
You all did love him once, not without cause ;

What cause withholds you, then, to mourn for him?
O judgment, thou art fled to brutish beasts,
And men have lost their reason!—Bear with me;
My heart is in the coffin there with Cæsar,
And I must pause till it come back to me.

    1 *Citizen.* Methinks, there is much reason in his sayings.

    2 *Citizen.* If thou consider rightly of the matter,
Cæsar has had great wrong.

    3 *Citizen.*   Has he, masters?
I fear there will a worse come in his place.

    4 *Citizen.* Mark'd ye his words? He would not take the
        crown;
Therefore 'tis certain he was not ambitious.

    1 *Citizen.* If it be found so, some will dear abide it.

    2 *Citizen.* Poor soul! his eyes are red as fire with weeping.

    3 *Citizen.* There's not a nobler man in Rome than Antony.

    4 *Citizen.* Now mark him, he begins again to speak.

    Antony. But yesterday the word of Cæsar might
Have stood against the world: now lies he there,
And none so poor to do him reverence.
O masters! if I were dispos'd to stir
Your hearts and minds to mutiny and rage,
I should do Brutus wrong, and Cassius wrong,
Who, you all know, are honourable men:
I will not do them wrong; I rather choose
To wrong the dead, to wrong myself, and you,
Than I will wrong such honourable men.
But here's a parchment, with the seal of Cæsar;
I found it in his closet; 'tis his will:
Let but the commons hear this testament
(Which, pardon me, I do not mean to read),
And they would go and kiss dead Cæsar's wounds,
And dip their napkins in his sacred blood;
Yea, beg a hair of him for memory,
And, dying, mention it within their wills,

Bequeathing it, as a rich legacy,
Unto their issue.

4 Citizen. We'll hear the will.   Read it, Mark Antony.

All. The will, the will! we will hear Cæsar's will.

Antony. Have patience, gentle friends ; I must not read it :
It is not meet you know how Cæsar lov'd you.
You are not wood, you are not stones, but men ;
And, being men, hearing the will of Cæsar,
It will inflame you, it will make you mad.
'Tis good you know not that you are his heirs ;
For if you should, O, what would come of it ?

4 Citizen. Read the will! we'll hear it, Antony!
You shall read us the will! Cæsar's will!

Antony. Will you be patient?   Will you stay a while?
I have o'ershot myself, to tell you of it.
I fear I wrong the honourable men,
Whose daggers have stabb'd Cæsar : I do fear it.

4 Citizen. They were traitors!   Honourable men!

All. The will! the testament!

2 Citizen. They were villains, murderers! The will! Read
the will!

Antony. You will compel me, then, to read the will?
Then make a ring about the corpse of Cæsar,
And let me show you him that made the will.
Shall I descend?   And will you give me leave?

All. Come down.

2 Citizen. Descend.   [*He comes down from the pulpit.*

3 Citizen. You shall have leave.

4 Citizen. A ring : stand round.

1 Citizen. Stand from the hearse ; stand from the body.

2 Citizen. Room for Antony!—most noble Antony!

Antony. Nay, press not so upon me ; stand far off.

All. Stand back! room! bear back!

Antony. If you have tears, prepare to shed them now.
You all do know this mantle : I remember

The first time ever Cæsar put it on ;
'Twas on a summer's evening, in his tent,
That day he overcame the Nervii.
Look ! in this place, ran Cassius' dagger through :
See what a rent the envious Casca made :
Through this the well-beloved Brutus stabb'd ;
And, as he pluck'd his cursed steel away,
Mark how the blood of Cæsar follow'd it,
As rushing out of doors, to be resolv'd
If Brutus so unkindly knock'd, or no ;
For Brutus, as you know, was Cæsar's angel :
Judge, O you gods, how dearly Cæsar lov'd him !
This was the most unkindest cut of all ;
For, when the noble Cæsar saw him stab,
Ingratitude, more strong than traitors' arms,
Quite vanquish'd him : then burst his mighty heart ;
And, in his mantle muffling up his face,
Even at the base of Pompey's statua,
Which all the while ran blood, great Cæsar fell.
O, what a fall was there, my countrymen !
Then I, and you, and all of us fell down,
Whilst bloody treason flourish'd over us.
O, now you weep ; and, I perceive, you feel
The dint of pity : these are gracious drops.
Kind souls, what ! weep you, when you but behold
Our Cæsar's vesture wounded ? Look you here,
Here is himself, marr'd, as you see, with traitors.

   1 *Citizen.* O piteous spectacle !
   2 *Citizen.* O noble Cæsar !
   3 *Citizen.* O woful day !
   4 *Citizen.* O traitors, villains !
   1 *Citizen.* O most bloody sight !
   2 *Citizen.* We will be reveng'd ; revenge ! about,—seek,—
burn,—fire,—kill,—slay !—let not a traitor live.
   Antony. Stay, countrymen.

1 *Citizen.* Peace there! Hear the noble Antony.

2 *Citizen.* We'll hear him, we'll follow him, we'll die with him.

Antony. Good friends, sweet friends, let me not stir you up
To such a sudden flood of mutiny.
They that have done this deed are honourable:
What private griefs they have, alas! I know not,
That made them do it; they are wise and honourable,
And will, no doubt, with reasons answer you.
I come not, friends, to steal away your hearts:
I am no orator, as Brutus is;
But, as you know me all, a plain blunt man,
That love my friend; and that they know full well
That gave me public leave to speak of him.
For I have neither wit, nor words, nor worth,
Action, nor utterance, nor the power of speech,
To stir men's blood: I only speak right on;
I tell you that which you yourselves do know,
Show you sweet Cæsar's wounds, poor, poor dumb mouths,
And bid them speak for me: but, were I Brutus,
And Brutus Antony, there were an Antony
Would ruffle up your spirits, and put a tongue
In every wound of Cæsar, that should move
The stones of Rome to rise and mutiny.

All. We'll mutiny.

1 *Citizen.* We'll burn the house of Brutus.

3 *Citizen.* Away, then! come, seek the conspirators.

Antony. Yet hear me, countrymen; yet hear me speak.

All. Peace, ho! Hear Antony, most noble Antony.

Antony. Why, friends, you go to do you know not what.
Wherein hath Cæsar thus deserved your loves?
Alas, you know not:—I must tell you, then.
You have forgot the will I told you of.

Citizen. Most true;—the will:—let's stay, and hear the will.

Antony. Here is the will, and under Cæsar's seal.

To every Roman citizen he gives,
To every several man, seventy-five drachmas.
  2 Citizen. Most noble Cæsar!—we'll revenge his death.
  3 Citizen. O royal Cæsar!
  Antony. Hear me with patience.
  All. Peace, ho!
  Antony. Moreover, he hath left you all his walks,
His private arbours, and new-planted orchards,
On this side Tiber: he hath left them you,
And to your heirs forever; common pleasures,
To walk abroad, and recreate yourselves.
Here was a Cæsar: when comes such another?
  1 Citizen. Never, never!—Come, away, away!
We'll burn his body in the holy place,
And with the brands fire the traitors' houses.
Take up the body.
  2 Citizen. Go, fetch fire.
  3 Citizen. Pluck down benches.
  4 Citizen. Pluck down forms, windows, anything.
                  [Exeunt Citizens, with the body.
  Antony. Now let it work. Mischief, thou art afoot,
Take thou what course thou wilt!—How now, fellow?

          Enter a Servant.

  Servant. Sir, Octavius is already come to Rome.
  Antony. Where is he?
  Servant. He and Lepidus are at Cæsar's house.
  Antony. And thither will I straight to visit him.
He comes upon a wish. Fortune is merry,
And in this mood will give us anything.
  Servant. I heard him say, Brutus and Cassius
Are rid like madmen through the gates of Rome.
  Antony. Belike they had some notice of the people,
How I had mov'd them. Bring me to Octavius. *[Exeunt.*

Scene III. *The same. A Street.*

Enter Cinna *the Poet.*

Cinna. I dream'd to-night that I did feast with Cæsar,
And things unlucky charge my fantasy.
I have no will to wander forth of doors,
Yet something leads me forth.

Enter Citizens.

1 *Citizen.* What is your name?
2 *Citizen.* Whither are you going?
3 *Citizen.* Where do you dwell?
4 *Citizen.* Are you a married man, or a bachelor?
2 *Citizen.* Answer every man directly.
1 *Citizen.* Ay, and briefly.
4 *Citizen.* Ay, and wisely.
3 *Citizen.* Ay, and truly, you were best.
Cinna. What is my name?   Whither am I going?   Where
do I dwell?   Am I a married man, or a bachelor?   Then to
answer every man directly and briefly, wisely and truly.
Wisely, I say, I am a bachelor.
2 *Citizen.* That's as much as to say, they are fools that
marry:—you'll bear me a bang for that, I fear.   Proceed;
directly.
Cinna. Directly, I am going to Cæsar's funeral.
1 *Citizen.* As a friend, or an enemy?
Cinna. As a friend.
2 *Citizen.* That matter is answered directly.
4 *Citizen.* For your dwelling,—briefly.
Cinna. Briefly, I dwell by the Capitol.
3 *Citizen.* Your name, sir, truly.
Cinna. Truly, my name is Cinna.
1 *Citizen.* Tear him to pieces, he's a conspirator.
Cinna. I am Cinna the poet, I am Cinna the poet.

4 *Citizen.* Tear him for his Bad verses, tear him for his bad verses.

Cinna. I am not Cinna the conspirator.

2 *Citizen.* It is no matter, his name's Cinna; pluck but his name out of his heart, and turn him going.

3 *Citizen.* Tear him, tear him! Come, brands, ho! fire-brands! To Brutus', to Cassius'; burn all. Some to Decius' house, and some to Casca's; some to Ligarius': away! go!

[*Exeunt.*

SITE OF THE ROMAN FORUM.

ROMAN SOLDIERS.

ACT IV.

SCENE I. *The same. A Room in Antony's House.* ANTONY, OCTAVIUS, *and* LEPIDUS, *seated at a Table.*

Antony. These many, then, shall die; their names are prick'd.

Octavius. Your brother too must die. Consent you, Lepidus?

Lepidus. I do consent.

Octavius.   Prick him down, Antony.

Lepidus. Upon condition Publius shall not live,
Who is your sister's son, Mark Antony.

Antony. He shall not live: look, with a spot I damn him.
But, Lepidus, go you to Cæsar's house;
Fetch the will hither, and we shall determine
How to cut off some charge in legacies.
　Lepidus. What, shall I find you here?
　Octavius. Or here, or at the Capitol.　　　[*Exit Lepidus.*
　Antony. This is a slight, unmeritable man,
Meet to be sent on errands: is it fit,
The three-fold world divided, he should stand
One of the three to share it?
　Octavius.　　　　　　So you thought him;
And took his voice who should be prick'd to die,
In our black sentence and proscription.
　Antony. Octavius, I have seen more days than you;
And though we lay these honours on this man,
To ease ourselves of divers slanderous loads,
He shall but bear them as the ass bears gold,
To groan and sweat under the business,
Either led or driven, as we point the way;
And, having brought our treasure where we will,
Then take we down his load, and turn him off,
Like to the empty ass, to shake his ears,
And graze in commons.
　Octavius.　　　　　You may do your will;
But he's a tried and valiant soldier.
　Antony. So is my horse, Octavius; and, for that,
I do appoint him store of provender.
It is a creature that I teach to fight,
To wind, to stop, to run directly on;
His corporal motion govern'd by my spirit.
And, in some taste, is Lepidus but so;
He must be taught, and train'd, and bid go forth:—
A barren-spirited fellow; one that feeds
On objects, arts, and imitations
Which, out of use, and stal'd by other men,

Begin his fashion.   Do not talk of him,
But as a property.—And now, Octavius,
Listen great things.   Brutus and Cassius
Are levying powers : we must straight make head ;
Therefore let our alliance be combin'd,
Our best friends made, our means stretch'd ;
And let us presently go sit in council,
How covert matters may be best disclos'd,
And open perils surest answered.

   Octavius. Let us do so : for we are at the stake,
And bay'd about with many enemies ;
And some that smile have in their hearts, I fear,
Millions of mischiefs.   *[Exeunt.*

    Scene II.   *Before the Tent of Brutus, in the Camp near
                      Sardis.*

Drum.   *Enter* Brutus, Lucilius, Titinius, *and Soldiers :*
    Pindarus *meeting them :* Lucius *at a distance.*

   Brutus. Stand, ho !

   Lucilius. Give the word, ho ! and stand.

   Brutus. What now, Lucilius ? is Cassius near ?

   Lucilius. He is at hand, and Pindarus is come
To do you salutation from his master.
                [Pindarus gives a Letter to Brutus.

   Brutus. He greets me well.—Your master, Pindarus,
In his own change, or by ill officers,
Hath given me some worthy cause to wish
Things done undone ; but, if he be at hand,
I shall be satisfied.

   Pindarus.   I do not doubt
But that my noble master will appear
Such as he is, full of regard and honour.

   Brutus. He is not doubted.—A word, Lucilius :
How he receiv'd you, let me be resolv'd.

Lucilius. With courtesy, and with respect enough ;
But not with such familiar instances,
Nor with such free and friendly conference,
As he hath us'd of old.
    Brutus.   Thou hast describ'd
A hot friend cooling. Ever note, Lucilius,
When love begins to sicken and decay,
It useth an enforced ceremony.
There are no tricks in plain and simple faith ;
But hollow men, like horses hot at hand,
Make gallant shew and promise of their mettle ;
But when they should endure the bloody spur,
They fall their crests, and, like deceitful jades,
Sink in the trial. Comes his army on?
    Lucilius. They mean this night in Sardis to be quarter'd ;
The greater part, the horse in general,
Are come with Cassius.   *[March within.*
    Brutus.   Hark, he is arriv'd :— ●
March gently on to meet him.

      Enter CASSIUS *and* Soldiers.

    Cassius. Stand, ho !
    Brutus. Stand, ho !   Speak the word along.
    Within. Stand.
    Within. Stand.
    Within. Stand.
    Cassius. Most noble brother, you have done me wrong.
    Brutus. Judge me, you gods !   Wrong I mine enemies?
And, if not so, how should I wrong a brother?
    Cassius. Brutus, this sober form of yours hides wrongs ;
And when you do them—
    Brutus.   Cassius, be content ;
Speak your griefs softly,—I do know you well.
Before the eyes of both our armies here,
Which should perceive nothing but love from us,
                  G

Let us not wrangle.   Bid them move away;
Then in my tent, Cassius, enlarge your griefs,
And I will give you audience.

    Cassius.   Pindarus,
Bid our commanders lead their charges off
A little from this ground.

    Brutus. Lucius, do you the like; and let no man
Come to our tent, till we have done our conference.
Lucilius and Titinius, guard our door.   [*Exeunt.*

Scene III. *Within the Tent of Brutus.*

Enter Brutus *and* Cassius.

    Cassius. That you have wrong'd me doth appear in this:
You have condemn'd and noted Lucius Pella
For taking bribes here of the Sardians;
Wherein my letter, praying on his side,
Because I knew the man, was slighted off.

    Brutus. You wrong'd yourself, to write in such a case.

    Cassius. In such a time as this, it is not meet
That every nice offence should bear his comment.

    Brutus. Let me tell you, Cassius, you yourself
Are much condemn'd to have an itching palm,
To sell and mart your offices for gold
To undeservers.

    Cassius.   I an itching palm?
You know that you are Brutus that speak this,
Or, by the gods, this speech were else your last.

    Brutus. The name of Cassius honours this corruption,
And chastisement doth therefore hide his head.

    Cassius. Chastisement!

    Brutus. Remember March, the ides of March remember!
Did not great Julius bleed for justice' sake?
What villain touch'd his body, that did stab,
And not for justice?   What! shall one of us.

That struck the foremost man of all this world,
But for supporting robbers, shall we now
Contaminate our fingers with base bribes,
And sell the mighty space of our large honours
For so much trash as may be grasped thus?
I had rather be a dog, and bay the moon,
Than such a Roman.
 Cassius.   Brutus, bay not me;
I'll not endure it: you forget yourself,
To hedge me in. I am a soldier, I,
Older in practice, abler than yourself
To make conditions.
 Brutus.   Go to; you are not, Cassius.
 Cassius. I am.
 Brutus. I say you are not.
 Cassius. Urge me no more, I shall forget myself;
Have mind upon your health, tempt me no further.
 Brutus. Away, slight man!
 Cassius. Is't possible?
 Brutus.   Hear me, for I will speak.
Must I give way and room to your rash choler?
Shall I be frighted when a madman stares?
 Cassius. O ye gods! ye gods! Must I endure all this?
 Brutus. All this? Ay, more. Fret till your proud heart
   break;
Go shew your slaves how choleric you are,
And make your bondmen tremble. Must I budge?
Must I observe you? Must I stand and crouch
Under your testy humour? By the gods,
You shall digest the venom of your spleen,
Though it do split you; for, from this day forth,
I'll use you for my mirth, yea, for my laughter,
When you are waspish.
 Cassius.   Is it come to this?
 Brutus. You say you are a better soldier:

Let it appear so ; make your vaunting true,
And it shall please me well.   For mine own part,
I shall be glad to learn of noble men.

 Cassius. You wrong me every way, you wrong me, Brutus ;
I said an elder soldier, not a better :
Did I say better ?

 Brutus.   If you did, I care not.   [me.

 Cassius. When Cæsar liv'd, he durst not thus have mov'd

 Brutus. Peace, peace! you durst not so have tempted him.

 Cassius. I durst not ?

 Brutus. No.

 Cassius. What? durst not tempt him ?

 Brutus.   For your life you durst not.

 Cassius. Do not presume too much upon my love ;
I may do that I shall be sorry for.

 Brutus. You have done that you should be sorry for.
There is no terror, Cassius, in your threats ;
For I am arm'd so strong in honesty,
That they pass by me as the idle wind,
Which I respect not.   I did send to you
For certain sums of gold, which you denied me ;—
For I can raise no money by vile means :
By heaven, I had rather coin my heart,
And drop my blood for drachmas, than to wring
From the hard hands of peasants their vile trash
By any indirection.—I did send
To you for gold to pay my legions,
Which you denied me.   Was that done like Cassius?
Should I have answer'd Caius Cassius so ?
When Marcus Brutus grows so covetous,
To lock such rascal counters from his friends,
Be ready, gods, with all your thunderbolts,
Dash him to pieces !

 Cassius.   I denied you not.

 Brutus. You did.

Cassius.   I did not : he was but a fool
That·brought my answer back.—Brutus hath riv'd my heart :
A friend should bear a friend's infirmities,
But Brutus makes mine greater than they are.
   Brutus. I do not, till you practise them on me.
   Cassius. You love me not.
   Brutus.   I do not like your faults.
   Cassius. A friendly eye could never see such faults.
   Brutus. A flatterer's would not, though they do appea⁀
As huge as high Olympus.
   Cassius. Come, Antony, and young Octavius, come,
Revenge yourselves alone on Cassius !
For Cassius is aweary of the world :
Hated by one he loves ; brav'd by his brother ;
Check'd like a bondman ; all his faults observ'd,
Set in a note-book, learn'd and conn'd by rote,
To cast into· my teeth.   O, I could weep
My spirit from mine eyes !—There is my dagger,
And here my naked breast ; within, a heart
Dearer than Plutus' mine, richer than gold :
If that thou beest a Roman, take it forth.
I, that denied thee gold, will give my heart :
Strike, as thou didst at Cæsar ; for, I know,
When thou didst hate him worst, thou lov'dst him better
Than ever thou lov'dst Cassius.
   Brutus.   Sheathe your dagger :·
Be angry when you will, it shall have scope ;
Do what you will, dishonour shall be humour.
O Cassius, you are yoked with a lamb,
That carries anger as the flint bears fire ;
Who, much enforced, shows a hasty spark,
And straight is cold again.
   Cassius.   Hath Cassius liv'd
To be but mirth and laughter to his Brutus,
When grief, and blood ill-temper'd, vexeth him ?

Brutus. When I spoke that, I was ill-temper'd too.
Cassius. Do you confess so much? Give me your hand.
Brutus. And my heart too.
Cassius.   O Brutus!—
Brutus.   What's the matter?
Cassius. Have you not love enough to bear with me,
When that rash humour which my mother gave me
Makes me forgetful?
Brutus.   Yes, Cassius; and from henceforth,
When you are over-earnest with your Brutus,
He'll think your mother chides, and leave you so.
                                [*Noise within.*
Poet [*Within*]. Let me go in to see the generals:
There is some grudge between 'em; 'tis not meet
They be alone.
Lucilius [*Within*]. You shall not come to them.
Poet [*Within*]. Nothing but death shall stay me.

    Enter Poet, *followed by* LUCILIUS *and* TITINIUS.

Cassius. How now? What's the matter?
Poet. For shame, you generals? What do you mean?
Love, and be friends, as two such men should be;
For I have seen more years, I'm sure, than ye.
Cassius. Ha, ha! how vilely doth this cynic rhyme!
Brutus. Get you hence, sirrah! saucy fellow, hence!
Cassius. Bear with him, Brutus; 'tis his fashion.
Brutus. I'll know his humour when he knows his time.
What should the wars do with these jigging fools!
Companion, hence!
Cassius. •   Away, away! be gone!   [*Exit Poet.*
Brutus. Lucilius and Titinius, bid the commanders
Prepare to lodge their companies to-night.
Cassius. And come yourselves, and bring Messala with you,
Immediately to us.   [*Exeunt Lucilius and Titinius.*
Brutus.   •   Lucius, a bowl of wine.

Cassius. I did not think you could have been so angry.

Brutus. O Cassius, I am sick of many griefs !

Cassius. Of your philosophy you make no use,
If you give place to accidental evils.

Brutus. No man bears sorrow better.—Portia is dead.

Cassius. Ha ! Portia ?

Brutus. She is dead.

Cassius. How scap'd I killing, when I cross'd you so ?—
O insupportable and touching loss !—
Upon what sickness ?

Brutus.   Impatient of my absence,
And grief that young Octavius with Mark Antony
Have made themselves so strong ;—for with her death .
That tidings came.—With this she fell distract,
And, her attendants absent, swallow'd fire.

Cassius. And died so ?

Brutus. Even so.

Cassius. O ye immortal gods !

Enter LUCIUS, *with wine and tapers.*

Brutus. Speak no more of her. — Give me a bowl of
    wine.—
In this I bury all unkindness, Cassius.   *[Drinks.*

Cassius. My heart is thirsty for that noble pledge.—
Fill, Lucius, till the wine o'erswell the cup ;
I cannot drink too much of Brutus' love.   *[Drinks.*

Enter TITINIUS, *with* MESSALA.

Brutus. Come in, Titinius.—Welcome, good Messala.—
Now sit we close about this taper here,
And call in question our necessities.

Cassius. Portia, art thou gone ?

Brutus.   No more, I pray you.—
Messala, I have here received letters,
That young Octavius and Mark Antony

Come down upon us with a mighty power,
Bending their expedition toward Philippi.

Messala. Myself have letters of the self-same tenour.

Brutus. With what addition?

Messala. That by proscription and bills of outlawry,
Octavius, Antony, and Lepidus
Have put to death an hundred senators.

Brutus. Therein our letters do not well agree:
Mine speak of seventy senators that died
By their proscriptions, Cicero being one.

Cassius. Cicero one?

Messala. Cicero is dead,
And by that order of proscription.—
Had you your letters from your wife, my lord?

Brutus. No, Messala.

Messala. Nor nothing in your letters writ of her?

Brutus. Nothing, Messala.

Messala. That, methinks, is strange.

Brutus. Why ask you? Hear you aught of her in yours?

Messala. No, my lord.

Brutus. Now, as you are a Roman, tell me true.

Messala. Then like a Roman bear the truth I tell:
For certain she is dead, and by strange manner.

Brutus. Why, farewell, Portia.—We must die, Messala.
With meditating that she must die once,
I have the patience to endure it now.

Messala. Even so great men great losses should endure.

Cassius. I have as much of this in art as you,
But yet my nature could not bear it so.

Brutus. Well, to our work alive. What do you think
Of marching to Philippi presently?

Cassius. I do not think it good.

Brutus. Your reason?

Cassius. This it is:—
'Tis better that the enemy seek us:

So shall he waste his means, weary his soldiers,
Doing himself offence ; whilst we, lying still,
Are full of rest, defence, and nimbleness.
  Brutus. Good reasons must, of force, give place to better.
The people 'twixt Philippi and this ground
Do stand but in a forc'd affection ;
For they have grudg'd us contribution.
The enemy, marching along by them,
By them shall make a fuller number up,
Come on refresh'd, new-added, and encourag'd ;
From which advantage shall we cut him off
If at Philippi we do face him there,
These people at our back.
  Cassius.   Hear me, good brother.
  Brutus. Under your pardon.—You must note beside,
That we have tried the utmost of our friends.
Our legions are brim-full, our cause is ripe :
The enemy increaseth every day ;
We, at the height, are ready to decline.
There is a tide in the affairs of men,
Which, taken at the flood, leads on to fortune ;
Omitted, all the voyage of their life
Is bound in shallows, and in miseries.
On such a full sea are we now afloat ;
And we must take the current when it serves,
Or lose our ventures.
  Cassius.   Then, with your will, go on ;
We'll along ourselves, and meet them at Philippi.
  Brutus. The deep of night is crept upon our talk,
And nature must obey necessity,
Which we will niggard with a little rest.
There is no more to say ?
  Cassius.   No more. Good night !
Early to-morrow will we rise, and hence.
  Brutus. Lucius, my gown. [*Exit Lucius.*] Farewell, good
    Messala !—

Good night, Titinius !—Noble, noble Cassius,
Good night, and good repose !
    Cassius.   O my dear brother,
This was an ill beginning of the night :
Never come such division 'tween our souls !
Let it not, Brutus.

Enter LUCIUS, *with the gown.*

    Brutus.   Everything is well.
    Cassius. Good night, my lord !
    Brutus.   Good night, good brother !
    Titinius, Messala. Good night, lord Brutus !
    Brutus.   Farewell, every one !—
              [*Exeunt Cassius, Titinius, and Messala.*
Give me the gown.   Where is thy instrument?
    Lucius. Here, in the tent.
    Brutus.   What ! thou speak'st drowsily ?
Poor knave, I blame thee not ; thou art o'er-watch'd.
Call Claudius, and some other of my men ;
I'll have them sleep on cushions in my tent.
    Lucius. Varro and Claudius !

Enter VARRO *and* CLAUDIUS.

    Varro.   Calls my lord?
    Brutus. I pray you, sirs, lie in my tent, and sleep ;
It may be, I shall raise you by and by
On business to my brother Cassius.
    Varro. So please you, we will stand, and watch your
        pleasure.
    Brutus. I will not have it so : lie down, good sirs ;
It may be·I shall otherwise bethink me.—
Look, Lucius, here's the book I sought for so ;
I put it in the pocket of my gown.   [*Servants lie down.*
    Lucius. I was sure your lordship did not give it me.
    Brutus. Bear with me, good boy ; I am much forgetful.

Canst thou hold up thy heavy eyes a while,
And touch thy instrument a strain or two?
   Lucius. Ay, my lord, an't please you.
   Brutus.   It does, my boy:
I trouble thee too much, but thou art willing.
   Lucius. It is my duty, sir.
   Brutus. I should not urge thy duty past thy might;
I know young bloods look for a time of rest.
   Lucius. I have slept, my lord, already.
   Brutus. It was well done; and thou shalt sleep again;
I will not hold thee long: if I do live,
I will be good to thee.   [*Music and a song.*
This is a sleepy tune.—O murderous slumber,
Lay'st thou thy leaden mace upon my boy,
That plays thee music?—Gentle knave, good night;
I will not do thee so much wrong to wake thee.
If thou dost nod, thou break'st thy instrument:
I'll take it from thee; and, good boy, good night.—
Let me see, let me see;—is not the leaf turn'd down,
Where I left reading?   Here it is, I think.   [*He sits down.*

Enter the Ghost of CÆSAR.

How ill this taper burns!—Ha! who comes here?
I think it is the weakness of my eyes
That shapes this monstrous apparition.
It comes upon me.—Art thou anything?
Art thou some god, some angel, or some devil,
That mak'st my blood cold, and my hair to stare?
Speak to me what thou art.
   Ghost. Thy evil spirit, Brutus.
   Brutus.   Why com'st thou?
   Ghost. To tell thee, thou shalt see me at Philippi.
   Brutus. Well; then I shall see thee again?
   Ghost.   Ay, at Philippi.
                              [*Ghost vanishes.*

Brutus. Why, I will see thee at Philippi then.—
Now I have taken heart, thou vanishest:
Ill spirit, I would hold more talk with thee.—
Boy! Lucius!—Varro! Claudius! Sirs, awake!—
Claudius!

Lucius. The strings, my lord, are false.

Brutus. He thinks he still is at his instrument.—
Lucius, awake!

Lucius. My lord!

Brutus. Didst thou dream, Lucius, that thou so criedst out?

Lucius. My lord, I do not know that I did cry.

Brutus. Yes, that thou didst. Didst thou see anything?

Lucius. Nothing, my lord.

Brutus. Sleep again, Lucius.—Sirrah, Claudius!
Fellow thou! awake!

Varro. My lord!

Claudius. My lord!

Brutus. Why did you so cry out, sirs, in your sleep?

Varro, Claudius. Did we, my lord?

Brutus.   Ay: saw you anything?

Varro. No, my lord, I saw nothing.

Claudius.   Nor I, my lord.

Brutus. Go, and commend me to my brother Cassius;
Bid him set on his powers betimes before,
And we will follow.

Varro, Claudius. It shall be done, my lord.   [*Exeunt.*

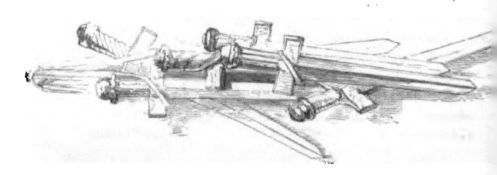

SCENE I. *The Plains of Philippi.*

Enter OCTAVIUS, ANTONY, *and their Army.*

Octavius. Now, Antony, our hopes are answered.
You said the enemy would not come down,
But keep the hills and upper regions.
It proves not so : their battles are at hand ;
They mean to warn us at Philippi here,
Answering before we do demand of them.

    Antony. Tut! I am in their bosoms, and I know
Wherefore they do it : they could be content
To visit other places ; and come down

With fearful bravery, thinking by this face
To fasten in our thoughts that they have courage;
But 'tis not so.

Enter a Messenger.

Messenger.   Prepare you, generals:
The enemy comes on in gallant shew;
Their bloody sign of battle is hung out,
And something to be done immediately.
  Antony. Octavius, lead your battle softly on,
Upon the left hand of the even field.
  Octavius. Upon the right hand I; keep thou the left.
  Antony. Why do you cross me in this exigent?
  Octavius. I do not cross you; but I will do so.   [*March.*

Drum.   Enter BRUTUS, CASSIUS, *and their Army;* LUCILIUS,
       TITINIUS, MESSALA, *and others.*

  Brutus. They stand, and would have parley.
  Cassius. Stand-fast, Titinius: we must out and talk.
  Octavius. Mark Antony, shall we give sign of battle?
  Antony. No, Cæsar, we will answer on their charge.
Make forth; the generals would have some words.
  Octavius. Stir not until the signal.
  Brutus. Words before blows; is it so, countrymen?
  Octavius. Not that we love words better, as you do.
  Brutus. Good words are better than bad strokes, Octavius.
  Antony. In your bad strokes, Brutus, you give good words:
Witness the hole you made in Cæsar's heart,
Crying, "Long live! Hail, Cæsar!"
  Cassius.   Antony,
The posture of your blows are yet unknown;
But for your words, they rob the Hybla bees,
And leave them honeyless.
  Antony.   Not stingless too.
  Brutus. O, yes, and soundless too;

For you have stolen their buzzing, Antony,
And, very wisely, threat before you sting.
·*Antony.* Villains, you did not so, when your vile daggers
Hack'd one another in the sides of Cæsar:
You shew'd your teeth like apes, and fawn'd like hounds,
And bow'd like bondmen, kissing Cæsar's feet;
Whilst damned Casca, like a cur, behind,
Struck Cæsar on the neck. O you flatterers!
   Cassius. Flatterers!—Now, Brutus, thank yourself:
This tongue had not offended so to-day,
If Cassius might have rul'd.
   Octavius. Come, come, the cause: if arguing make us sweat,
The proof of it will turn to redder drops.
Look, I draw a sword against conspirators;
When think you that the sword goes up again?—
Never, till Cæsar's three and thirty wounds
Be well aveng'd; or till another Cæsar
Have added slaughter to the sword of traitors.
   Brutus. Cæsar, thou canst not die by traitors' hands,
Unless thou bring'st them with thee.
   Octavius.   So I hope;
I was not born to die on Brutus' sword.
   Brutus. O, if thou wert the noblest of thy strain,
Young man, thou couldst not die more honourable.
   Cassius. A peevish schoolboy, worthless of such honour,
Join'd with a masker and a reveller.
   Antony. Old Cassius still!
   Octavius.   Come, Antony; away!—
Defiance, traitors, hurl we in your teeth.
If you dare fight to-day, come to the field;
If not, when you have stomachs.
        [Exeunt Octavius, Antony, and their Army.
   Cassius. Why now, blow wind, swell billow, and swim bark!
The storm is up, and all is on the hazard.
   Brutus. Ho! Lucilius; hark, a word with you.

Lucilius.   My, lord ! [*Brutus and Lucilius talk apart.*
Cassius. Messala,—
Messala.   What says my general ?
Cassius.   Messala,
This is my birth-day ; as this very day
Was Cassius born.   Give me thy hand, Messala :
Be thou my witness, that, against my will,
As Pompey was, am I compell'd to set
Upon one battle all our liberties.
You know that I held Epicurus strong,
And his opinion ; now I change my mind,
And partly credit things that do presage.
Coming from Sardis, on our former ensign
Two mighty eagles fell, and there they perch'd,
Gorging and feeding from our soldiers' hands ;
Who to Philippi here consorted us :
This morning are they fled away and gone,
And in their steads do ravens, crows, and kites
Fly o'er our heads, and downward look on us,
As we were sickly prey ; their shadows seem
A canopy most fatal, under which
Our army lies, ready to give up the ghost.
     Messala. Believe not so.
     Cassius.   I but believe it partly
For I am fresh of spirit, and resolv'd
To meet all perils very constantly.
     Brutus. Even so, Lucilius.
     Cassius.   Now, most noble Brutus,˙
The gods to-day stand friendly, that we may,
Lovers in peace, lead on our days to age !
But, since the affairs of men rest still incertain,
Let's reason with the worst that may befall.
If we do lose this battle, then is this
The very last time we shall speak together :●
What are you then determined to do ?

Brutus. Even by the rule of that philosophy,
By which I did blame Cato for the death
Which he did give himself. I know not how,
But I do find it cowardly and vile,
For fear of what might fall, so to prevent
The time of life,—arming myself with patience,
To stay the providence of some high powers
That govern us below.
   Cassius. Then, if we lose this battle,
You are contented to be led in triumph
Thorough the streets of Rome?
   Brutus. No, Cassius, no : think not, thou noble Roman,
That ever Brutus will go bound to Rome ;
He bears too great a mind. But this same day
Must end that work the ides of March begun ;
And whether we shall meet again, I know not.
Therefore, our everlasting farewell take :—
For ever, and for ever, farewell, Cassius !
If we do meet again, why we shall smile ;
If not, why then, this parting was well made.
   Cassius. For ever, and for ever, farewell, Brutus !
If we do meet again, we'll smile indeed ;
If not, 'tis true, this parting was well made.
   Brutus. Why then, lead on.—O that a man might know
The end of this day's business ere it come !
But it sufficeth that the day will end,
And then the end is known.—Come, ho ! away!   [*Exeunt.*

SCENE II. *The same. The Field of Battle.*

Alarum. Enter BRUTUS *and* MESSALA.

   Brutus. Ride, ride, Messala, ride, and give these bills
Unto the legions on the other side.   [*Loud alarum.*
Let them set on at once ; for I perceive
But cold demeanour in Octavius' wing,

H

And sudden push gives them the overthrow.
Ride, ride, Messala : let them all come down.   [*Exeunt.*

SCENE III.   *The same.   Another part of the Field.*

Alarums.   Enter CASSIUS *and* TITINIUS.

Cassius.   O, look, Titinius, look, the villains fly !
Myself have to mine own turn'd enemy :
This ensign here of mine was turning back ;
I slew the coward, and did take it from him.
    Titinius.   O Cassius, Brutus gave the word too early ;
Who, having some advantage on Octavius,
Took it too eagerly : his soldiers fell to spoil,
Whilst we by Antony are all enclos'd.

Enter PINDARUS.

Pindarus.   Fly further off, my lord, fly further off ;
Mark Antony is in your tents, my lord !
Fly, therefore, noble Cassius, fly far off.
    Cassius.   This hill is far enough.   Look, look, Titinius ;
Are those my tents, where I perceive the fire ?
  Titinius.   They are, my lord.
    Cassius.   Titinius, if thou lov'st me,
Mount thou my horse, and hide thy spurs in him,
Till he have brought thee up to yonder troops
And here again ; that I may rest assur'd,
Whether yond troops are friend or enemy.
    Titinius.   I will be here again even with a thought. [*Exit.*
    Cassius.   Go, Pindarus, get higher on that hill ;
My sight was ever thick ; regard Titinius,
And tell me what thou not'st about the field.—
                                        [*Pindarus goes up.*
This day I breathed first : time is come round,
And where I did begin, there shall I end ;
My life is run his compass.—Sirrah, what news ?

Pindarus [*Above*]. O my lord!

Cassius. What news?

Pindarus. Titinius is enclosed round about
With horsemen, that make to him on the spur;—
Yet he spurs on.—Now they are almost on him.
Now, Titinius!
Now some light:—O, he lights too:—He's ta'en;—and,
   hark!
They shout for joy.   [*Shout.*

Cassius.   Come down, behold no more.—
O, coward that I am, to live so long,
To see my best friend ta'en before my face!

          PINDARUS *comes down.*

Come hither, sirrah!
In Parthia did I take thee prisoner;
And then I swore thee, saving of thy life,
That, whatsoever I did bid thee do,
Thou shouldst attempt it. Come now, keep thine oath!
Now be a freeman; and with this good sword,
That ran through Cæsar's bowels, search this bosom.
Stand not to answer: here, take thou the hilts;
And when my face is cover'd, as 'tis now,
Guide thou the sword.—Cæsar, thou art reveng'd,
Even with the sword that kill'd thee.   [*Dies.*

Pindarus. So, I am free; yet would not so have been,
Durst I have done my will. O Cassius!
Far from this country Pindarus shall run,
Where never Roman shall take note of him.   [*Exit.*

    Enter TITINIUS, *with* MESSALA.

Messala. It is but change, Titinius; for Octavius
Is overthrown by noble Brutus' power,
As Cassius' legions are by Antony.

Titinius. These tidings will well comfort Cassius.

Messala. Where did you leave him?

Titinius.   All disconsolate,
With Pindarus his bondman, on this hill.

Messala. Is not that he, that lies upon the ground?

Titinius. He lies not like the living. O my heart!

Messala. Is not that he?

Titinius.   No, this was he, Messala,
But Cassius is no more.—O setting sun!
As in thy red rays thou dost sink to night,
So in his red blood Cassius' day is set;
The sun of Rome is set! Our day is gone;
Clouds, dews, and dangers come; our deeds are done!
Mistrust of my success hath done this deed.

Messala. Mistrust of good success hath done this deed.
O hateful Error, Melancholy's child!
Why dost thou show to the apt thoughts of men
The things that are not? O Error, soon conceiv'd,
Thou never com'st unto a happy birth,
But kill'st the mother that engender'd thee.

Titinius. What, Pindarus! Where art thou, Pindarus?

Messala. Seek him, Titinius, whilst I go to meet
The noble Brutus, thrusting this report
Into his ears: I may say, thrusting it;
For piercing steel, and darts envenomed,
Shall be as welcome to the ears of Brutus
As tidings of this sight.

Titinius.   Hie you, Messala,
And I will seek for Pindarus the while.   [*Exit Messala.*
Why didst thou send me forth, brave Cassius?
Did I not meet thy friends? and did not they
Put on my brows this wreath of victory,
And bid me give it thee? Didst thou not hear their shouts?
Alas! thou hast misconstru'd everything.
But hold thee, take this garland on thy brow;
Thy Brutus bid me give it thee, and I

Will do his bidding.—Brutus, come apace,
And see how I regarded Caius Cassius.—
By your leave, gods :—this is a Roman's part :
Come, Cassius' sword, and find Titinius' heart.　　　[*Dies.*

Alarum.　Enter MESSALA, *with* BRUTUS, *young* CATO, STRA-
　　TO, VOLUMNIUS, *and* LUCILIUS.

Brutus. Where, where, Messala, doth his body lie ?
Messala. Lo, yonder ; and Titinius mourning it.
Brutus. Titinius' face is upward.
Cato.　　　　　　　　　　　　He is slain.
Brutus. O Julius Cæsar, thou art mighty yet !
Thy spirit walks abroad, and turns our swords
In our own proper entrails.　　　　　[*Low alarums.*
Cato.　　　　　　　　　　Brave Titinius !
Look, whe'r he have not crown'd dead Cassius !
Brutus. Are yet two Romans living such as these ?—
The last of all the Romans, fare thee well !
It is impossible that ever Rome
Should breed thy fellow.—Friends, I owe more tears
To this dead man, than you shall see me pay.—
I shall find time, Cassius, I shall find time.—
Come, therefore, and to Thassos send his body :
His funerals shall not be in our camp,
Lest it discomfort us.—Lucilius, come ;—
And come, young Cato ; let us to the field.—
Labeo and Flavius, set our battles on :—
'Tis three o'clock ; and, Romans, yet ere night
We shall try fortune in a second fight.　　　　[*Exeunt.*

SCENE IV.　*Another part of the Field.*

·*Alarum.　Enter, fighting, Soldiers of both Armies ; then* BRU-
　　TUS, CATO, LUCILIUS, *and others.*

Brutus. Yet, countrymen, O, yet hold up your heads !

Cato. What bastard doth not? Who will go with me?
I will proclaim my name about the field :—
I am the son of Marcus Cato, ho!
A foe to tyrants, and my country's friend ;
I am the son of Marcus Cato, ho!   [*Charges the enemy.*
   Brutus. And I am Brutus, Marcus Brutus, I ;
Brutus, my country's friend ; know me for Brutus!
      [*Exit, charging the enemy. Cato is overpowered, and
      falls.*
Lucilius. O young and noble Cato, art thou down?
Why, now thou diest as bravely as Titinius ;
And mayst be honour'd, being Cato's son.
   1 *Soldier.* Yield, or thou diest.
   Lucilius.   . Only I yield to die :
There is so much, that thou wilt kill me straight ;
                    [*Offering money.*
Kill Brutus, and be honour'd in his death.
   1 *Soldier.* We must not.—A noble prisoner!
   2 *Soldier.* Room, ho! Tell Antony, Brutus is ta'en.
   1 *Soldier.* I'll tell the news.—Here comes the general.—

Enter ANTONY.

Brutus is ta'en, Brutus is ta'en, my lord.
   Antony. Where is he?
   Lucilius. Safe, Antony ; Brutus is safe enough.
I dare assure thee, that no enemy
Shall ever take alive the noble Brutus :
The gods defend him from so great a shame !
When you do find him, or alive or dead,
He will be found like Brutus, like himself.
   Antony. This is not Brutus, friend ; but, I assure you,
A prize no less in worth. Keep this man safe ;
Give him all kindness : I had rather have
Such men my friends than enemies. Go on,
And see whe'r Brutus be alive or dead ;

And bring us word unto Octavius' tent
How everything is chanc'd.   [*Exeunt.*

SCENE V.   *Another part of the Field.*

Enter BRUTUS, DARDANIUS, CLITUS, STRATO, *and* VOLUMNIUS.

Brutus. Come, poor remains of friends, rest on this rock.
Clitus. Statilius shew'd the torch-light ; but, my lord,
He came not back : he is or ta'en or slain.
Brutus. Sit thee down, Clitus.   Slaying is the word ;
It is a deed in fashion.   Hark thee, Clitus.—   [*Whispering.*
Clitus. What ! I, my lord ?   No, not for all the world.
Brutus. Peace, then ! no words.
Clitus.   I'll rather kill myself.
Brutus. Hark thee, Dardanius !   [*Whispers him.*
Dardanius.   Shall I do such a deed ?
Clitus. O Dardanius !
Dardanius. O Clitus !
Clitus. What ill request did Brutus make to thee ?
Dardanius. To kill him, Clitus.   Look, he meditates.
Clitus. Now is that noble vessel full of grief,
That it runs over even at his eyes.
Brutus. Come hither, good Volumnius ; list a word.
Volumnius. What says my lord ?
Brutus.   Why, this, Volumnius :
The ghost of Cæsar hath appear'd to me
Two several times by night : at Sardis once ;
And, this last night, here in Philippi fields.
I know my hour is come.
Volumnius.   Not so, my lord.
Brutus. Nay, I am sure it is, Volumnius.
Thou seest the world, Volumnius, how it goes ;
Our enemies have beat us to the pit :   [*Low alarums.*
It is more worthy to leap in ourselves
Than tarry till they push us.   Good Volumnius,

Thou know'st that we two went to school together;
Even for that our love of old, I prithee,
Hold thou my sword hilts whilst I run on it.
   Volumnius. That's not an office for a friend, my lord.
                                   [Alarum still.
   Clitus. Fly, fly, my lord! there is no tarrying here.
   Brutus. Farewell to you;—and you;—and you, Volum-
Strato, thou hast been all this while asleep;   [nius.—
Farewell to thee too, Strato.—Countrymen,
My heart doth joy, that yet in all my life
I found no man but he was true to me.
I shall have glory by this losing day,
More than Octavius and Mark Antony
By this vile conquest shall attain unto.
So, fare you well at once: for Brutus' tongue
Hath almost ended his life's history.
Night hangs upon my eyes; my bones would rest,
That have but labour'd to attain this hour.
               [Alarum.   Cry within, Fly, fly, fly!
   Clitus. Fly, my lord, fly!
   Brutus.   Hence! I will follow.
       [Exeunt Clitus, Dardanius, and Volumnius.
I prithee, Strato, stay thou by thy lord.
Thou art a fellow of a good respect;
Thy life hath had some smatch of honour in it:
Hold then my sword, and turn away thy face
While I do run upon it.   Wilt thou, Strato?
   Strato. Give me your hand first: fare you well, my lord.
   Brutus. Farewell, good Strato.—Cæsar, now be still:
I kill'd not thee with half so good a will.
          [He runs on his sword, and dies.

  Alarum.   Retreat.   Enter OCTAVIUS, ANTONY, MESSALA,
        LUCILIUS, *and their Army.*
   Octavius. What man is that?

Messala. My master's man.—Strato, where is thy master?

Strato. Free from the bondage you are in, Messala :
The conquerors can but make a fire of him ;
For Brutus only overcame himself,
And no man else hath honour by his death.

Lucilius. So Brutus should be found.—I thank thee, Brutus,
That thou hast prov'd Lucilius' saying true.

Octavius. All that serv'd Brutus, I will entertain them.
Fellow, wilt thou bestow thy time with me?

Strato. Ay, if Messala will prefer me to you.

Octavius. Do so, good Messala.

Messala. How died my master, Strato?

Strato. I held the sword, and he did run on it.

Messala. Octavius, then take him to follow thee,
That did the latest service to my master.

Antony. This was the noblest Roman of them all.
All the conspirators, save only he,
Did that they did in envy of great Cæsar ;
He only, in a general honest thought
And common good to all, made one of them.
His life was gentle ; and the elements
So mix'd in him, that Nature might stand up,
And say to all the world, " This was a man !"

Octavius. According to his virtue let us use him,
With all respect and rites of burial.
Within my tent his bones to-night shall lie,
Most like a soldier, ordered honourably.—
So, call the field to rest ; and let's away,
To part the glories of this happy day.   [*Exeunt.*

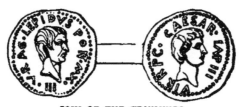

COIN OF THE TRIUMVIRS.

ROMAN MATRON.

NOTES.

ABBREVIATIONS USED IN THE NOTES.

Abbott (or Gr.), Abbott's *Shakespearian Grammar* (third edition).
Adv. of L., Bacon's *Advancement of Learning*.
A. S., Anglo-Saxon.
B. and F., Beaumont and Fletcher.
C., Craik's *English of Shakespeare* (Rolfe's edition).
Cf. (*confer*), compare.
Coll., Collier.
Crit. Exam.,Wm. Sidney Walker's *Critical Examination of the Text of Shakespeare* (London, 1860).
D., Dyce.
F., Fowler's *English Language* (8vo edition).
F. Q., Spenser's *Faërie Queene*.
Foll., following.
H., Hudson.
Hen. VIII. (followed by reference to *page*), Rolfe's edition of *Henry VIII.*
Id. (*idem*), the same.
J., Johnson.
K., Knight.
Mer., Rolfe's edition of *The Merchant of Venice.*
N., North's *Plutarch.*
P. L., Milton's *Paradise Lost.*
Prol., Prologue.
Rich., Richardson's Dictionary (London, 1838).
S., Shakespeare.
Shep. Cal., Spenser's *Shepherd's Calendar.*
Sr., Singer.
St., Staunton.
Temp. (followed by reference to *page*), Rolfe's edition of *The Tempest.*
Theo., Theobald.
V., Verplanck.
Var. ed., the *Variorum* edition of Shakespeare (1821).
W., White.
Warb.,Warburton.
Wb., Webster's Dictionary (revised quarto edition of 1864).
Worc., Worcester's Dictionary (quarto edition).

The abbreviations of the names of Shakespeare's Plays will be readily understood ; as *T. N.* for *Twelfth Night, Cor.* for *Coriolanus*, 3 *Hen. VI.* for *The Third Part of King Henry the Sixth*, etc. *P. P.* refers to *The Passionate Pilgrim* ; *V. and A.* to *Venus and Adonis* ; *L. C.* to *A Lover's Complaint* ; and *Sonn.* to the *Sonnets.*

PLEBEIANS.

NOTES.

ACT I.

Scene I.—In the folio of 1623 the play is divided into acts, but not into scenes, and there is no list of *dramatis personæ*. The heading of Act I. is as follows : "*Actus Primus. Scæna Prima. Enter Flauius, Murellus, and certaine Commoners ouer the Stage.*" The spelling *Murellus* is found throughout the play, except in one instance (i. 2), where we find "*Murrellus* and *Flauius*, for pulling Scarffes off *Cæsars* Images, are put to silence." The name in North's Plutarch is *Marullus*, and Theo. made the correction here.

Being mechanical. "Cobblers, tapsters, or such like base mechanical people" (N.). S. uses both *mechanic* and *mechanical* as noun and as adjective. Cf. *M. N. D.* iii. 2 : "rude mechanicals ;" 2 *Hen. IV.* v. 5 : "by most mechanical and dirty hand ;" *Cor.* v. 3 : "Rome's mechanics ;" *A. and C.* v. 2 : "mechanic slaves."

Ought not walk. On the omission of *to*, see Gr. 349.

A labouring day. As C. remarks, *labouring* here is not the participle, but the verbal noun (or gerund) used as an adjective. Cf. the expressions *a walking-stick, a writing-desk,* etc. The participle in *-ing* is *active,* and it remains so when used as an adjective ; as in *a labouring man,* etc. When used as a noun, which rarely occurs in English, it denotes the *agent.* Thus "the erring" means *those who err,* as *amans* in Latin means a *lover.* The verbal noun in *-ing,* on the other hand, denotes the *act* (as "labouring is wearisome"), like the Latin gerund *amandi,* etc. This verbal noun is commonly called a "participial noun" in our English grammars, but it has no etymological connection with the participle. In early English (as in A. S.) the two had different forms. The ending of the participle was *ande* (*and*), *ende* (*end*), or *inde,* and that of the verbal noun was *ing* or *ung ;* but the former went out of use, and the latter came to do service for both. This change began before the year 13co, but in the time of Chaucer the old participial ending was still occasionally used, and it is found in Scotch writers even to the end of the sixteenth century.

The following are examples of the participle and the verbal noun used with their appropriate endings in the same sentence :

> "Hors, or hund, or othir thing
> That war plesa*nd* to their liki*ng*."—*Barbour* (1357).

> "Full low inclina*nd* to their queen full clear
> Whom for their noble nourishi*ng* they thank."—*Dunbar* (*Ellis's Spec.*).

What trade art thou? Either *trade* is equivalent to *tradesman* (as C. makes it), or *of* is understood. Cf. Gr. 202. On the use of *thou* and *you* in S., see Gr. 232.

1 *Citizen.* The folio has "*Car.*" (that is, *Carpenter*), and for 2 *Citizen* either "*Cobl.*" or "*Cob.*" (*Cobbler*).

Answer me directly. That is, explicitly, without ambiguity. Cf. below (iii. 3): "Answer every man directly." It is hardly necessary to say that *cobbler* meant not only a mender of shoes, but a clumsy workman at any trade ; and the latter sense is not wholly unknown even now.

A mender of bad soles. "An immemorial quibble, doubtless" (C.). Cf. *M. of V.* iv. 1: "Not on thy sole, but on thy soul, harsh Jew." Malone quotes Fletcher's *Woman Pleased:*

> "If thou dost this, there shall be no more shoe-mending ;
> Every man shall have a special care of his own *soul,*
> And carry in his pocket his two confessors."

What trade, thou knave? The folio gives this speech to *Flavius* (as do K. and H.), but the "Mend *me,* thou saucy fellow?" shows that it belongs to *Marullus.*

Be not out with me, etc. The play upon *out with* and *out* (*at the toes*) is obvious.

But withal, etc. This is the folio reading, and may well enough be retained. "What the cobbler means to say is, that although he meddles not with tradesmen's matters or women's matters, he is withal (making at the same time his little pun) a surgeon to old shoes" (W.). K., Coll., and H. print "but with all. I am," etc. C., D., and the Camb. ed. have "but with awl. I am," etc.

As proper men, etc. See *Mer.* p. 132 (note on *A proper man's picture*), and cf. *Temp.* ii. 2 : "as proper a man as ever went on four legs," and "any emperor that ever trod on neat's-leather."

But wherefore art not, etc. On the ellipsis, see Gr. 401.

His triumph. This was in honour of his successes in Spain, whence he had returned late in the preceding September, after defeating the sons of Pompey at the battle of Munda (March 17th, B.C. 45). It was Cæsar's fifth and last triumph.

Many a time. Trench (*English Past and Present*) explains "many a man" as a corruption of "many of men ;" but Abbott (see Gr. 85) shows that the "many" is probably used as an adverb. Cf. the German *mancher* (adj.) *Mann* with *manch* (adv.) *ein Mann*, etc. In A. S. the idiom was *many man*, not *many a man*.

Pass the streets. Cf. *A. and C.* i. 4 : "to reel the streets at noon." See Gr. 198.

And when you saw his chariot but appear. That is, saw but his chariot appear. See Gr. 129 and 420.

That Tiber trembled, etc. On this common ellipsis of *so* before *that*, see

. **ROMAN HIGHWAY ON THE BANKS OF THE TIBER.**

Gr. 283. The river is here personified as feminine; as also in the next scene: "The troubled Tiber chafing with her shores." Cf. Milton, *P. L.* iii. 359:

> —"the river of bliss through midst of Heaven
> Rolls o'er Elysian flowers her amber stream."

Be gone! On these brief "interjectional lines," see Gr. 512.

That needs must. On *needs*, see *Mer.* p. 141, and Gr. 25.

Tiber banks. This use of proper names as adjectives is common in S. Cf. below, v. 1: "Here in Philippi fields." For other examples, see Gr. 22.

Whe'r. This contraction is often found in S., and the *th* appears to have been "softened" in some cases where the word is written in full, as also, perhaps, in *either, neither, hither, other*, etc. See Gr. 466.

Deck'd with ceremonies. This is the reading of the folio, and is retained by all the editors except W., who has "ceremony." If "ceremonies" is what S. wrote, it must mean "honorary ornaments" (Malone), or what are afterwards called "Cæsar's trophies," and described as "scarfs" hung on his images.

The feast of Lupercal. The Lupercal was a cavern in the Palatine Hill, sacred to Lupercus, the old Italian god of fertility, who came to be identified with Pan by Greek writers and their Roman followers. Thus Virgil (*Æn.* viii. 344) speaks of the place as

> —"sub rupe Lupercal
> Parrhasio dictum Panos de more Lycæi."

Here the feast of the *Lupercalia* was held every year, in the month of February. After certain sacrifices and other rites, the *Luperci* (or priests of Lupercus) ran through the city wearing only a cincture of goatskin, and striking with leather thongs all whom they met. This performance was a symbolic purification of the land and the people. The festal day was called *dies februata* (from *februare*, to purify), the month in which it occurred *Februarius*, and the god himself *Februus*.

Who else would soar. On *who=for he*, etc., see Gr. 263.

SCENE II.—The heading in the folio is, "*Enter Cæsar, Antony for the Course, Calphurnia, Portia, Decius, Cicero, Brutus, Cassius, Caska, a Soothsayer: after them Murellus and Flauius.*" *Calphurnia* is the name of Cæsar's wife throughout the play, and also in North's *Plutarch* (eds. of 1579 and 1612*), though C. and W. say that it is *Calpurnia* in the latter authority. W. prints *Calpurnia*, which was the classical form of the name.

Decius. His true name was *Decimus Brutus.* "The error, however, is as old as the edition of Plutarch's Greek text produced by Henry Stephens in 1572;† and it occurs likewise in the accompanying Latin translation, and both in Amyot's and Dacier's French, as well as in North's English. It is also found in Philemon Holland's translation of *Suetonius*, published in 1606. Lord Stirling, in his *Julius Cæsar*, probably misled in like manner by North, has fallen into the same mistake" (C.). It may be noted, also, that it was this Decimus Brutus who had been the special

---

* In some of the later editions (as in that of 1676, now before me) the name is changed to *Calpurnia*.   † Ἐν δὲ τούτῳ Δέκιος Βροῦτος ἐπίκλησιν 'Αλβῖνος. *Vit. Cæs.* p. 1354.

favourite of Cæsar, and not Marcus Junius Brutus, as represented in the play.

In Antonius' way. The folio has "in *Antonio's* way;" and in other names ending in *-ius* it often gives the Italian form in *-io*, which was more familiar to the actors of the time.

Antony was the head or chief of a third "college" of *Luperci* that had been added to the original two in honour of Cæsar.

When he doth run his course. Cf. N.* (*Life of Cæsar*): "At that time the feast Lupercalia was celebrated, the which in old time, men say, was the feast of Shepheards or Herdmen, and is much like unto the feast of Lycæians in Arcadia. But, howsoever it is, that day there are divers noble men's sons, young men (and some of them Magistrates themselves that govern them), which run naked through the City, striking in sport them they meet in their way with Leather thongs, hair and all on, to make them give place. And many noble Women and Gentlewomen also, go of purpose to stand in their way, and do put forth their hands to be stricken, as Scholars hold them out to their Schoolmaster, to be stricken with the ferula; perswading themselves that, being with Child, they shall have good delivery; and so, being barren, that it will make them to conceive with Child. . . . Antonius, who was Consull at that time, was one of them that ran this holy course."

Set on. See *Hen. VIII.* p. 180, and cf. below (v. 2): "Let them set on at once."

The Ides of March. In the Roman calendar the Ides fell on the 15th of March, May, July, and October, and on the 13th of the other months.

A soothsayer bids. The *Var.* ed. and C. put a comma after *soothsayer*, as if there were an ellipsis of *who* (Gr. 244). On the measure of this line, see Gr. 460.

Sennet. See *Hen. VIII.* p. 176.

That gentleness . . . as. See Gr. 280, and cf. below, "Under these hard conditions as this time," etc.

Merely upon myself. Altogether upon myself. See *Temp.* p. 111, note on *We are merely cheated.* Cf. Bacon, *Adv. of L.* ii. 1, 4: "narrations which are merely and sincerely natural;" *Id.* ii. 25, 9: "which do make men merely aliens and disincorporate from the Church of God;" *Essay* 27: "it is a mere and miserable solitude to want true friends."

Passions of some difference. "With a fluctuation of discordant opinions and desires" (J.).

Proper to myself. Peculiar to myself; my own. See Gr. 16, and *Temp.* p. 133, note on *Their proper selves.*

My behaviours. Cf. *M. Ado*, ii. 3: "in all outward behaviours," etc.

Mistook your passion. See *Mer.* p. 141, note on *Not undertook*, or Gr. 343. On *passion*=feeling, see *Mer.* p. 157, note on *Masters of passion.*

Cogitations. Thoughts. Cf. Bacon, *Adv. of L.* i. Introd.: "I may excite your princely cogitations to visit the excellent treasure of your own mind," etc. See also *Daniel*, vii. 28.

The eye sees not itself. Cf. *T. and C.* iii. 3:

* All the quotations from North's *Plutarch* in these Notes are from the edition of 1676.

I

—"nor doth the eye itself,
That most pure spirit of sense, behold itself."

Steevens quotes Sir John Davies, *Nosce Teipsum* (1599):

—"the mind is like the eye,
*   *   *   *   *   *
Not seeing itself, when other things it sees."

But by reflection by some other things. This is the folio reading, retained by K. and H. Pope read "from some other things;" D. has "from some other thing" (so H. in *school* ed.); and W., "by some other thing." If "by" is what S. wrote, it is probably *equivalent* to "by means of" or "from." Cf. the peculiar uses of *by* noted in Gr. 146. Even now we may say "being reflected by some other thing."

Mirrors. Walker and D. read "mirror."

Of the best respect. Cf. below, v. 5: "Thou art a fellow of a good respect."

Therefore, good Brutus, etc. "The eager, impatient temper of Cassius, absorbed in his own one idea, is vividly expressed by his thus continuing his argument as if without appearing to have even heard Brutus's interrupting question; for such is the only interpretation which his *therefore* would seem to admit of" (C.).

Jealous on me. Distrustful or suspicious of me. See *Mer.* p. 143 (note on *Glad on't*), or Gr. 180.

A common laugher. The folio has "common Laughter." Pope substituted "laugher," which has been adopted by all the more recent editors. As C. remarks, "neither word seems to be perfectly satisfactory." A friend, who has been a careful student of S., suggests "lover" as being in harmony with the context.

To stale with ordinary oaths, etc. Johnson (followed by W.) explains this, "to invite every new protester to my affection by the stale, or allurement, of customary oaths." On this sense of *stale*, see *Temp.* p. 137. But here (as C. and H. suggest) the word doubtless means "to make stale," or common. Cf. below, iv. 2: "staled by other men;" *A. and C.* ii. 3: "Age cannot wither her, nor custom stale Her infinite variety," etc.

And after scandal them. Cf. *Cor.* iii. 1: "Scandal'd the suppliants for the people," where, as here, it means to defame or traduce. For a different meaning, cf. *Temp.* iv. 1: "Her and her blind boy's scandal'd company;" *Cymb.* iii. 4: "Sinon's weeping Did scandal many a holy tear." On *after*, see Gr. 26.

honour in one eye, etc. Johnson explains this as follows: "When ▮▮▮us first names *honour* and *death*, he calmly declares them *indifferent*, but as the image kindles in his mind, he sets *honour* above life." Coleridge says: "Warburton would read *death* for *both*; but I prefer the old text. There are here three things—the public good, the individual Brutus's honour, and his death. The latter two so balanced each other that he could decide for the first by equipoise; nay—the thought growing—that honour had more weight than death. That Cassius understood it as Warburton is the beauty of Cassius as contrasted with Brutus." Craik remarks: "It does not seem to be necessary to suppose any such change or growth either of the image or the sentiment. What Brutus means by saying that he will look upon honour and death indifferently, if they present themselves together, is merely that, for the sake of the honour, he will not mind the death, or the risk of death, by which it may be accompanied; he will look as fearlessly and steadily upon the one as upon the other. He will think the honour to be cheaply purchased even by the loss of life; that price will never make him falter or hesitate in clutching at such a prize. He must be understood to set honour above life from the first; that he should ever have felt otherwise for a moment would have been the height of the unheroic."

On *indifferently*, cf. Bacon, *Adv. of L.* ii. Introd.: "I for my part shall be indifferently glad either to perform myself, or accept from another, that duty of humanity." See also *Hen. VIII.* p. 177, note on *No judge indifferent.*

Your outward favour. Your face, or personal appearance. So below, ii. 1: "By any mark of favour." Cf. Bacon, *Ess.* 27 (ed. of 1625): "For, as *S. James* saith, they are as Men, *that looke sometimes into a Glasse, and presently forget their own Shape, & Favour.*" See also *Proverbs*, xxxi. 30.

The troubled Tiber chafing, etc. See Gr. 376. *Chafe* (the Latin *calefacere*, through the Fr. *échauffer* and *chauffer*) meant, first, to warm; then, to ▉▉ by rubbing; and then simply to rub—either literally, as here, or in a ▉▉urative sense=to irritate; as in *Hen. VIII.* i. 1: "What, are you chaf'd?" Cf. 2 *Samuel*, xvii. 8.

In this passage, as in "Tiber trembled underneath her banks" (i. 1), some editors have changed "her" to "his," because *Tiber* is masculine in Latin; but, as C. remarks, "this is to give us both language and a conception different from Shakespeare's." It was not the Roman river-god that he had in mind in these personifications of the stream.

THE RIVER-GOD TIBER.

With lusty sinews. With vigorous sinews. Cf. *Temp.* ii. 1 : "lush and lusty." *Lusty* is "from the Saxon *lust* in its primary sense of eager desire, or intense longing, indicating a corresponding intensity of bodily vigour" (*Bible Word-Book*). See *Judges*, iii. 29.

Arrive the point. Cf. 3 *Hen. VI.* v. 3 : "have arriv'd our coast;" Milton, *P. L.* ii. 409 : "Ere he arrive The happy isle." See Gr. 198.

The old Anchises, etc. On the measure, see Gr. 501.

His coward lips, etc. "There can, I think, be no question that Warburton is right in holding that we have here a pointed allusion to a soldier flying from his colours. The lips would never otherwise be made to fly from their colour, instead of their colour from them. The figure is quite in Shakespeare's manner and spirit" (C.).

And that same eye whose bend. Cf. *A. and C.* ii. 2 :

> "Her gentlewomen, like the Nereids,
> So many mermaids, tended her i' th' eyes,
> And made their bends adornings."

His lustre. That is, *its* lustre. See *Temp.* p. 120, note on *With it's sweet air.* Gr. 228.

Of such a feeble temper. That is, "temperament, constitution" (D.). Cf. *M. of V.* i. 2 : "a hot temper leaps o'er a cold decree."

What should be in that Cæsar? On *should*, see Gr. 325.

More than yours. In the folio, "more then yours;" and *then* is the invariable form in that edition, as in Bacon, Hooker, etc. Usage had varied. Wiclif has *than* for both *than* and *then*, while Tyndale has *then* for both. Milton has *than* for *then* in the *Hymn on the Nativity*, 88 :

> "Full little thought they than
> That the mighty Pan
> Was kindly come to live with them below."

Noble bloods. Cf. iv. 3 : "I know young bloods look for a time of rest ;" *K. John,* ii. 1 : "As many and as well-born bloods," etc.

The great flood. A Roman would mean by this the deluge of Deucalion.

Fam'd with. Famed for. Cf. the peculiar uses of *with* in Gr. 193, 194.

That her wide walls. The folio has "That her wide Walkes," which K. and H. retain. Collier, C., D., and W. adopt Rowe's correction of "walls."

Now is it Rome indeed and room enough. "Evidence this that 'Rome' was pronounced *room*, or 'room' *rome*" (W.). Cf. below, iii. 1 : "No Rome of safety for Octavius yet ;" *K. John,* iii. 1 : "I have room with Rome to curse a while." St. quotes Prime, *Commentary on Galatians* (1587): "Rome is too narrow a Room for the Church of God." In 1 *Hen. VI.* iii. 1, the Bishop of Winchester says, "Rome shall remedy this," and Warwick replies, "Roam thither then." W. infers from this play upon *Rome* and *roam* (together with the fact that *room* was often spelled *rome*) that all three words were pronounced with the long sound of *o ;* but it is not impossible that *oa* was sometimes pronounced *oo*. In our day *loom* is the rustic pronunciation of *loam*. It is more probable, however, that C. and Earle (*Philology of English Tongue*, 1871) are right in assuming that in S.'s day the modern pronunciation of *Rome* was beginning to be heard, although the other was more common.

OLD WALLS OF ROME.

But one only man. See Gr. 130. Cf. Hooker, *Eccl. Pol.* i. 25: "one only God ;" i. 10, 14: "one only family," etc.

There was a Brutus once. Lucius Junius Brutus, who brought about the expulsion of Tarquinius Superbus.

The eternal devil. J. thought that S. wrote "infernal devil." Steevens says: "I would continue to read *eternal devil*. L. J. Brutus (says Cassius) would as soon have submitted to the perpetual dominion of a demon as to the lasting government of a king." Abbott (Gr. p. 16) considers it one of the exceptions to the exactness with which the poet used words that were "the recent inventions of the age." Cf. *Oth.* iv. 2: "eternal villain ;" *Ham.* i. 5: "this eternal blazon."

I am nothing jealous. I am nowise doubtful. See Gr. 55. Cf. above, "be not jealous on me." See also *T. of S.* iv. 5:

> "Come, go along, and see the truth hereof;
> For our first merriment hath made thee jealous."

I have some aim. Some guess, or conjecture. Cf. *T. G. of V.* iii. 1: "fearing lest my jealous aim might err," etc.

For this present. See *Hen. VIII.* p. 200, note on *At this present.*

So with love. On *so* (=if, provided that), see Gr. 133.

Chew upon this. "We have lost the Saxon word in this application, but we retain the metaphor, only translating *chew* into the Latin equivalent, *ruminate*" (C.).

Brutus had rather be, etc. See *Mer.* p. 132, note on *I had rather to be married.* The superlative *rathest* is found in Bacon, *Colours of Good and Evil,* i.: "whome next themselves they would rathest commend."

Than to repute. See *Temp.* p. 131 (note on *Than to suffer*), or Gr. 350.

What hath proceeded worthy note. What hath happened. On the ellipsis, see Gr. 198 a.

But look you, Cassius. Here *Cassius* is a trisyllable, as in several other instances.

Such ferret and such fiery eyes. The ferret has red eyes.

As we have seen him. That is, seen him look with. See Gr. 384.

Crossed in conference, etc. Opposed in debate. Walker and D. read "senator."

Let me have men about me that are fat, etc. Cf. N. (*Life of Cæsar*): "*Cæsar* also had *Cassius.* in great jealousie, and suspected him much : whereupon he said upon a time to his friends, what will *Cassius* do, think ye ? I like not his pale looks. Another time, when *Cæsars* friends complained unto him of *Antonius* and *Dolabella,* that they pretended some mischief towards him : he answered them again, As for those fat men and smooth combed heads, quoth he, I never reckon of them ; but these pale visaged and carrion lean People, I fear them most, meaning *Brutus* and *Cassius.*" So also, in *Life of Brutus:* "For, intelligence being brought him one day that *Antonius* and *Dolabella* did conspire against him : he answered, That these fat long haired men made him not afraid, but the lean and whitely faced fellows, meaning that by *Brutus* and *Cassius.*"

Such as sleep o' nights. The folio has "a-nights." See Gr. 182, and cf. 176 and 24.

Yond. Printed "Yond'" by K., W., and H., but it is not a contraction of *yonder.* See *Temp.* p. 121, note on *What thou seest yond.*

Well given. Well disposed. Cf. *2 Hen. VI.* iii. 1: "too well given," etc. In *I Hen. IV.* iii. 3, we have both "virtuously given" and "given to virtue."

Liable to fear. Liable to the imputation of fear.

He hears no music. Cf. *M. of V.* v. 1: "The man that hath not music in himself," etc.

Seldom he smiles. He seldom smiles. Cf. just below, "for always I am Cæsar," and see Gr. 421.

Such men as he be never at heart's ease. On *be,* see *Mer.* p. 134, note on *There be land-rats,* and Gr. 300. On *at,* see Gr. 144.

Whiles. See *Mer.* p. 133, or Gr. 137.

Tell us what hath chanc'd. W. says that the folio has "*had* chanc'd," but he must have been looking at the next speech of Brutus. Here the folio reading is, "I *Caska,* tell vs what hath chanc'd to day ;" there, "I should not then aske *Caska* what had chanc'd."

Why, there was a crown offer'd him. The editors generally quote here

Plutarch's *Life of Cæsar*, but it seems to me that the account given in the
Life of Antonius is more in keeping with Casca's way of telling the story :
" When he [Antony] was come to *Cæsar*, he made his fellow Runners with
him lift him up, and so he did put his Lawrell Crown upon his head, sig-
nifying thereby that he had deserved to be King. But *Cæsar* making as
though he refused it, turned away his head. The People were so rejoiced
at it, that they all clapped their hands for joy. *Antonius* again did put it
on his head : *Cæsar* again refused it ; and thus they were striving off and
on a great while together. As oft as *Antonius* did put this Lawrell Crown
unto him, a few of his followers rejoyced at it : and as oft also as *Cæsar*
refused it, all the People together clapped their hands. . . . *Cæsar* in a
rage arose out of his Seat, and plucking down the choller of his Gown
from his neck, he shewed it naked, bidding any man strike off his head
that would. This Lawrell Crown was afterwards put upon the head of
one of *Cæsar's* Statues or Images, the which one of the Tribunes pluckt
off. The People liked his doing therein so well, that they waited on him
home to his house, with great clapping of hands. Howbeit *Cæsar* did
turn them out of their offices for it." According to the *Life of Cæsar*, his
" tearing open his Doublet Coller," and offering his throat to be cut, was
among his friends *in his own house*, and on a different occasion, namely,
when " the Consuls and Prætors, accompanied with the whole Assembly
of the Senate, went unto him in the Market-place, where he was set by
the Pulpit for Orations, to tell him what honours they had decreed for
him in his absence," and he offended them by " sitting still in his Majesty, disdaining to rise up unto them when they came in." The historian
adds that, " afterwards to excuse his folly, he imputed it to his disease,
saying, that their wits are not perfect which have this disease of the fall-
ing-Evill, when standing on their feet they speak to the common People,
but are soon troubled with a trembling of their Body, and a suddain dim-
ness and giddiness." The Lupercalia and the offering of the crown are
then described as occurring *after* this insult to " the Magistrates of the
Commonwealth."

Ay, marry, was't. On *Marry*, see *Mer.* p. 138.

The rabblement shouted. The folio has " howted," which is doubtless a
misprint for " showted," as the word is spelled just above in " mine honest Neighbours showted." The *Var.* ed., K., and H. have " hooted," but
that word is not consistent with the context, as it expresses " insult, not
applause."

He swooned. The folio has " hee swoonded," and below, " what, did
Cæsar swound ?"

At mouth. For the ellipsis of *the*, see Gr. 90.

'*Tis very like*, etc. *Like* for *likely*, as very often. The folio reads, " 'Tis
very like he hath the Falling sicknesse," and Coll. adheres to that pointing. But Brutus knew that Cæsar was subject to these epileptic attacks.
Cf. N. : " For, concerning the constitution of his body, he was lean, white,
and soft skinned, and often subject to head-ach, and other while to the
falling-sickness (the which took him the first time, as it is reported, in
CORDUBA, a City of SPAIN), but yet therefore yielded not to the disease
of his body, to make it a cloak to cherish him withall, but contrarily, took

the pains of War, as a Medicine to cure his sick body, fighting alwaies with his disease, travelling continually, living soberly, and commonly lying abroad in the Field."

Tag-rag. Cf. *Cor.* iii. 1 : "Will you hence, before the tag return?" "This," says Nares, "is, perhaps, the only instance of *tag* without his companions *rag* and *bobtail,* or at least one of them." Coll. quotes John Partridge, 1566 :

"To walles they goe, both tagge and ragge,
Their citie to defende."

No true man. No honest man. Cf. *M. for M.* iv. 2 : "Every true man's apparel fits your thief;" *L. L. L.* iv. 3 : "a true man or a thief;" *Cymb.* ii. 3 : "hangs both thief and true man," etc.

Pluck'd me ope his doublet. On *me,* see *Mer.* p. 135, note on *Pill'd me,* and Gr. 220. On *ope,* see Gr. 343, 290.

An I had been. The folio has "and I had beene." See Gr. 101 foll.

A man of any occupation. "A mechanic, one of the plebeians to whom he offered his throat" (J.). Cf. *Cor.* iv. 6 : "the voice of occupation and The breath of garlic-eaters." But may it not mean, as W. suggests, "a man of action, a busy man?"

At a word. At his word. Elsewhere the phrase =*in* a word. Cf. *Cor.* i. 3 : "No, at a word, madam ;" *M. Ado,* ii. 1 : "At a word, I am not." See also *M. W.* i. 1 ; 2 *Hen. IV.* iii. 2, etc.

I am promised forth. Cf. *M. of V.* ii. 5 : "I am bid forth to supper," and "I have no mind of feasting forth to-night." See Gr. 41.

He was quick mettle. Collier's MS. corrector has "mettled." Walker suggests "metal," referring to "blunt" in the preceding line. The folio has "mettle," not only here, but below in "Thy Honourable Mettle," and also in i. 1 ("their basest mettle"), in ii. 1 ("th' insuppressiue Mettle of our Spirits"), and iv. 2 ("promise of Mettle"). But in *Temp.* ii. 1, "No vse of Mettall, Corne, or Wine ;" *M. of V.* i. 3 : "A breede of barraine mettall ;" *Id.* iv. 1 : "but no mettall can . . . beare halfe the keennesse," etc. The two words are etymologically one.

This rudeness is a sauce to his good wit, etc. Cf. *Lear,* ii. 2 :

"This is some fellow,
Who, having been prais'd for bluntness, doth affect
A saucy roughness."

Thou art noble. On *thou,* see Gr. 233.

From that it is disposed. From that *to which* it is disposed. See Gr. 244 (cf. 394).

So firm that cannot. See Gr. 279.

Doth bear me hard. "Does not like me, bears me a grudge" (C.). Cf. ii. 1 : "Caius Ligarius doth bear Cæsar hard ;" iii. 1 : "if you bear me hard." The expression occurs nowhere else in S.

He should not humour me. "He (that is, Brutus) should not cajole me as I do him" (Warb.). "'Cæsar loves Brutus, but if Brutus and I were to change places, his love should not humour me,' should not take hold of my affection, so as to make me forget my principles" (J.). C. adopts the former explanation, but the latter is perhaps to be preferred.

In several hands. Referring to "writings" below. Cf. Gr. 419 *a.*

Seat him sure. See Gr. 223 and 1. On the rhyming couplet at the end of a scene, see Gr. 515.

SCENE III.—*Brought you Cæsar home?* On *bring*=accompany, escort, cf. *Oth.* iii. 4: "I pray you, bring me on the way a little," etc. See also *Genesis*, xviii. 16; *Acts*, xxi. 5; *2 Corinth.* i. 16.

The sway of earth. "The whole weight or momentum of this world" (J.). "The balanced swing of earth" (C.).

Unfirm. S. uses both *infirm* and *unfirm*—each four times. See *Mer.* p. 155, note on *Uncapable*, or Gr. 442.

To be exalted with. That is, in the effort to rise to that height; or, possibly, *so as* to rise to the clouds.

A tempest dropping fire. The folio has "a Tempest-dropping-fire," and I believe that some editor has explained the expression as "a tempest-dropping fire."

Incenses them to send destruction. Here *destruction* is a quadrisyllable. This making two syllables of the termination *-ion* is frequent at the end of a line, but rare in any other position. See Gr. 479.

Anything more wonderful. Abbott (Gr. 6) explains this as "more wonderful than usual;" C., "anything more that was wonderful." Cf. *Cor.* iv. 6:

> "The slave's report is seconded, and more,
> More fearful, is delivered."

You know him well by sight. This is a stumbling-block to some of the commentators. D. suggests "you'd know him," and C. "you knew him," in the sense of "would have known him." But it is nothing strange that both Cicero and Casca should happen to know a particular slave by sight, and it is natural enough that Casca, in referring to him here, should say, And you yourself know the man.

On this whole passage, cf. N. (*Life of Cæsar*): "Certainly, destiny may easier be foreseen than avoided, considering the strange and wonderfull Signs that were said to be seen before *Cæsars* death. For, touching the Fires in the Element, and Spirits running up and down in the night, and also the solitary Birds to be seen at noon days sitting in the great Market-place, are not all these Signs perhaps worth the noting, in such a wonderfull chance as happened? But *Strabo* the philosopher writeth, that divers men were seen going up and down in fire: and furthermore, that there was a Slave of the Souldiers that did cast a marvellous burning flame out of his hand, insomuch as they that saw it thought he had been burnt: when the Fire was out, it was found he had no hurt. *Cæsar* self also doing Sacrifice unto the gods, found that one of the Beasts which was sacrificed had no Heart: and that was a strange thing in nature: how a Beast could live without a Heart."

A lion Who, etc. See *Mer.* p. 144, *Temp.* pp. 111, 124, 133, or Gr. 264. The folio has "glaz'd vpon me." Pope substituted "glar'd," and Collier's MS. corrector has the same. Cf. *Lear*, iii. 6: "Look, how he stands and glares!"

Without annoying me. Cf. *Rich. III.* v. 3: "Good angels guard thee from the boor's annoy!" Chaucer (*Persones Tale*) speaks of a man as

"Against the Capitol I met a Lion."

annoying his neighbour by burning his house, or poisoning him, and the like. .

Drawn upon a heap. Crowded together. Cf. *T. A.* ii. 4: "All on a heap," etc. For *heap* applied to persons, see *Rich. III.* ii. 1: "Among this princely heap."

These are their reasons. "That such and such are their reasons" (C.). Cf. below, ii. 1: "Would run to these and these extremities." Collier's MS. corrector has "seasons."

Climate. Region, clime. Cf. Bacon, *Adv. of L.* i. 6, 10: "the southern stars were in that climate unseen." The word is used as a verb in *W. T.* v. 1: "whilst you Do climate here."

Clean from the purpose. On *clean,* cf. *Psalm* lxxvii. 8; *Isaiah,* xxiv. 19, etc. On *from*=away from, see Gr. 158. Cf. below, "from quality and kind."

Is not to walk in. See Gr. 405.

What night is this! C. reads "What a night," but this is a needless marring of the metre. Cf. *T. G. of V.* i. 2:

> "What fool is she that knows I am a maid,
> And would not force the letter to my view !"

and *T. N.* ii. 5 :

> "*Fabian.* What dish o' poison has she dressed him !
> *Sir Toby.* And with what wing the staniel checks at it !"

For other examples, see Gr. 86.

Submitting me. Exposing myself. Gr. 223.

The thunder-stone. "The imaginary product of the thunder, which the ancients called *Brontia,* mentioned by Pliny (*N. H.* xxxvii. 10) as a species of gem, and as that which, falling with the lightning, does the mischief.

It is the fossil commonly called the Belemnite, or Finger-stone, and now known to be a shell. We still talk of the *thunder-bolt*, which, however, is commonly confounded with the lightning. The *thunder-stone* was held to be quite distinct from the lightning, as may be seen from *Cymb.* iv. 2 :

> "'*Guiderius.* Fear no more the lightning-flash.
> *Arviragus.* Nor the all-dreaded thunder-stone.'

It is also alluded to in *Oth.* v. 2 :

> "'Are there no stones in heaven
> But what serve for the thunder?'" (C.)

Case yourself in wonder. The folio has "cast your selfe in wonder," which is retained by Coll., C., St., H., and the Camb. ed. D. (2d ed.) and W. have "case," which was independently suggested by Swynfen Jervis and M. W. Williams. Cf. *M. Ado*, iv. 1 : "attir'd in wonder."

Why birds and beasts, etc. That is, why they change their natures. See above, on *From that it is dispos'd.* Cf. *Lear*, ii. 2 : "Quite from his nature."

Why old men fool, etc. "Why old men become fools, and children prudent" (W.). The folio reads, "Why Old men, Fooles, and Children calculate;" and so K., C., and H. Coll. and St. have "Why old men fools" —that is, why we have old men fools. D. (2d ed.), W., and the Camb. ed. read "Why old men fool," which was suggested by W. N. Lettsom (Walker's *Crit. Exam.* vol. i. p. 250). On *fool*, see Gr. 290.

Their ordinance. What they were ordained to be.

Unto some monstrous state. "That is, I suppose, some monstrous or unnatural state of things, not some overgrown commonwealth" (C.). It may, however, mean some unnatural commonwealth. On the measure of this line and the next but one, see Gr. 511.

As doth the lion in the Capitol. "That is, roars in the Capitol as doth the lion" (C.).

Than thyself or me. On *me*, see Gr. 210.

Prodigious. Portentous; as always in S. except in *T. G. of V.* ii. 3 : "the prodigious son" (Launce's blunder for "prodigal son"). Cf. B. and F., *Philaster*, v. 1 : "like a prodigious meteor;" and see Gr. p. 13.

Thews and limbs. Here *thews* means muscular powers, as in the two other instances (2 *Hen. IV.* iii. 2, and *Ham.* i. 3) in which S. uses the word. It is from the A. S. *theow* or *theoh*, whence also *thigh*, and must not be confounded with the obsolete *thews*=manners, or qualities of mind, which is from the A. S. *theaw.* This latter *thews* is common in Chaucer, Spenser, and other early writers; the former is found very rarely before S.'s day.

Woe the while. See Gr. 137 (cf. 230).

Govern'd with. On *with*, see Gr. 193.

Can be retentive, etc. "Can retain or confine the spirit" (C.).

Never lacks power. Here *power* is a dissyllable. Gr. 480.

So every bondman, etc. There is a play on *bond;* as in *Rich. III.* iv. 4 : "Cancel his bond of life, dear God, I pray!" Cf. also *Cymb.* v. 4 : "take my life, And cancel these cold bonds" (that is, his *chains*); *Macb.* iii. 2 :

> "And with thy bloody and invisible hand
> Cancel and tear to pieces tnat great bond
> Which keeps me pale!"

My answer must be made. "I shall be called to account, and must an, swer as for seditious words" (J.).

Such a man That is no fleering tell-tale. On *such . . . that,* see Gr. 279. *Fleering* here =deceitful, or treacherous. Cf. South (quoted by Worc.) : "A treacherous fleer on the face of deceivers."

Hold, my hand. Here, take my hand. St. omits the comma after "Hold." C. interprets the passage thus : " Have, receive, take hold (of it) ; there is my hand." But *hold* is probably a mere interjection, as often in S., and not an imperative with object "understood." Cf *Macb.* ii. 1 : "Hold, take my sword ;" *Rich. II.* ii. 2 : "Hold, take my ring," etc. This *hold* is of course identical with the *reflexive* verb which we have below (v. 3) : "But hold thee, take this garland," etc.

Be factious, etc. "*Factious* seems here to mean *active*" (J.). Coleridge says, "I understand it thus : You have spoken as a conspirator ; be so in *fact,* and I will join you." It may, however, have its ordinary meaning, as it does in every other instance in S. *Griefs* here =*grievances.* Cf. iii. 2 : " What private griefs they have ;" iv. 2 : " Speak your griefs softly," and " Enlarge your griefs."

As who goes farthest. On *who,* see Gr. 257.

Honourable-dangerous. See Gr. 2. Walker and D. print "bloody-fiery" just below.

Pompey's porch. A large building connected with Pompey's Theatre.

The element. The heaven, or sky. Cf. N. (*Life of Pompey*) : "When Pompey saw the dust in the element" (that is, in the air) ; and in the quotation above (note on *You know him well by sight*) we have " the Fires in the Element." See also Milton, *Comus,* 298 :

> "I took it for a faery vision
> Of some gay creatures of the element,
> That in the colours of the rainbow live,
> And play in the plighted clouds."

In favour's like. In aspect is like. The folio reads, "Is Fauors, like the Worke we haue in hand." J. proposed "In favour's," which K., D., W., H., and Camb. ed. adopt. Steevens suggested "'It favours,' or 'Is favour'd ;'" and Reed, "Is fev'rous," quoting in support of it *Macb.* ii. 3 : "the earth Was feverous, and did shake." C. is "strongly inclined to adopt Reed's ingenious conjecture."

To find out you. To find you out. See Gr. 240.

One incorporate To our attempt. "One united with us in our enterprise" (C.). Cf. Bacon, *Adv. of L.* ii. 2, 12 : "not incorporate into the history." See Gr. 342 and 187. The folio has "To our Attempts," which is retained by K., C., H., and Camb. ed. D. and W. adopt Walker's correction, "attempt."

There's two or three. See *Temp.* p. 122, note on *There is no more such shapes,* or Gr. 335.

Where Brutus may but find it. On *but,* see Gr. 128.

Upon old Brutus' statue. Cf. N. (*Life of Brutus*) : "But for *Brutus,* his friends and Countreymen, both by divers procurements and sundry rumors of the City, and by many bills also, did openly call and procure him to do that he did. For under the image of his ancestor *Junius Brutus* (that drave the Kings out of ROME) they wrote: O, that it pleased the gods thou wert now alive, *Brutus!* and again, That thou were here among us now! His tribunal or chair, where he gave audience during the time he was Prætor, was full of such bills: *Brutus* thou art asleep, and art not *Brutus* indeed."

Bestow. See *Mer.* p. 140.

Three parts of him Is ours. See Gr. 333.

Pompey's theatre. This was the first stone theatre that had been built at Rome, and was modelled after one that Pompey had seen at Mitylene. It was large enough to accommodate forty thousand spectators. At its opening in B.C. 55, the games exhibited by Pompey lasted many days, and consisted of dramatic representations, contests of gymnasts and of gladiators, and fights of wild beasts. Five hundred African lions were killed, and eighteen elephants were brought into the arena, most of which fell before Gætulian huntsmen.

You have right well conceited. "To *conceit* is only another form of our still familiar to *conceive*" (C.). Cf. below, iii. 1: "one of two bad ways you must conceit me;" *Oth.* iii. 3: "one that so imperfectly conceits." The noun *conceit* was also equivalent to *conception*, as in *M. of V.* i. 1: "profound conceit" (deep thought). Cf. Bacon, *Essay* 6: "It pusleth & perplexeth the Conceits of many."

POMPEY.

ACT II.

SCENE I.—The heading in the folio is, "*Enter Brutus in his Orchard.*" *Orchard* in S. is "generally synonymous with garden" (D.). The word is the A. S. *ortgeard,* or *wyrtgeard* (wort-yard or plant-yard), not a tautological compound of the Latin *hortus* and the A. S. *geard,* as Earle (*Philology of English Tongue,* Clarendon Press series, 1871) and others have made it. Below (iii. 2) the "private arbours and new-planted orchards" are the "*gardens* and arbours" of N.

What, Lucius! See *Mer.* p. 141 (note on *What, Jessica!*), *Temp.* p. 119 (note on *Come, thou tortoise! when?*), and Gr. 73 *a.* Conf. just below, "When, Lucius, when?"

How near to day. How near it is to day. Gr. 403.

It must be by his death, etc. Coleridge remarks : "This speech is singular—at least, I do not at present see into Shakespeare's motive, his *rationale,* or in what point of view he meant Brutus's character to appear. For surely—(this, I mean, is what I say to myself, with my present *quantum* of insight, only modified by my experience in how many instances I have ripened into a perception of beauties where I had before descried faults)—surely nothing can seem more discordant with our historical preconceptions of Brutus, or more lowering to the intellect of the Stoico-Platonic tyrannicide, than the tenets here attributed to him—to him, the stern Roman republican ; namely, that he would have no objection to a king, or to Cæsar, a monarch in Rome, would Cæsar but be as good a monarch as he now seems disposed to be! How, too, could Brutus say that he found no personal cause—none in Cæsar's past conduct as a man ? Had he not crossed the Rubicon ? Had he not entered Rome as a conqueror ? Had he not placed his Gauls in the Senate ? Shakespeare, it may be said, has not brought these things forward. True—and this is just the ground of my perplexity. What character did Shakespeare mean his Brutus to be ?"

But for the general. "For the community, or the people" (C.). Cf. *M. for M.* ii. 4 : "the general, subject to a well-wish'd king ;" *Ham.* ii. 2 : "caviare to the general ;" *T. and C.* i. 3 : "good or bad unto the general." But here it may be simply "for the general *cause.*"

Crown him?—That. Be that so ; suppose that done.

Do danger. Do what is dangerous ; do mischief.

Remorse. Mercy, or pity. See *Mer.* p. 156, and *Temp.* p. 140.

Common proof. A thing commonly proved, a common experience. Cf. *Cymb.* iii. 3 :

> "Out of your proof you speak ; we, poor unfledg'd,
> Have never wing'd from view o' th' nest, nor know not
> What air's from home."

Climber-upward. On the "noun-compounds" of S., see Gr. 430.

Upmost. Like *inmost, outmost,* or *utmost,* etc. Mrs. Clarke does not give the word, but has *utmost* in this passage, following what is probably a slip of the type in Knight's edition. We find *upmost* in Dryden (Worc.).

The base degrees. The lower steps of the ladder. Cf. *Hen. VIII.* ii. 4 : "You have . . . Gone slightly o'er low steps, and now are mounted," etc.

Will bear no colour, etc. Can find no pretext in what he now is. On *colour*, cf. *Hen. VIII.* p. 160.

As his kind. "Like the rest of his species" (Mason).

And kill him in the shell. "It is impossible not to feel the expressive effect of the hemistich here. The line itself is, as it were, killed in the shell" (C.).

The Ides of March. The folio has "the first of March." Theo. made the correction.

Where I have took. See *Mer.* p. 141 (note on *Not undertook*), or Gr. 343.

My ancestors. D. reads "My ancestor."

March is wasted fifteen days. This is the folio reading, changed to "fourteen days" by Theo. and all the recent editors except W., who remarks that "in common parlance Lucius is correct"—and so in *Roman* parlance, he might have added.

Like a phantasma. Like a vision. S. uses this form of the word nowhere else. He has *phantasm* twice, but only in the sense of something *fantastical.* See *L. L. L.* iv. 1: "A phantasm, a Monarcho, and one that makes sport," etc.; *Id.* v. 1: "I abhor such fanatical phantasms."

The genius and the mortal instruments. "The commentators have written and disputed lavishly upon these celebrated words. Apparently, by the *genius* we are to understand the contriving and immortal mind, and most probably the *mortal instruments* are the earthly passions. The best light for the interpretation of the present passage is reflected from the one below, where Brutus says—

> "'Let our hearts, as subtle masters do,
> Stir up their servants to an act of rage,
> And after seem to chide 'em.'

The *servants* here may be taken to be the same with the *instruments* in the passage before us. It has been proposed to understand by the *mortal instruments* the bodily powers or organs; but it is not obvious how these could be said to hold consultation with the genius or mind. Neither could they in the other passage be so fitly said to be stirred up by the heart" (C.).

According to J., the poet "is describing the *insurrection* which a conspirator feels agitating the *little kingdom* of his own mind; when the *genius*, or power that watches for his protection, and the *mortal instruments*, the passions, which excite him to a deed of honour and danger, are in council and debate; when the desire of action, and the care of safety, keep the mind in continual fluctuation and disturbance."

Malone indorses Johnson's interpretation, but understands *mortal* to mean *deadly*, as often in S.

A writer in the *Edinburgh Review* (Oct. 1869) makes *genius* "the spirit, ruling intellectual power, rational soul, as opposed to the irascible nature," and *mortal instruments* "the bodily powers through which it works." This is perhaps to be preferred to Craik's explanation. I cannot believe that *genius* has here the meaning which J. ascribes to it, and which it has in some other passages of our poet; as in *C. of E.* v. 1:

> "One of these men is genius to the other;
> And so of these. Which is the natural man,
> And which the spirit?"

The state of man. The folio has "the state of a man," which K. and C. retain ; all the other recent editors omit "a."

On the whole passage, cf. *T. and C.* ii. 3 :

> —"'twixt his mental and his active parts
> Kingdom'd Achilles in commotion rages,
> And batters 'gainst himself."

Your brother Cassius. Cassius had married Junia, the sister of Brutus.

There are more with him. The folio has "moe with him." See *Mer.* p. 129, note on *I'll tell thee more.*

I may discover. On *may*, see *Mer.* p. 133 (note on *May you stead me ?*) and Gr. 307. On the ellipsis of *so*, see Gr. 283.

By any mark of favour. See above (i. 2), on *Your outward favour.*

Sham'st thou, etc. Cf. *W. T.* ii. 1 : "What she should shame to know ;" *Macb.* ii. 1 :

> "My hands are of your colour, but I shame
> To wear a heart so white."

For if thou path, etc. The folio reads, "For if thou path thy natiue semblance on," which (with a comma after "path") may be explained "If thou walk in thy true form" (J.). Drayton uses *path* as a *transitiv* verb in his *Polyolbion :* "Where from the neighbouring hills her passage Wey doth path," and again in his *Epistle from Duke Humphrey*, etc. "Pathing young Henry's unadvised ways." It is not unlikely, however that *path* is a misprint here. Southern and Coleridge independently suggested "put," which Walker pronounces "certainly" right, and which D adopts. W. is inclined to the opinion that S. wrote "hadst."

We are too bold, etc. "We intrude too boldly or unceremoniously upor your rest" (C.).

Shall I entreat a word ? See *Introduction*, p. 13.

Here, as I point my sword. On *as*, see Gr. 112.

Which is a great way, etc. Which must be far to the south, when we consider the time of year. On *weighing*, see Gr. 378.

Your hands all over. "That is, all included" (C.).

No, not an oath. Cf. N. (*Life of Brutus*): "The onely name and grea' Calling of *Brutus*, did bring on the most of them to give consent to thi' conspiracy ; who having never taken Oaths together, nor taken nor giver any caution or assurance, nor binding themselves one to another by any religious Oaths, they all kept the matter so secret to themselves, and could so cunningly handle it, that notwithstanding, the gods did reveal i' by manifest signs and tokens from above, and by Predictions of Sacrifices yet all this would not be believed."

If not the face of men. The folio reading, retained by K., C., D., W., H. and Camb. ed. Warburton proposed "fate of men ;" Mason, "faith ;" and Steevens, "faiths."

The time's abuse. The abuses of the time.

Idle bed. Bed of idleness ; as we say "a sick bed." Cf. *T. and C.* i. 3 "upon a lazy bed."

By lottery. As chance may determine. Steevens thought there migh' be an allusion to the custom of *decimation*—"the selection by lot of ever' tenth soldier, in a general mutiny, for punishment." Cf. *T. of A.* v. 5: "By decimation, and a tithed death."

What need we any spur. On *what,* see Gr. 253.

Than secret Romans. Than *that of* Romans pledged to secrecy. Gr. 390.

Will not palter. Will not shuffle or equivocate. Cf. *A. and C.* iii. 11: "dodge And palter in the shifts of lowness;" *Cor.* iii. 1: "This paltering Becomes not Rome;" *Macb.* v. 7:

> "And be these juggling fiends no more believ'd,
> That palter with us in a double sense;
> That keep the word of promise to our ear,
> And break it to our hope."

Cautelous. Wary, crafty. Cf. *Cor.* iv. 1: "cautelous baits and practice." These are the only instances of the word in S. He uses the noun *cautel* in *Ham.* i. 3: "no soil nor *cautel* doth besmirch The virtue of his will." Cotgrave (*French Dict.*, 1611) defines *cautelle* thus: "A wile, cautell, sleight; a craftie reach, or fetch, guilefull deuise or endeuor; also, craft, subtiltie, trumperie, deceit, cousenage." Cf. Bacon, *Adv. of L.* ii. 21, 9: "frauds, cautels, impostures."

The even virtue. "The firm and steady virtue" (C.).

The insuppressive metal. Here *insuppressive* is used in a "passive" sense, =not to be suppressed. Cf. *A. Y. L.* iii. 2: "The fair, the chaste, and *unexpressive* she;" *T. and C.* iii. 3: "the *uncomprehensive* (unknown) deeps;" *A. W.* i. 2: "his *plausive* (plausible, specious) words;" *T. G. of V.* iv. 4: "I can make *respective* (respectable) in myself," etc. See Gr. 3.

To think that. On the use of the infinitive, see Gr. 356.

Did need an oath. Ever could need an oath. Gr. 370.

A several bastardy. "A special or distinct act of baseness, or of treason against ancestry and honourable birth" (C.). See *Temp.* p. 131, note on *Several.*

His silver hairs. Cicero was then about sixty years old. There is an obvious play upon *silver* and *purchase.*

Let us not break with him. That is, broach the matter to him. See *Hen. VIII.* p. 197.

Cf. N. (*Life of Brutus*): "For this cause they durst not acquaint *Cicero* with their conspiracy, although he was a man whom they loved dearly, and trusted best; for they were afraid that he, being a coward by nature, and age also having encreased his fear, he would quite turn and alter all their purpose, and quench the heat of their enterprise, the which specially required hot and earnest execution."

We shall find of him A shrewd contriver. On *of*=in, see Gr. 172. On *shrewd*=evil, mischievous, see *Hen. VIII.* p. 202. Wiclif (*Genesis*, vi. 12) translates the *iniquitate* of the Vulgate by "shrewdnes." Cf. Chaucer, *Tale of Melibœus:* "The prophete saith: Flee shrewdnesse, and do goodnesse; seek pees, and folwe it, in as muchel as in thee is;" *Id.:* "And Seint Poule the Apostle sayth in his Epistle, whan he writeth unto the Romaines, that the juges beren not the spere withouten cause, but they beren it to punish the shrewes and misdoers, and for to defende the goode men."

As to annoy us. See above (i. 3), on *Without annoying me.*

K

CICERO.

And envy afterwards. Here *envy*=malice, as often. See *Mer.* p. 151,
note on *Envious.*

Let us be sacrificers, etc. On the measure, see Gr. 468; and also fo
Our purpose necessary, etc., just below.

This shall make, etc. *Make* is equivalent to "make to seem." C
adopts the "mark" of Collier's MS. corrector.

Yet I fear him. Steevens read "do fear," which C. says "improves
if it is not absolutely required by, the sense or expression as well as th
prosody." It is adopted by no other editor, so far as I know.

Take thought, and die. Thought used to mean "anxiety, melancholy;"
and to *think,* or *take thought,* "to be anxious, despondent." Cf. *A. and C*
iii. 2 : *"Cleopatra.* What shall we do, Enobarbus ? *Enobarbus.* Think, an
die ;" Holland, *Camden's Ireland:* "the old man for very thought an
grief of heart pined away and died ;" Bacon, *Hist. of Hen. VII.:* "Hawi
. . . . dyed with thought, and anguish." See also 1 *Samuel,* ix. 5, an
Matthew, vi. 25.

There is no fear in him. That is, nothing for us to fear. *Fear* is else
where used for the *cause* or *object* of fear ; as in *M. N. D.* v. 1 :

> "Or in the night, imagining some fear,
> How easy is a bush suppos'd a bear !"

Count the clock. Of course this is an anachronism, as the *clepsydræ,* o
water-clocks, of the Romans did not strike the hours.

Hath stricken. S. uses *struck* (or *strook*), *strucken* (or *stroken*), an
stricken. See Gr. 344.

Whether Cæsar will come forth. Here the folio prints "Whether" in full, though the word is metrically equivalent to the "whe'r" in "See whe'r their basest metal," etc. (i. 1). Gr. 466.

Quite from the main opinion. Quite contrary to the fixed (or predominant) opinion. Cf. above (i. 3), "from quality and kind;" and *T. N.* v. 1: "Write from it (that is, differently from it), if you can," etc. Mason proposed to read "mean opinion."

Fantasy. "Fancy, or imagination, with its unaccountable anticipations and apprehensions, as opposed to the calculations of reason" (C.).

Ceremonies. "Omens or signs deduced from sacrifices, or other *cere-monial* rites" (Malone). Cf. Bacon, *Adv. of L.* ii. 10, 3: "ceremonies, characters, and charms," where the word means superstitious rites.

These apparent prodigies. These manifest portents. *Apparent* is used in its emphatic sense (*clearly* appearing), not in its weaker one (*merely* appearing, or *seeming*). Cf. 1 *Hen. IV.* ii. 4: "this open and apparent shame;" *K. John,* iv. 2:

> "It is apparent foul play; and 'tis shame
> That greatness should so grossly offer it."

See also Bacon, *Ess.* xl. (ed. 1625): "Overt, and Apparent vertues bring forth Praise; But there be Secret and Hidden Vertues, that bring Forth Fortune."

That unicorns, etc. Steevens says: "Unicorns are said to have been taken by one who, running behind a tree, eluded the violent push the animal was making at him, so that his horn spent its force on the trunk, and stuck fast, detaining the beast till he was dispatched by the hunter." Cf. Spenser, *F. Q.* ii. 5, 10:

> "Like as a Lyon, whose imperiall powre
> A prowd rebellious Unicorn defyes,
> T' avoide the rash assault and wrathful stowre
> Of his fiers foe, him to a tree applyes,
> And when him ronning in full course he spyes,
> He slips aside; the whiles that furious beast
> His precious horne, sought of his enimyes,
> Strikes in the stocke, ne thence can be releast,
> But to the mighty victor yields a bounteous feast."

See also *T. of A.* iv. 3: "wert thou the unicorn, pride and wrath would confound thee, and make thine own self the conquest of thy fury."

"Bears," adds Steevens, "are reported to have been surprised by means of a mirror, which they would gaze on, affording their pursuers an opportunity of taking a surer aim. This circumstance, I think, is mentioned by Claudian. Elephants were seduced into pitfalls, lightly covered with hurdles and turf, on which a proper bait to tempt them was exposed. See Pliny's *Natural History,* book viii."

Most flattered. "At the end of a line *ed* is often sounded after *er*" (Gr. 474). On the metre of the next line, see Gr. 512.

Doth bear Cæsar hard. See above (i. 2), on *Cæsar doth bear me hard.* On the relations of this Caius (or, rather, Quintus) Ligarius to Cæsar, cf. N. (*Life of Brutus*): "Now amongst *Pompey's* friends, there was one called *Caius Ligarius,* who had been accused unto *Cæsar* for taking part with *Pompey,* and *Cæsar* discharged him. But *Ligarius* thanked not *Cæsar* so much for his discharge, as he was offended with him for that he was brought in danger by his tyrannicall power. And, therefore, in his heart he was alway his mortall enemy, and was besides very familiar with *Brutus*, who went to see him being sick in his bed, and said unto him : *Ligarius* in what a time art thou sick ! *Ligarius* rising up in his bed, and taking him by the right hand, said unto him : *Brutus* (said he) if thou hast any great enterprise in hand worthy of thyself, I am whole."

Go along by him. That is, by his house (on your way home). Cf. below (iv. 3): "The enemy, marching along by them." Pope read "Go along to him," and was followed by the other editors before Malone, who restored "by."

Look fresh and merrily. That is, freshly and merrily. Cf. *T. N.* v. 1: "Apt and willingly." For other examples, see Gr. 397.

Let not our looks put on our purposes. That is, "such expression as would betray our purposes." C. compares the exhortation of Lady Macbeth to her husband (*Macb.* i. 5):

> "To beguile the time,
> Look like the time: bear welcome in your eye,
> Your hand, your tongue ; look like the innocent flower,
> But be the serpent under it."

But the sentiment takes its boldest form from the lips of Macbeth himself in the first fervour of his weakness exalted into determined wickedness (i. 7):

> "Away, and mock the time with fairest show :
> False face must hide what the false heart doth know."

Formal constancy. "Constancy in outward form or aspect" (C.).

The honey-heavy dew of slumber. See Gr. 430. The folio reads, "the hony-heauy-Dew of Slumber," for which Collier's MS. corrector (followed by H.) substitutes "heavy honey-dew." D. in his first edition has "honey heavy dew" (which he explains as "honeyed and heavy"), but in his second he adopts "heavy honey-dew." K., W., and the Cambridge ed. have "honey-heavy dew." W. adds : "that is, slumber as refreshing as dew, and whose heaviness is sweet." There does not seem to be sufficient reason for rejecting the old reading, though it is not improbable that S. wrote "heavy honey-dew." It may be noted in favour of the latter (though I am not aware that any former editor has mentioned it) that "honey-dew" occurs in *T. A.* iii. 1:

> —"the honey-dew
> Upon a gather'd lily almost wither'd."

On the other hand, cf. *Rich. III.* iv. 1 : "enjoy the golden dew of sleep."

Thou hast no figures, etc. "Pictures created by imagination or apprehension" (C.). Cf. *M. W.* iv. 2 : "if it be but to scrape the figures out of your husband's brains." On the double negative, see Gr. 406.

Enter PORTIA. Cf. N. (*Life of Brutus*): "Now *Brutus*, who knew very well, that for his sake all the noblest, valiantest, and most couragious men of ROME did venture their lives, weighing with himself the greatness of the danger : when he was out of his house, he did so frame and fashion his countenance and lookes, that no man could discern he had anything to trouble his mind. But when night came that he was in his own house

then he was clean changed : for either care did wake him against his will
when he would have slept, or else oftentimes of himself he fell into such
deep thoughts of this enterprise, casting in his mind all the dangers that
might happen : that his Wife lying by him, found that there was some
marvellous great matter that troubled his mind, not being wont to be in
that taking, and that he could not well determine with himself. . . . This
young Lady being excellently well seen in Philosophy, loving her Husband
well, and being of a noble courage, as she was also wise : because she
would not ask her Husband what he ayled, before she had made some
proof by herself : she took a little Razor, such as Barbers occupy to pare
mens nails, and causing her Maids and Women to go out of her Chamber
gave herself a great gash withall in her thigh, that she was straight all of
a gore bloud : and incontinently after, a vehement Feaver took her, by
reason of the pain of her wound. Then perceiving her Husband was
marvellously out of quiet, and that he could take no rest, even in her
greatest pain of all, she spake in this sort unto him : 'I being, O *Brutus*
(said she) the daughter of *Cato*, was married unto thee ; not to be thy
bedfellow, and Companion in bed and at board onely, like a Harlot, but
to be partaker also with thee of thy good and evill Fortune. Now for
thy self, I can find no cause of fault in thee touching our match : but for
my part, how may I show my duty towards thee, and how much I would do
for thy sake, if I cannot constantly bear a secret mischance or grief with
thee, which requireth secresie and fidelity. I confess, that a Womans wit
commonly is too weak to keep a secret safely : but yet (*Brutus*) good ed-
ucation, and the company of vertuous men, have some power to reform
the defect of nature. And for my self, I have this benefit moreover, that
I am the Daughter of *Cato*, and Wife of *Brutus*. This notwithstanding,
I did not trust to any of these things before, untill that now I have found
by experience, that no pain or grief whatsoever can overcome me.' With
those words she shewed him her wound on her thigh, and told him what
she had done to prove her self. *Brutus* was amazed to hear what she
said unto him, and lifting up his hands to Heaven, he besought the god-
desses to give him the grace he might bring his enterprise to so good
pass, that he might be found a Husband, worthy of so noble a Wife as
Porcia : so he then did comfort her the best he could."

Stole from my bed. On *stole*, see *Mer.* p. 141 (note on *Not undertook*), or
Gr. 343.

Wafture. The folio has "wafter." S. uses the word nowhere else.

That impatience. Here *impatience* has four syllables. See above (i. 3),
on *Incenses them to send destruction.* Gr. 479.

Hath his hour. Here *his*=its, as often. Gr. 228.

Prevail'd on your condition. Influenced your temper or state of mind.
See *Mer.* p. 133, note on *Condition.*

Dear my lord. See Gr. 13. Cf. the French *cher monsieur*, etc.

Is Brutus sick ? "For *sick*, the correct English adjective to express all
degrees of suffering from disease, and which is universally used in the
Bible and by Shakespeare, the Englishman of Great Britain has poorly
substituted the adverb *ill*" (W.). Cf. *Genesis*, xlviii. 1 : 1 *Samuel*, xix. 14 ;
xxx. 13, etc.

Is it physical ?   Trench (*Glossary,* etc.) says : " Though *physical* has not dissociated itself from *physics,* it has from *physic* and *physician,* being used now as simply the equivalent for *natural.*"   Cf. the only other instance in which S. uses the word, *Cor.* i. 5 :

> "The blood I drop is rather physical
> Than dangerous to me."

To walk unbraced.   Cf. above (i. 3) : "And thus unbraced," etc.   W. has " unbrac'd," which is probably a misprint.   It is " vnbraced" in the folio.

Rheumy.   Moist, damp.   S. uses the word only here.

Some sick offence.   " Some pain, or grief, that makes you sick" (C.).

I charm you.   I conjure you.   Pope substituted " charge"—a needless and prosaic alteration.

But, as it were, in sort or limitation.   Only in a manner, or in some lim- ited sense.

As dear to me as are the ruddy drops, etc.   Gray has imitated this in *The Bard :* " Dear as the ruddy drops that warm my heart."   Some crit- ics see here an anticipation of Harvey's discovery of the circulation of the blood ; but it must be recollected that vague notions of such a circulation prevailed before Harvey's day.

A woman well-reputed, etc.   St. reads, "A woman, well-reputed Cato's daughter ;" that is, daughter of the much-esteemed Cato.

Being so father'd, etc.   As Abbott remarks (Gr. 290), " any noun or ad- jective could be converted into a verb by the Elizabethan authors."

All the charactery, etc.   The word *charactery* occurs also in *M. W.* v. 5 : " Fairies use flowers for their charactery," and with the same accent as here.

Who's that knocks ?   On the ellipsis, see Gr. 244.

Vouchsafe good morrow, etc.   Vouchsafe *to receive,* etc.   Gr. 382.

To wear a kerchief.   The word *kerchief* (French *couvrir,* to cover, and *chef,* the head) is here used in its original sense of a covering for the head. Cf. *M. W.* iii. 3 : "A plain kerchief, Sir John ; my brows become nothing else."   As Malone remarks, S. here gives to Rome the manners of his own time, it being a common practice in England for sick people to wear a kerchief on their heads.   Cf. Fuller, *Worthies :* " if any there be sick, they make him a posset, and tye a kerchief on his head, and if that will not mend him, then God be merciful to him."

Thou, like an exorcist.   " Here, and in all other places where the word occurs in S., to *exorcise* means to raise spirits, not to lay them" (Mason). See *Cymb.* iv. 2 ; *A. W.* v. 3 ; *2 Hen. VI.* i. 4.

Mortified spirit.   The former word makes *four* syllables ; the latter, as often, only *one.*   On *mortified*=deadened, cf. *Hen. V.* i. 1 :

> "The breath no sooner left his father's body,
> But that his wildness, mortified in him,
> Seem'd to die too."

To whom it must be done.   See Gr. 208, and cf. 394.

SCENE II.—*Nor heaven nor earth have been.*   On the plural verb, cf. Gr. 408.

Thrice hath Calphurnia in her sleep cried out, etc.   Cf. N. (*Life of Cæsar*):

" He heard his wife *Calpurnia*, being fast asleep, weep and sigh, and put forth many fumbling* lamentable speeches : for she dreamed that *Cæsar* was slain, and that she had him in her Arms. . . . Insomuch that *Cæsar* rising in the morning, she prayed him if it were possible, not to go out of the doors that day, but to adjourn the Session of the Senate untill another day. And if that he made no reckoning of her Dream, yet that he would search further of the Soothsayers by their Sacrifices, to know what should happen him that day. Thereby it seemed that *Cæsar* likewise did fear or suspect somewhat, because his Wife *Calpurnia* untill that time was never given to any fear and superstition : and that then he saw her so troubled in mind with this Dream she had. But much more afterwards, when the Soothsayers having sacrificed many Beasts one after another, told him that none did like them :† then he determined to send *Antonius* to adjourn the Session of the Senate. But in the mean time came *Decius Brutus*, surnamed *Albinus*, in whom *Cæsar* put such confidence, that in his last Will and Testament he had appointed him to be his next Heir, and yet was of the conspiracy with *Cassius* and *Brutus:* he, fearing that if *Cæsar* did adjourn the Session that day, the conspiracy would be betrayed, laughed at the Soothsayers, and reproved *Cæsar*, saying, that he gave the Senate occasion to mislike with him, and that they might think he mocked them, considering that by his commandment they were assembled, and that they were ready willingly to grant him all things, and to proclaim him King of all his Provinces of the Empire of ROME out of ITALY, and that he should wear his Diadem in all other places both by Sea and Land. And further-more, that if any man should tell them from him, they should depart for that present time, and return again when *Calpurnia* should have better Dreams, what would his Enemies and ill-willers say, and how could they like of his Friends words ?"

Do present sacrifice. That is, immediate sacrifice. Cf. the use of *pres-ently=*immediately, on which see *Mer.* p. 131.

Opinions of success. That is, of the issue (what is to succeed or follow). Cf. *Rich. III.* iv. 4 : " dangerous success of bloody wars ;" Hall, *Hen. IV.:* " the aliance had so vnfortunate successe ;" Sidney, *Arcadia:* " and straight my heart misgaue me some euil successe," etc. See also *Joshua*, i. 8.

I never stood on ceremonies. I never regarded auguries. See above (ii. 1), on *Ceremonies.*

Fierce fiery warriors fought. The folio has " fight," which K., C., and H. retain. " Fought" was proposed by D., and is adopted by W. and the Camb. ed.

Hurtled. Cf. Gray, *The Fatal Sisters:*

> " Iron sleet of arrowy shower
> Hurtles in the darken'd air."

Horses did neigh. The folio has " Horsses do neigh," which is correct-ed in the second folio. K. retains " do," on the ground that " the tenses are purposely confounded, in the vague terror of the speaker ;" but, as C. remarks, " no degree of mental agitation ever expressed itself in such a jumble and confusion of tenses as this—not even insanity or drunkenness."

---

* This is the word in the edition (of 1676) before me ; as quoted by K., it is " grum-bling." † That is, none of the victims did *please* them, or give good omens.

And ghosts did shriek, etc.   Cf. the passage from *Hamlet* (i. 1) quoted on page 27.

Beyond all use.   That is, all that we are used to.

Whose end is purpos'd.   The completion of which is designed (C.).

Cowards die many times, etc.   See *Introduction,* p. 17.

They would not have you to stir.   For the *to,* see Gr. 349.

Cæsar should be a beast.   On *should*=would, see Gr. 322.

We are two lions.   The folio has, "We heare two Lyons."   The correction is Upton's, and is adopted by Coll., C., D., W., and Cambridge ed. Theo. proposed "were," and is followed by K. and H.

To be afeard.   See *Mer.* p. 144.

That is enough to satisfy the senate.   That is, enough *for me to do* towards that end (C.).

She dream'd to-night she saw my statua.   Here *to-night* means last night, as in *M. of V.* ii. 6: "For I did dream of money-bags to-night."   See *Mer.* p. 142.

In this line the folio has "Statue," and also in iii. 2: "Euen at the Base of *Pompeyes* Statue;" but in both passages the editors, almost without exception, have given "statua," a form of the word common in the time of S. in both poetry and prose.   Bacon, for example, uses it in *Essays* 27, 37, and 45, in *Adv. of L.* ii. 1, 2 ; 22, 1 ; 23, 36 ("a statua of Cæsar's"), and repeatedly (if not uniformly) elsewhere.   It is not unlikely that S. wrote "statua" when he employed the word as a trisyllable, and "statue" in other cases.   See C. p. 246 fol., or Gr. 487.

Lusty Romans.   See above (i. 2), on *With lusty sinews.*

And evils imminent.   This is the folio reading, altered by Hanmer and Collier's MS. corrector to "Of evils imminent."   C. and D. (*second ed.*) adopt this emendation, but K., H., W., and the Camb. ed. retain "And."

For tinctures, stains, etc.   "*Tinctures* and *stains* are understood both by Malone and Steevens as carrying an allusion to the practice of persons dipping their handkerchiefs in the blood of those whom they regarded as martyrs.   And it must be confessed that the general strain of the passage, and more especially the expression 'shall *press* for tinctures,' etc., will not easily allow us to reject this interpretation.   Yet does it not make the speaker assign to Cæsar by implication the very kind of death Calphurnia's apprehension of which he professes to regard as visionary?   The pressing for tinctures and stains, it is true, would be a confutation of so much of Calphurnia's dream as seemed to imply that the Roman people would be delighted with his death—

> "'Many lusty Romans
> Came smiling, and did bathe their hands in it.'

Do we refine too much in supposing that this inconsistency between the purpose and the language of Decius is intended by the poet, and that in this brief dialogue between him and Cæsar, in which the latter suffers himself to be so easily won over—persuaded and relieved by the very words that ought naturally to have confirmed his fears—we are to feel the presence of an unseen power driving on both the unconscious prophet and the blinded victim?" (C.)

Apt to be render'd.   Likely to be made in reply.

Love to your proceeding. Affectionate interest in your prosperity or advancement. Cf. *Rich. III.* iv. 4 :

> " Be opposite all planets of good luck
> To my proceeding, if with dear heart's love," etc.

And reason to my love is liable. " ' Reason,' or propriety of conduct and language, is subordinate to my love" (J.). In other words, My love leads me to indulge in a freedom of speech that my reason would restrain.

'Tis strucken eight. See above (ii. 1), on *Hath stricken.*

Long o' nights. It is "a-nights" in the folio. See above (i. 2), on *Such as sleep o' nights.*

So to most noble Cæsar. On *so*, see Gr. 65.

To be thus waited for. See Gr. 356.

An hour's talk. Here *hour's* is a dissyllable. See *Hen. VIII.* p. 197, or Gr. 480.

That every like is not the same. " That to be like a thing is not always to be that thing"(C.). There is a reference to Cæsar's " We, *like* friends."

The heart of Brutus yearns to think upon. The folio has " earnes," another form of the same word. Cf. Spenser, *F. Q.* iii. 10, 21 : "And ever his faint hart much earned at the sight," where it is used in the same sense as here. In *F. Q.* i. 1, 3 (" his heart did earne To prove his puissance"), i. 6, 25 (" he for revenge did earne"), iv. 12, 24, etc., it is used in its current sense. In S. "yearn" always* means either to pain (transitive) or to be pained, to grieve (intransitive). Cf. *Hen. V.* ii. 3 : " For Falstaff he is dead, And we must yearn therefore ;" *Id.* iv. 3 : " It yearns me not if men my garments wear ;" *Rich. II.* v. 5 : " O, how it yearned my heart," etc. On the position of *upon*, see Gr. 203.

SCENE III.—*Look about you.* On *you* following *thou*, see Gr. 235.

Security gives way to. That is, leaves the way open to. Cf. *Hen. VIII.* iii. 2 : " the time Gives way to us."

Thy lover. See *Mer.* p. 153.

Out of the teeth of emulation. Safe from the attacks of envy. Conf. *T. and C.* ii. 3 : " Whilst emulation in the army crept." In the Rheims version of the Bible (1582), *Acts* vii. 9 reads, "And the patriarchs through emulation sold Joseph into Egypt." Bacon, like S., uses the word in both a good and a bad sense.

Contrive. Cf. *M. of V.* iv. 1 : " Thou hast contriv'd against the very life ;" 1 *Hen. VI.* i. 3 : " Thou that contriv'dst to murder," etc. In *T. of S.* i. 2 (" Please you we may contrive this afternoon"), *contrive* is used in the sense of wear away, spend (Latin *contero, contrivi*), and Walker makes it have a similar meaning (sojourning, *conterentes tempus*) in *A. and C.* i. 2 : " our contriving friends in Rome." Cf. Spenser, *F. Q.* ii. 9, 48 : " Three ages, such as mortall men contrive."

---

* In *Per.* iii. 4, some editors have "yearning time ;" but "yeaning" (or "eaning," which is the word in the folio of 1664) is the preferable reading. D. speaks of "yearning" (which was proposed by Steevens) as a "ridiculous reading." H. adopts it, but says that "either word suits the text well enough."

SCENE IV.—*O constancy.* "Firmness or resolution" (C.). Cf. *Macb.* ii. 1 : "Your constancy Hath left you unattended" (that is, your firmness has forsaken you).

To keep counsel. To keep a secret. Cf. *Ham.* iii. 2 : "the players cannot keep counsel ; they'll tell all ;" *A. W.* iii. 7 : "what to your sworn counsel (secrecy) I have spoken." So above (ii. 1) : "Tell me your counsels, I will not disclose 'em." See Wb. s. v.

A bustling rumour. Here *rumour*=murmur, noise. Cf. *K. John,* v. 4 : "the noise and rumour of the field." Drayton uses *rumorous* similarly : "the rumorous sound Of the sterne billowes." ●

Sooth, madam. See *Mer.* p. 127, note on *In sooth.*

Enter Soothsayer. Here Rowe (followed by W.) substituted "Artemidorus." Tyrwhitt says that it should be "Artemidorus, who is seen and accosted by Portia in his passage from his first stand to one more convenient." The folio may be wrong, but the case is hardly clear enough to justify a change.

I'll get me to a place more void. I'll betake myself to a place more open (as opposed to "narrow"). On *get me,* see Gr. 296, 223.

Ay me! It is "Aye me!" in the folio, but all the editors except C. and D. (second ed.) have "Ah me!" The latter, as C. remarks, is a phrase that S. nowhere uses. Cf. Milton, *Lycidas,* 56, 154 ; *Comus,* 511 ; *P. L.* iv. 86 ; x. 813, etc. Neither Worc. nor Wb. recognizes this *ay.* The *affirmative* particle *ay* or *aye* is uniformly printed "I" in the folio ;" as in the second line of the next scene : "I *Cæsar,* but not gone."

Brutus hath a suit, etc. "This she addresses in explanation to the boy, whose presence she had for a moment forgotten" (C.).

COINS STRUCK ON THE DEATH OF CÆSAR.

ACT III.

SCENE I.—Here, as in *Ham.* and *A. and C.* (see quotations on pp. 28, 29), the death of Cæsar is represented as taking place in the Capitol, instead of the Curia of Pompey. Cf. N. (*Life of Brutus*): "Furthermore, they [the conspirators] thought also that the appointment of the place where the Councill should be kept, was chosen of purpose by divine Providence, and made all for them. For it was one of the Porches about the Theater, in the which there was a certain place full of Seats for men to sit in; where also was set up the image of *Pompey*, which the City had made and consecrated in honour of him, when he did beautifie that part of the City with the Theater he built, with divers Porches about it. In this lace was the assembly of the Senate appointed to be, just on the fifteenth of the Moneth *March*, which the ROMANS call, *Idus Martias:* so that it seemed some god of purpose had brought *Cæsar* thither to e slain, for revenge of *Pompey's* death."

See also N. (*Life of Cæsar*): "And one *Artemidorus* also born in the Isle of GNIDOS, a Doctor of Rhetorick in the Greek Tongue, who by means of his Profession was very familiar with certain of *Brutus* Confederates; and therefore knew the most part of all their practices against *Cæsar*, came and brought him a little Bill written with his own hand, of all that he meant to tell him. He marking how *Cæsar* received all the Supplications that were offered him, and that he gave them straight to his men that were about him pressed nearer to him, and said: *Cæsar*, read this Memorial to your self, and that quickly, for they be matters of great weight, and touch you nearly. *Cæsar* took it of him, but could never read it, though he many times attempted it, for the number of People that did salute him."

What touches us ourself, etc. Collier's MS. corrector alters this to "That touches us? Ourself shall be last serv'd." C. adopts this "specious but entirely needless change," as W. calls it.

I wish your enterprise to-day may thrive. Cf. N. (*Life of Brutus*): "Another Senatour called *Popilius Læna*, after he had saluted *Brutus* and *Cassius* more friendly than he was wont to do, he rounded* softly in their ears, and told them: I pray the goddess you may go through with that you have taken in hand; but withall, dispatch I read† you, for your enterprise is bewrayed. When he had said, he presently departed from them, and left them both afraid that their conspiracy would out."

Look, how he makes to Cæsar: mark him. See how he presses towards Cæsar. *Mark* is a dissyllable here. Gr. 485.

Cassius or Cæsar never shall turn back, etc. This is the folio reading, retained by K., D., H., and Camb. ed. Malone proposed "Cassius on Cæsar," which is adopted by C. and W. But, as Ritson remarks, "Cassius says, if the plot be discovered, at all events either he or Cæsar shall never return alive; for, if the latter cannot be killed, he is determined to

* See *Hen. VIII.* p. 168, foot-note.
† *Read*, or *rede*, meant to advise or counsel. We have the noun in *Ham.* i. 3: "And recks not his own read."

slay himself." C., commenting on this, says that "to *turn back* cannot mean to return alive, or to return in any way." But see *Rich. III.* iv. 4: "Ere from this war thou turn a conqueror;" *T. A.* v. 2: "And tarry with him till I turn again;" *A. Y. L.* iii. 1:

> "Bring him dead or living
> Within this twelvemonth, or turn thou no more
> To seek a living in our territory."

Cassius, be constant, etc. Cf. N. (*Life of Brutus*): "And when *Cassius* and certain other clapped their hands on their Swords to draw them, *Brutus* marking the countenance and gesture of *Læna,* and considering that he did use himself rather like an humble and earnest suiter, then like an accuser: he said nothing to his Companion (because there were many amongst them that were not of the conspiracy), but with a pleasant countenance encouraged *Cassius.* And immediately after, *Læna* went from *Cæsar,* and kissed his hand: which shewed plainly that it was for some matter concerning himself, that he had held him so long in talk."

He draws Mark Antony out of the way. Cf. N. (*Life of Brutus*): "*Trebonius* on the other side, drew *Antonius* aside, as he came into the house where the Senate sate, and held him with a long talk without."

He is address'd. He is ready. Cf. *M. of V.* ii. 9: "And so have I address'd me" (prepared myself); *2 Hen. IV.* iv. 4: "Our navy is address'd;" *M. N. D.* v. 1: "the Prologue is address'd," etc.

Casca, you are the first that rears your hand. Cf. *Temp.* ii. 1: "When I rear my hand." On the construction, see Gr. 247.

Are we all ready? In the folio (so in K. and the Camb. ed.) these words begin Cæsar's speech. Ritson proposed to add them to Cinna's speech, but Collier's MS. corrector assigns them to Casca, "in whose mouth they form a very natural rejoinder to what Cinna has just said." This latter arrangement is adopted by C., D., W., and H. C. evidently had the impression that the folio gives this, and the following speech to Casca, not to Cæsar.

On the remainder of this scene, cf. N. (*Life of Brutus*): "So when he was set, the Conspiratours flocked about him, and amongst them they presented one *Tullius Cimber,*[*] who made humble suit for the calling home again of his Brother that was banished. They all made as though they were intercessours for him, and took *Cæsar* by the hands, and kissed his head and breast. *Cæsar* at the first, simply refused their kindness and entreaties: but afterwards, perceiving they still pressed on him, he violently thrust them from him. Then *Cimber,* with both his hands plucked *Cæsar's* Gown over his shoulders, and *Casca* that stood behind him, drew his Dagger first and strake *Cæsar* upon the shoulder, but gave him no great wound. *Cæsar* feeling himself hurt, took him straight by the hand he held his Dagger in, and cried out, in Latine, O traytor *Casca,* what doest thou? *Casca* on the other side cried in Greek, and called his Brother to help him. So divers running on a heap together to flie upon *Cæsar,* he looking about him to have fled, saw *Brutus* with a Sword drawn in his hands ready to strike at him: then he let *Casca's* hand go, and casting his

---

[*] In the *Life of Cæsar* he is called *Metellus Cimber,* and in Suetonius (i. 82) *Cimber Tullius.*

Gown over his face, suffered every man to strike at him that would. Then the Conspiratours thronging one upon another, because every man was desirous to have a cut at him, so many Swords and Daggers lighting upon one body, one of them hurt another, and among them *Brutus* caught a blow on his hand, because he would make one in murthering of him, and all the rest also were every man of them bloudied. *Cæsar* being slain in this manner, *Brutus* standing in the middest of the house, would have spoken and staied the other Senatours that were not of the conspiracy, to have told them the reason why they had done this fact. But they as men both afraid and amazed, fled, one upon anothers neck in hast to get out at the door, and no man followed them. For it was set down, and agreed between them, that they should kill no man but *Cæsar* onely, and should intreat all the rest to look to defend their liberty."

Most puissant Cæsar. S. generally uses *puissant* and *puissance* as dissyllables, but sometimes as trisyllables. Cf. two lines in 2 *Hen. IV.* i. 3 : "Upon the power and puissance of the king," and "And come against us in full puissance." So in Spenser we find (*F. Q.* iv. 11, 15) "Of puissant Nations which the world possest," and (*F. Q.* v. 2, 7) "For that he is so puissant and strong."

These couchings. Collier's MS. corrector has "crouchings," which C. says "does not admit of a doubt." But Sr. remarks that "*couching* had the same meaning as *crouching;* thus Huloet : 'Cowche, like a dogge; *procumbo, prosterno.*'" Cf. also *Genesis,* xlix. 14. K., D., W., H., and Camb. ed. retain "couchings."

Into the law of children. The folio reads "the lane of Children," a misprint which J. corrected.

Be not fond, etc. Be not so foolish as to think, etc. See *Mer.* pp. 146, 152, and Gr. 281. On *such . . . that,* see Gr. 279.

Low-crooked curtsies. Collier's MS. corrector has "Low-crouched," which C. adopts. But "*low-crooked* is the same as *low-crouched;* for Huloet has '*crooke-backed* or *crowche-backed,*' and to *crook* was to bow" (Sr.). See *Temp.* p. 120, note on *Curtsied.*

Know Cæsar doth not wrong, etc. Ben Jonson, in his *Discoveries,* speaking of Shakespeare, says : "Many times he fell into those things could not escape laughter; as when he said in the person of Cæsar, one speaking to him, 'Cæsar, thou dost me wrong,' he replied, 'Cæsar did never wrong but with just cause.'" And he ridicules the expression again in his *Staple of News :* "Cry you mercy; you never did wrong but with just cause." C. believes that the words stood originally as Jonson has given them; but, as Collier suggests, Jonson was probably speaking only from memory, which, as he himself says, was "shaken with age now, and sloth," and misquoted the passage.

The repealing of my banish'd brother. That is, his recall. Both the verb and the noun (see the next speech) are often used by S. in this sense. Cf. *Rich. II.* iv. 1 : "Till Norfolk be repeal'd : repeal'd he shall be ;" *Cor.* v. 5 : "Repeal him with the welcome of his mother ;" *Id.* iv. 1 : "A cause for thy repeal ;" *Lucrece,* 640 : "I sue for exiled majesty's repeal."

But I am constant, etc. Cf. i. 2 : "But always I am Cæsar."

Apprehensive. Endowed with apprehension or intelligence. Compare

2 *Hen. IV.* iv. 3: "Makes it (the brain) apprehensive, quick, forgetive (inventive);" B. and F., *Philaster*, v. 1: "as I did grow More and more apprehensive," etc.

Holds on his rank, etc. Continues to "hold his place" (like the star), resisting every attempt to move him. "Unshaked of motion" might mean unshaken in his motion (Gr. 173), but that would not be in keeping with the simile of the pole-star.

Et tu, Brute! "There is no ancient Latin authority, I believe, for this famous exclamation, although in Suetonius, i. 82, Cæsar is made to address Brutus Καὶ σὺ, τέκνον; (And thou too, my son?). It may have occurred as it stands here in the Latin play on the same subject which is record-ed to have been acted at Oxford in 1582; and it is found in *The True Tragedy of Richard Duke of York*, first printed in 1595, on which the *Third Part of King Henry the Sixth* is founded, as also in a poem by S. Nicholson, entitled *Acolastus his Afterwit*, printed in 1600, in both of which nearly contemporary productions we have the same line—'*Et tu, Brute?* Wilt thou stab Cæsar too?'" (C.)

Publius, good cheer. On the literal meaning of *cheer*, see *Mer.* p. 152.

Lest that the people. On *that* as a "conjunctional affix," see Gr. 287.

Abide this deed. That is, answer for it, be held responsible for it. Cf. below (iii. 2): "If it be found so, some will dear abide it." *Aby* was used in the same sense; as in *M. N. D.* iii. 2: "Lest to thy peril thou aby it dear." This *aby* is frequent in Spenser. See *F. Q.* ii. 8, 28: "His life for dew revenge should deare abye;" *Id.* iii. 4, 38; iii. 10, 3; iv. 1, 53; iv. 6, 8, etc.

As it were doomsday. As *if* it were. Gr. 107.

Why, he that cuts off, etc. The folio gives this speech to Casca, but some of the editors have transferred it to Cassius. As H. remarks, "the sen-timent is in strict keeping with what Casca says in i. 3: 'So every bond-man in his own hand bears,' etc."

In states unborn. The folio has "State," and just below "lye along;" both corrected in second folio.

On Pompey's basis lies along. Lies prostrate at the base of Pompey's statue. Cf. *Cor.* v. 6: "When he lies along,"etc. See also *Judges*, vii. 13.

The most boldest. See Gr. 11. Cf. below (iii. 2): "the most unkindest cut of all."

Be resolv'd. Have his doubts resolved or removed; be satisfied. Cf. below (iii. 2): "As rushing out of doors, to be resolv'd," etc.; and (iv. 2): "How he receiv'd you, let me be resolv'd."

Thorough the hazards. See *Mer.* p. 144, note on *Throughfares.*

Tell him, so please him come. See Gr. 133, 297, and 349.

We shall have him well to friend. See *Temp.* p. 124, note on *A paragon to their queen.* Gr. 189.

My misgiving still Falls shrewdly to the purpose. My suspicions are al-ways shrewd enough to hit the mark. On *still*, see *Mer.* p. 128.

Who else is rank. "Who else may be supposed to have *overtopped* his equals, and *grown too high* for public safety" (J.). Cf. *Hen. VIII.* i. 2: "Ha! What, so rank?"

Of half that worth as. See Gr. 280.

I do beseech ye, if you bear me hard. On the pronouns, see Gr. 236. For *bear me hard,* see note on the same phrase, i. 2.

Live a thousand years. Cf. *M. of V.* iii. 2 : " Live thou, I live ;" and see Gr. 361.

Apt to die. Ready or disposed to die.

No mean of death. On *mean*=means, see *Hen. VIII.* p. 201.

The choice and master spirits. C. thinks that *choice* may be either noun or adjective, but it is pretty certainly the latter. We have the expression " choice spirits" in 1 *Hen. VI.* v. 3.

As fire drives out fire. The first *fire* is a dissyllable, the second a monosyllable. See Gr. 480, and cf. 475. For the simile, cf. *R. and J.* i. 2 : " one fire burns out another's burning ;" *Cor.* iv. 7 : " One fire drives out one fire ;" *T. G. of V.* ii. 4 : " Even as one heat another heat expels," etc.

Our arms, in strength of malice, etc. The passage stands thus in the folio :

> " Our Armes in strength of malice, and our Hearts
> Of Brothers temper, do receiue you in,
> With all kinde loue, good thoughts, and reuerence."

Pope read " exempt from malice ;" Capell (followed by D. and H.), " no strength of malice ;" Collier's MS. corrector, " in strength of welcome," which C. adopts. Sr. suggested " in strength of amity." K. and W. retain the folio reading, and the latter remarks : " The difficulty found in this passage, which even Mr. Dyce suspects to be corrupt, seems to result from a forgetfulness of the preceding context.

> " ' Though now we must appear *bloody and cruel,*
> As *by our hands,* and this our present act,
> You see we do ; yet you see but our hands,
> And this the bleeding business they have done.
> *Our hearts* you see not ; they are pitiful ;
> And pity to the general wrong of Rome,' etc.

So (*Brutus* continues) our arms, even in the intensity of their hatred to *Cæsar's* tyranny, and our hearts in their brotherly love to all Romans, do receive you in."

And then we will deliver. On *deliver* (=declare, relate), see *Temp.* p. 144, and *Hen. VIII.* pp. 163, 176.

Let each man render, etc. " Give me back in return for mine" (C.).

Though last, not least in love. Cf. *Lear,* i. 1 : "Although the last, not least in our dear love." Spenser has the expression " though last, not least" in *Colin Clout's Come Home Again,* published in 1595.

You must conceit me. See above (i. 3), on *You have right well conceited.*

Dearer than thy death. See *Temp.* p. 124, note on *The dear'st of the loss.*

Here wast thou bayed. That is, " brought to bay," or hemmed in by enemies as a hart by the hounds.

Crimson'd in thy lethe. " Crimson'd in the stream that bears thee to oblivion" (W.). Collier's MS. corrector alters " lethe" to " death," which C. adopts. Collier himself, in his second edition, restores " lethe," which is also given by K., D., St., H., and Camb. ed.

O world, thou wast the forest to this hart, etc. Coleridge doubted the genuineness of these two lines, both on account of the rhythm, " which is not Shakespearian," and because they interrupt the sense and connection and "the Shakespearian link of association." He adds: "I venture to say there is no instance in Shakespeare fairly like this. Conceits he has; but they not only rise out of some word in the lines before, but also lead to the thought in the lines following. Here the conceit is a mere alien: Antony forgets an image when he is even touching it, and then recollects it, when the thought last in his mind must have led him away from it."

Strucken by many princes. The folio has "stroken," and in the preceding speech "strooke" for "struck." Gr. 344.

It is cold modesty. That is, moderation. Cf. *T. of S.*, Induction, sc. 1: "If it be husbanded with modesty."

But what compact. On the accent of *compact*, see Gr. 490.

Will you be prick'd. That is, marked off. Cf. below (iv. 1): "their names are prick'd," and "Prick him down, Antony," which is explained by Antony's "look, with a spot I damn him." See also 2 *Hen. IV.* iii. 2.

So full of good regard. "So full of what is entitled to favourable regard" (C.). Cf. i. 2: "many of the best respect."

Produce his body. Bear forth his body; "using *produce* in its radical sense" (W.).

By your pardon. By your leave, I will explain.

Have all true rites. Pope (and Collier's MS. corrector) read "due rites," but, as Coll. says, "the change seems rather for the worse." Walker and D., however, adopt it.

In the tide of times. "In the course of times" (J.). As C. remarks, "*tide* and *time* properly mean the same thing." Cf. Spenser, *F. Q.* i. 2, 29: "and rest their weary limbs a tide;" *Id.* iii. 6, 21: "mine may be your paine another tide;" *Id.* iii. 9, 32: "glad of so fitte tide Him to commend to her," etc. The word still has this sense in certain compounds; as *eventide, springtide*, etc.

Woe to the hands. The folio has "hand," which K. and H. retain; but above (iii. 1) Antony says, "Now, whilst your purpled hands do reek."

A curse shall light upon the limbs of men.· This is the folio reading, retained by K., W., and H. W., however, is "almost sure" that S. wrote "the *sonnes* of men." Warb. proposed "line," Hanmer "kind," J. "lives" or "lymms,"* Collier's MS. corrector "loins" (which C. adopts), Walker "times," St. "tombs," and Swynfen Jervis (whom D. follows) "minds."

With the hands of war. Here *with*=by, as often. Gr. 193. Cf. in next seene "marr'd, as you see, with traitors." See also *Hen. VIII.* p. 193.

With Ate by his side. C. remarks that "this Homeric goddess had taken a strong hold of Shakespeare's imagination." See *M. Ado*, ii. 1: "the infernal Ate;" *L. L. L.* v. 2: "more Ates, more Ates;" *K. John*, iv. 1: "an Ate stirring him to blood and strife."

Cry "Havoc!" In old times this cry was the signal that no quarter was to be given. Cf. *Cor.* iii. 1:

---

* "That is," he adds, "these *bloodhounds* of men." S. uses the word in *Lear*, iii. 6:
"Mastiff, greyhound, mongrel grim,
Hound or spaniel, brach or lym."
The old copies have "him" or "hym," but there can be no doubt that these are misprints for "lym."

"Do not cry havoc, where you should but hunt
With modest warrant."

The dogs of war. Steele (*Tatler*, No. 137) suggests that by "the dogs of war" S. probably meant *fire, sword,* and *famine.* Cf. *Hen. V.* i. chorus :

"Then should the warlike Harry, like himself,
Assume the port of Mars ; and, at his heels,
Leash'd in like hounds, should Famine, Sword, and Fire
Crouch for employment."

See also 1 *Hen. VI.* iv. 2 :

"You tempt the fury of my three attendants,
Lean Famine, quartering Steel, and climbing Fire."

That this foul deed. So that, etc. Gr. 283.
Passion, I see, is catching. That is, emotion is contagious. See above (i. 2), on *I have much mistook your passion.*
For mine eyes. The folio has "from mine eyes ;" corrected in second folio. D. alters "began" in the next line to "begin."
No Rome of safety. See above (i. 2), on *Rome indeed, and room enough.*
According to the which. See *Mer.* p. 133, on *For the which.*

Scene II.—On this scene, and the next, cf. N. (*Life of Brutus*): "Now, at the first time when the murther was newly done, there were suddain outcries of People that ran up and down the City, the which indeed did the more increase the fear and tumult. But when they saw they slew no man, neither did spoil nor make havock of anything, then certain of the Senatours, and many of the People emboldening themselves, went to the Capitoll unto them. There a great number of men being assembled together one after another, *Brutus* made an Oration unto them to win the favour of the People, and to justify that they had done. All those that were by, said they had done well, and cried unto them, that they should boldly come down from the Capitoll : whereupon *Brutus* and his Companions came boldly down into the Market-place. The rest followed in Troop, but *Brutus* went foremost, very honourably compassed in round about with the noblest men of the City, which brought him from the Capitoll, through the Market-place, to the Pulpit for Orations. When the People saw him in the Pulpit, although they were a multitude of rake-hels of all sorts, and had a good will to make some stir : yet being ashamed to do it, for the reverence they bare unto *Brutus*, they kept silence to hear what he would say : when *Brutus* began to speak, they gave him quiet audience : Howbeit immediately after, they shewed that they were not all contented with the murther. For when another called *Cinna* would have spoken, and began to accuse *Cæsar*, they fell into a great uprore among them, and marvellously reviled him. Insomuch that the Conspiratours returned again into the Capitoll. There *Brutus* being afraid to be besieged, sent back again the Noblemen that came thither with him, thinking it no reason, that they which were no partakers of the murther, should be partakers of the danger. . . .
"Then *Antonius* thinking good his Testament should be read openly, and also that his body should be honourably buried, and not in hugger

L

mugger,* lest the People might thereby take occasion to be worse offended if they did otherwise : *Cassius* stoutly spake against it. But *Brutus*
went with the motion, and agreed unto it : wherein it seemeth he com-
mitted a second fault. For the first fault he did, was when he would not
consent to his fellow Conspiratours that *Antonius* should be slain : and
therefore he was justly accused, that thereby he had saved and strength-
ened a strong and grievous Enemy of their conspiracy. The second fault
was, when he agreed that *Cæsars* Funerals should be as *Antonius* would
have them, the which indeed marred all. For first of all, when *Cæsars*
Testament was openly read among them, whereby it appeared that he be-
queathed unto every Citizen of ROME seventy-five Drachma's a man ;
and that he left his Gardens and Arbors unto the People, which he had
on this side of the River Tyber, in the place where now the Temple of
Fortune is built : the people then loved him, and were marvellous sorry
for him. Afterwards when *Cæsars* body was brought into the Market-
place, *Antonius* making his Funerall Oration in praise of the dead, according to the ancient Custom of Rome, and perceiving that his words moved
the common People to compassion, he framed his Eloquence to make
their hearts yearn the more ; and taking *Cæsars* Gown all bloudy in his
hand, he layed it open to the sight of them all, shewing what a number
of cuts and holes it had upon it. Therewithall the People fell presently
into such a rage and mutiny, that there was no more order kept amongst
the common People. For some of them cried out, Kill the murtherers :
others plucked up Forms, Tables, and Stalls about the Market-place, as
they had done before at the funerals of *Clodius ;* and having laid them all
on a heap together, they set them on fire, and thereupon did put the Body
of *Cæsar*, and burnt it in the middest of the most holy places. And Furthermore, when the fire was thoroughly kindled, some here, some there,
took burning Fire-brands, and ran with them to the Murtherers houses
that killed him, to set them on fire. Howbeit, the Conspiratours foresee-
ing the danger, before had wisely provided for themselves, and fled. But
there was a Poet called *Cinna,* who had been no partaker of the conspiracy, but was alway one of *Cæsars* chiefest friends : he dreamed the night
before, that *Cæsar* bad him to supper with him, and that he refusing to go,
Cæsar was very importunate with him, and compelled him, so that at length
he led him by the hand into a great dark place, where being marvellously
afraid, he was driven to follow him in spite of his heart. This dream put
him all night into a Feaver, and yet notwithstanding, the next morning
when he heard that they carried *Cæsars* body to buriall, being ashamed
not to accompany his Funerals, he went out of his house, and thrust himself into the preass of the common People, that were in a great uproar.
And because some one called him by his name, *Cinna :* the People thinking he had been that *Cinna,* who in an Oration he made, had spoken very
ill of *Cæsar,* they falling upon him in their rage, slew him outright in the
Market-place."

Part the numbers. "Divide the multitude" (C.).

* Cf. *Ham.* iv. 5:

"And we have done but greenly
In hugger-mugger to inter him."

Shall be rendered. On *rendered* here and just below, see Gr. 474.

Be patient till the last. Many brief quotations from the folio have been given in the notes of this series of Shakespeare's plays, but the reader may like to see a longer extract, as an illustration of the orthography and typography of that edition. The speech of Brutus appears there as follows:

"*Bru.* Be patient till the last.
Romans, Countrey-men, and Louers, heare mee for my cause, and be silent, that you may heare. Beleeue me for mine Honor, and haue respect to mine Honor, that you may beleeue. Censure me in your Wisedom, and awake your Senses, that you may the better Iudge. If there bee any in this Assembly, any deere Friend of *Cæsars*, to him I say, that *Brutus* loue to *Cæsar*, was no lesse then his. If then, that Friend demand, why *Brutus* rose against *Cæsar*, this is my answer: Not that I lou'd *Cæsar* lesse, but that I lou'd Rome more. Had you rather *Cæsar* were liuing, and dye all *S*laues; then that *Cæsar* were dead, to liue all Free-men? As *Cæsar* lou'd mee, I weepe for him; as he was Fortunate, I reioyce at it; as he was Valiant, I honour him: But, as he was Ambitious, I slew him. There is Teares, for his Loue: Ioy, for his Fortune: Honor, for his Valour: and Death, for his Ambition. Who is heere so base, that would be a Bondman? If any, speak, for him haue I offended. Who is heere so rude, that would not be a Roman? If any, speak, for him haue I offended. Who is heere so vile, that will not loue his Countrey? If any, speake, for him haue I offended. I pause for a Reply.
All. None *Btutus*, none.
Brutus. Then none haue I offended. I haue done no more to *Cæsar*, then you shall do to *Brutus*. The Question of his death, is inroll'd in the Capitoll: his Glory not extenuated, wherein he was worthy: nor his offences enforc'd, for which he suffered death.

Enter Mark Antony, with Cæsars body.

Heere comes his Body, mourn'd by *Marke Antony*, who though he had no hand in his death, shall receiue the benefit of his dying, a place in the Cōmonwealth, as which of you shall not. With this I depart, that as I slewe my best Louer for the good of Rome, I haue the same Dagger for my selfe, when it shall please my Country to need my death.
All. Liue *Brutus*, liue, liue.
1. Bring him with Triumph home vnto his house.
2. Giue him a Statue with his Ancestors.
3. Let him be *Cæsar*.
4. *Cæsars* better parts,
Shall be Crown'd in *Brutus*.
1. Wee'l bring him to his House,
With Showts and Clamors.
Bru. My Country-men.
2. Peace, silence, *Brutus* speakes.
1. Peace ho.
Bru. Good Countrymen, let me depart alone,
And (for my sake) stay heere with *Antony*:
Do grace to *Cæsars* Corpes, and grace his Speech
Tending to *Cæsars* Glories, which *Marke Antony*
(By our permission) is allow'd to make.
I do intreat you, not a man depart,
Saue I alone, till *Antony* have spoke. *Exit*"

Upon this speech of Brutus, Knight, after quoting Hazlitt's remark (see *Introduction*, p. 13) that it is "not so good" as Antony's, comments as follows: " In what way is it not so good? As a specimen of eloquence, put by the side of Antony's, who can doubt that it is tame, passionless, severe, and therefore ineffective? But as an example of Shakespeare's wonderful power of characterization, it is beyond all praise. It was the consummate artifice of Antony that made him say, 'I am no orator, as Brutus is.' Brutus was *not* an orator. . . . He is a man of just intentions, of calm understanding, of settled purpose, when his principles are to become actions. But his notion of oratory is this :

> " 'I will myself into the pulpit first,
> And show the reason of our Cæsar's death.'

And he does show the *reason.* .... He expects that Antony will speak with equal moderation—all good of Cæsar—no blame of Cæsar's murderers ; and he thinks it an advantage to speak *before* Antony. He knew not what *oratory* really is. But Shakespeare knew, and he painted Antony."

So far as the mere *style* of the speech is concerned, I think that Warburton was right in considering it an " imitation of his famed laconic brevity." Cf. N. (*Life of Brutus*): " they do note in some of his Epistles, that he counterfeited that brief compendious manner of speech of the LACEDÆMONIANS. As when the War was begun, he wrote unto the PERGAMENIANS in this sort: I understand you have given *Dolabella* money : if you have done it willingly, you confess you have offended me ; if against your wills, show it then by giving me willingly. Another time again unto the SAMIANS: Your counsels be long, your doings be slow, consider the end. And in another Epistle he wrote unto the PATAREIANS : the XANTHIANS despising my good will, have made their Countrey a grave of despair, and the PATAREIANS that put themselves into my protection, have lost no jot of their liberty : and therefore whilest you have liberty, either chuse the judgement of the PATAREIANS, or the fortune of the XANTHIANS. These were *Brutus* manner of letters, which were honoured for their briefness." In the *Dialogus de Oratoribus* also it is said that Brutus's oratory was censured as "otiosum et disjunctum ;" and, as Verplanck remarks, " the *disjunctum*, the broken-up style, without oratorical continuity, is precisely that assumed by the dramatist."

I am not aware that any commentator has called attention to the fact that S. has made Brutus express himself in a somewhat similar style in the speech in i. 2, beginning : " That you do love me I am nothing jealous," etc.

And lovers. See above (ii. 3), on *Thy lover.*

Have respect to my honour. That is, look to it, consider it.

Censure me. That is, judge me. See *Hen. VIII.* p. 157, note on *No discerner,* etc. Cf. *Ham.* i. 3 : " Take each man's censure, but reserve thy judgment ;" Bacon, *Adv. of L.* ii. Introd. 15 : " many will conceive and censure that some of them are already done," etc.

There is tears. See *Temp.* p. 122, note on *There is no more such shapes.*

The question of his death. A statement of the reasons *why* he was put to death (the *answer* to that question).

Enforc'd. Cf. *A. and C.* v. 2, where, as here, the word is opposed to *extenuate :* " We will extenuate rather than enforce."

Shall now be crown'd. The folio (see extract above) has " Shall be." Pope added " now," and the emendation is generally adopted.

Do grace. Show respect, do honour.

Tending to Cæsar's glories. D. adopts Walker's suggestion of "glory."

Save I alone. The expression occurs also in *T. N.* iii. 1. Cf. below (v. 5), " save only he ;" *Sonn.* 109 : " Save thou," etc. Gr. 118.

I am beholding to you. See *Mer.* p. 135, note on *Beholding.* Gr. 372.

The evil that men do, etc. Cf. *Hen. VIII.* iv. 2 :
> "Men's evil manners live in brass; their virtues
> We write in water."

If it were so, etc. See Gr. 301.

When that the poor. See above (iii. 1), on *Lest that the people.*

Withholds you then to mourn. Withholds you from mourning. Cf. Gr. 356.

Has he, masters? Capell suggested "my masters," and C. reads "Has he not, masters?" If any change is to be made, the latter seems preferable.

Some will dear abide it. See above (iii. 1), on *Let no man abide this deed.*

There's not a nobler man. W. misprints "a bolder man."

And none so poor, etc. On the ellipsis of *as,* see Gr. 281.

The commons. The common people.

Their napkins. Their handkerchiefs. Cf. *T. A.* iii. 1 : "Thy napkin cannot drink a tear of mine;" *Ham.* v. 2 : "Here, Hamlet, take my napkin; rub thy brows;" *Oth.* iii. 3 :
> "I am glad I have found this napkin:
> This was her first remembrance from the Moor."

Malone says that the word is still used in this sense in Scotland.

I have o'ershot myself, etc. I have gone too far, etc. On *to tell,* see Gr. 356.

Stand far off. D. prints "far' off," and he is probably right in considering *far* as a contraction of *farther,* both here and in v. 3 : "fly far off." Cf. *W. T.* iv. 3 : "Far than Deucalion off." So *near* is often used for *nearer.* Cf. *Rich. II.* iii. 2 : "Nor near nor farther off, my gracious lord;" *Id.* v. 1 : "Better far off than near, be ne'er the near." For other examples, see Walker, *Crit. Exam.* vol. i. p. 190 foll.

That day he overcame the Nervii. On that day on which, etc. The *Var.* ed. and some others make this an independent sentence. The Nervii were the most warlike of the Belgic tribes, and their subjugation was one of the most important events in Cæsar's Gallic campaigns.

To be resolv'd. See above (iii. 1), on *Be resolv'd.*

Cæsar's angel. His *alter ego,* as it were, or one as intimately connected with him as his guardian angel. Boswell asks, "Does it not mean that Cæsar put his trust in him as he would in his guardian angel?" C. understands it as "simply his best beloved, his darling."

Pompey's statua. See above (ii. 2), on *She dream'd to-night she saw my statua.*

The dint of pity. The *impression* or influence of pity. S. uses the word only here and in *2 Hen. IV.* iv. 1 : "by dint of sword."

Marr'd, as you see, with traitors. Cf. iii. 1 : "quarter'd with the hands of war." Gr. 193.

We will be revenged, etc. The folio gives this speech to 2 *Citizen,* but perhaps D. is right in assuming that it belongs to the citizens generally.

What private griefs. What personal grievances. See above (i. 3), on *Be factious,* etc.

For I have neither wit, etc. The folio reads, "For I haue neyther writ nor words, nor worth." J. explains "writ" as "penned or premeditated oration," and Malone as "writing." The latter adds that "the editor of the second folio, who altered whatever he did not understand, substituted *wit* for *writ.*" Even K., though he gives "wit," thinks that "*writ* may be explained as a prepared writing." All the other recent editors, I believe, accept "wit" as indubitably the correct reading. On the meaning of *wit* in S., see *Hen. VIII.* p. 182.

Every several man. On *several*=separate, see *Temp.* p. 131.

Seventy-five drachmas. The drachma was a Greek coin worth very nearly the same as the French *franc,* or 18.6 cents. Plutarch gives seventy-five drachmas as the Greek equivalent for three hundred Roman sesterces, which was the amount named in the will. The sesterce (before the time of Augustus) was worth a little more than four cents. It must be borne in mind, however, that the value (or "purchasing power") of money was then much greater than now.

On this side Tiber. See Gr. 202. Cæsar's gardens were *beyond* the Tiber, as a Roman would say, or on the right bank of the river. Cf. Horace, *Sat.* i. 9, 18 : "Trans Tiberim longe cubat is prope Cæsaris hortos." S. copied the error from N., as will be seen above.

Left them you. The *you* is emphatic, which explains the inversion.

To walk abroad. For walking, etc. See Gr. 356.

And with the brands fire, etc. Another instance of *fire* as a dissyllable. Gr. 480.

How now, fellow? The accent of *fellow* is probably on the first syllable. See Gr. 453.

I heard him say. The folio reading. Capell and Collier's MS. corrector (followed by C.) read "them," and D. (*second* ed.) has "'em." K., W.; and H. retain "him."

Belike. Probably ; often used by S., but now obsolete.

Some notice of the people. Some information *respecting* (not *from*) the people.

SCENE III.—*Things unlucky.* The folio has "things vnluckily." Warb. substituted "unlucky," and is followed by D., St., H., W., and Camb. ed. Collier's MS. corrector gives "unlikely," which C. adopts. K. retains "unluckily," and W. is "not quite sure" that a change is called for. "The poet may mean that many things besides his dream of the feast charge his fancy unluckily."

Forth of doors. Cf. *Temp.* v. 1 : "thrust forth of Milan ;" 3 *Hen. VI.* ii. 2 : "forth of France," etc. Gr. 156.

Answer every man directly. See above (i. 1), on *Answer me directly.*

You were best. Originally the *you* was dative (*to* you it were best), but it came to be regarded as a nominative. Hence we find in S. "I were better" (2 *Hen. IV.* i. 2), "I were best" (1 *Hen. VI.* v. 3), "She were better" (*T. N.* i. 2), "Thou'rt best" (*Temp.* i. 2), etc. See Gr. 230, 352, and cf. 190. For a similar change in an old idiom, see *Mer.* p. 134, note on *If it please you.*

You'll bear me a bang. On the *me,* see Gr. 220.

My name is Cinna. Helvius Cinna. The conspirator was Cornelius Cinna.

Turn him going. Let him go. Cf. *A. Y. L.* iii. 1 : "Do this expediently, and turn him going."

To Brutus', to Cassius'. That is, to Brutus's house, etc. The folio prints : "to *Brutus*, to *Cassius*, burne all. Some to *Decius* House, and some to *Caska*'s ; some to *Ligarius :* Away, go." Note also the repeated "*Cæsars*" in the extract from the folio above. W., however, chooses to print "To Brutus, to Cassius," and "to Ligarius."

ANTONY'S HOUSE.

ACT IV.

SCENE I.—*The same. A Room in Antony's House.* The heading in the folio is simply "*Enter Antony, Octauius, and Lepidus.*" That the scene is laid at Rome is evident from the fact that Lepidus is sent to Cæsar's house for the will, and told that on his return he will find Antony and Octavius "Or here, or at the Capitol." Their actual place of meeting, however, was on a small island in the river Rhenus (now the *Reno*), near Bononia (*Bologna*).

Cf. N. (*Life of Antony*) : "thereupon all three met together (to wit, *Cæsar, Antonius* and *Lepidus*) in an Island environed round about with a little River, and there remained three days together. Now as touching all other matters, they were easily agreed, and did divide all the Empire of ROME between them, as if it had been their own Inheritance. But yet they could hardly agree whom they would put to death : for every one

of them would kill their Enemies, and save their Kinsmen and friends.
Yet at length, giving place to their greedy desire to be revenged of their
Enemies, they spurned all reverence of Blood, and holiness of friendship
at their feet. For *Cæsar* left *Cicero* to *Antonius* will, *Antonius* also for-
sook *Lucius Cæsar*, who was his Uncle by his Mother : and both of them ·
together suffered *Lepidus* to kill his own Brother *Paulus*. Yet some Writers affirm, that *Cæsar* and *Antonius* requested *Paulus* might be slain, and
that *Lepidus* was contented with it. In my Opinion there was never a
more horrible, unnatural, and crueller change then this was. For thus
changing murther for murther, they did aswell kill those whom they did
forsake and leave unto others, as those also which others left unto them
to kill : but so much more was their wickedness and cruelty great unto
their friends, for that they did put them to death being innocents, and
having no cause to hate them."

Their names are prick'd. See above (iii. 1), on *Will you be prick'd*, etc.

Who is your sister's son. As C. remarks, this is a mistake. The person
meant is Lucius Cæsar, and Mark Antony was *his* sister's son. Upton
suggested that S. wrote "You are his sister's son," but this is not at all
probable.

Unmeritable. Without merit, or "incapable of deserving" (C.). Cf.
Rich. III. iii. 7: "my desert Unmeritable shuns your high request." Gr. 3.

Under the business. Here, as not unfrequently, *business* appears to be a
trisyllable. Cf. *Rich. II.* ii. 1 : "To see this business. To-morrow next,"
etc. Gr. 479.

Graze in commons. Collier's MS. corrector has "on," which C. adopts.

In some taste. "In some measure or degree" (C.).

On objects, arts, and imitations, etc. The folio has a period after "imitations." K. substituted a comma, and thus made the passage plain
enough. Antony says that "Lepidus feeds not on objects, arts, and imitations generally, but on such of them as are out of use and staled (or
worn out) by other people, which, notwithstanding, begin his fashion (or
with which his following the fashion begins)." Theo. proposed " On ab-
ject orts and imitations," which D. adopts. St. has "abjects, orts, and
imitations," defining *abjects* as "things thrown away as useless." The
Camb. ed. adopts this reading. Coll., C., W., and H. follow K.

A property. "A thing quite at our disposal, and to be treated as we
please" (Steevens).

Listen great things. Cf. *Much Ado,* iii. 1: "To listen our purpose ;"
1 *Hen. VI.* v. 3: "vouchsafe to listen what I say," etc. Gr. 199.

Our best friends made, our means stretch'd. "A mutilated line, for which
the second folio gives 'Our best friends made, and our best means stretch'd
out ;' and Malone, with equal authority, if not equal fitness, 'Our best
friends made, our means stretch'd to the utmost' " (W.).

Are levying powers. That is, forces. Both *power* and *powers* were used
in this sense. Cf. below (iv. 3): "Come down upon us with a mighty
power ;" "bid him set on his powers ;" and (v. 3) "noble Brutus' power."
Puissance was used in the same sense ; as in *K. John*, iii. 1: "Cousin, go
draw our puissance together."

Go sit in council. Cf. *Ham.* ii. 1: "I will go seek the king," etc. Gr.

349. The folio has " Councell ;" K., D., H., and W., " council ;" C., " counsel."

And bay'd about with many enemies. See above (iii. 1), on *Here wast thou bay'd,* and on *With the hands of war.*

SCENE II.—*To do you salutation.* Cf. *Hen. V.* iv. 1 : " Do my good-morrow to them ;" and see Gr. 303.

He greets me well. This seems to mean, His greeting is friendly.

In his own change, etc. Either because of some change in himself, or through the misconduct of his officers. Warburton suggested " his own charge," and J. " ill offices."

Full of regard. Cf. above (iii. 1) : " so full of good regard."

Let me be resolv'd. See above (iii. 1), on *Be resolv'd.* .

But not with such familiar instances. As D. remarks, "*instance* is a word used by S. with various shades of meaning, which it is not always easy to distinguish—' motive, inducement, cause, ground ; symptom, prognostic ; information, assurance ; proof, example, indication.' " Here C. explains it as " assiduities."

Hot at hand. " That is, apparently, when held by the hand, or led ; or rather, perhaps, when acted upon only by the rein" (C.). Cf. *Hen. VIII.* v. 2 :

> —" those that tame wild horses
> Pace 'em not in their hands to make 'em gentle,
> But stop their mouths with stubborn bits, and spur 'em,
> Till they obey the manage."

They fall their crests. Cf. *T. and C.* i. 1 : " make him fall His crest." C. says that this transitive use of *fall* " is not common in S. ;" but it occurs no less than fifteen times. See *Temp.* pp. 127, 140, and *Mer.* p. 135.

Like deceitful jades. Cf. *Hen. V.* iii. 7 : " he is, indeed, a horse ; and all other jades you may call beasts ;" *Id.* iv. 2 : " their poor jades Lob down their heads," etc.

Cassius, be content. That is, *contain* (or restrain) yourself.

Enlarge your griefs. Set forth fully your grievances. On *griefs,* cf. i. 3 : " redress of all these griefs ;" iii. 2 : " What private griefs," etc.

Lucius, do you the like. The folio reads as follows :

> "*Lucillius,* do you the like, and let no man
> Come to our Tent, till we haue done our Conference.
> Let *Lucius* and *Titinius* guard our doore."

C. was the first to transpose *Lucius* and *Lucilius,* which both mends the measure and removes the absurdity of associating a servant-boy and an officer of rank in the guarding of the door. Cassius sends *his* servant Pindarus with a message to his division of the army, and Brutus sends his servant Lucius on a similar errand. The folio itself confirms this correction, since it makes *Lucilius* oppose the intrusion of the *Poet,* and at the close of the conference Brutus addresses "*Lucilius* and Titinius," who had evidently remained on guard together all the while. K., H., and the Camb. ed., however, retain the folio reading.

SCENE III.—Cf. N. (*Life of Brutus*): "Therefore, before they fell in hand with any other matter, they went into a little Chamber together, and bade every man avoid, and did shut the doors to them. Then they began to pour out their complaints one to the other, and grew hot and loud, earnestly accusing one another, and at length fell both a weeping. Their friends, that were without the Chamber, hearing them loud within and angry between themselves, they were both amazed and afraid also, lest it would grow to further matter : but yet they were commanded, that no man should come to them. Notwithstanding, one *Marcus Phaonius* [Favonius], that had been a friend and follower of *Cato* while he lived, and took upon him to counterfeit a Philosopher, not with wisdom and discretion, but with a certain bedlam and frantick motion : he would needs come into the Chamber, though the men offered to keep him out. But it was no boot to lett *Phaonius*, when a mad mood or toy took him in the head : for he was a hot hasty man, and suddain in all his doings, and cared for never a Senatour of them all. Now, though he used this bold manner of speech after the profession of the Cynick Philosophers, (as who would say, Dogs,) yet his boldness did no hurt many times, because they did but laugh at him to see him so mad. This *Phaonius* at that time, in despite of the Door-keepers, came into the Chamber, and with a certain scoffing and mocking gesture, which he counterfeited of purpose, he rehearsed the Verses which old *Nestor* said in *Homer :*

"*'My Lords, I pray you hearken both to me,*
For I have seen moe years than suchie three.'

Cassius fell a laughing at him : but *Brutus* thrust him out of the Chamber, and called him Dog and counterfeit Cynick. Howbeit his coming in brake their strife at that time, and so they left each other."

Coleridge says : " I know no part of Shakespeare that more impresses on me the belief of his genius being superhuman than this scene between Brutus and Cassius."

You have condemn'd and noted Lucius Pella. Cf. N. (*Life of Brutus*): "The next day after, *Brutus* upon complaint of the SARDIANS, did condemn and note *Lucius Pella* for a defamed Person, that had been a Prætor of the ROMANS, and whom *Brutus* had given charge unto : for that he was accused and convicted of robbery, and pilfery in his Office. This judgement much misliked *Cassius*, because he himself had secretly (not many days before) warned two of his friends, attainted and convicted of the like offences, and openly had cleared them : but yet he did not therefore leave to employ them in any manner of service as he did before. And therefore he greatly reproved *Brutus*, for that he would shew himself so straight and severe, in such a time as was meeter to bear a little, then to take things at the worst. *Brutus* in contrary manner answered, that he should remember the Id's of *March*, at which time they slew *Julius Cæsar*, who neither pilled nor polled* the Countrey, but only was a favourer and

---

* To *pill* is to pillage or rob, and to *poll* is to strip or plunder. Cf. *Rich. II.* ii. 1: "The commons hath he pill'd ;" Spenser, *State of Ireland:* "They will poll and spoyle soe outragiously, as the verye Enemye cannot doe much woorse." The two words are often joined, as here. Cf. Spenser, *F. Q.* v, 2, 6: "Which pols and pils the poore in piteous wize ;" Holinshed, *History of Ireland:* "Kildare did use to pill and poll his friendes, tenants, and reteyners."

suborner of all them that did rob and spoil, by his countenance and Authority."

Wherein my letter, etc. This is the reading of the second folio, and furnishes the simplest correction of the first, which gives

> "Wherein my Letters, praying on his side,
> Because I knew the man was slighted off."

K., D., H., and Camb. ed. read "letters . . . were slighted ;" W., "letter . . . was."

That every nice offence, etc. That every petty offence should bear *its* comment, or criticism.

Let me tell you, Cassius. Abbott (Gr. 483) makes *you* a dissyllable here. Capell (followed by D.) read "And let."

Condemn'd to have. Condemned as having, accused of having. Gr. 356.

To sell and mart. Cf. *W. T.* iv. 3 : "You have let him go, and nothing marted with him." See also *Cymb.* i. 7.

You are Brutus that speak this. The folio has "speakes."

For justice' sake. The folio prints "for Iustice sake." On the omis-sion of the apostrophe, see above (iii. 3), note on *To Brutus', to Cassius'.* Gr. 217.

Brutus, bay not me. "The folio has '*Brutus*, baite not me,' which, though corrected by Theo., is retained by Malone in direct opposition to common sense ; for the veriest child might perceive that the author in-tended Cassius to echo the word used by Brutus" (D.). C., W., and Camb. ed. have "bay ;" K. and H. "bait."

To make conditions. "To arrange the terms on which offices should be conferred" (C.).

Go to. See *Mer.* p. 136.

Have mind upon your health. Look to your safety.

Slight man. Cf. iv. 1 : "a slight, unmeritable man."

Is't possible? This interruption does not break the measure of what Brutus is saying. See Gr. 514.

Must I observe you? To *observe* is to treat with reverence, be obsequious to, etc. Cf. *2 Hen. IV.* iv. 2 : "For he is gracious, if he be observ'd." See also *Mark*, vi. 20, where most of the earlier versions have "gave him rev-erence."

I shall be glad to learn of noble men. This is the folio reading, followed by K., St., H., W., and Camb. ed. Collier's MS. corrector alters "noble" to "abler," which C. and D. (*second* ed.) adopt, referring to what Cassius has said—"Older in practice, abler than yourself," etc.

Which I respect not. That is, heed not, regard not. Cf. *M. N. D.* i. 1 : "For she respects me as her only son," etc.

Than to wring. Cf. i. 2 : "Brutus had rather be a villager, Than to re-pute," etc. Gr. 350.

By any indirection. By "indirect crooked ways" (*2 Hen. IV.* iv. 4) or "dishonest practice" (D.).

Rascal counters. Puttenham (*Art of English Poetry*, 1582) says : "*Ras-kall* is properly the hunter's term given to young deer, lean and out of season, and not to people." Conf. Drayton, *Polyolbion*, Song 13 : "The bucks and lusty stags among the rascals strewed." *Counters* were pieces of false coin used in casting accounts. Cf. *W. T.* iv. 2 : "I cannot do't without counters ;" *Cymb.* v. 4 : "pen, book, and counters," etc. Here the word is used contemptuously for money.

Be ready, gods, etc. The folio reads and points thus :

> " Be ready Gods with all your Thunder-bolts,
>   Dash him to peeces."

The modern editors generally retain the comma after " thunderbolts," but Coll. and W. omit it. C. thinks that *dash* is " probably to be understood as the infinitive," with *to* omitted, but I prefer to consider it as the imperative : Be ready with all your thunderbolts, *and* dash him to pieces.

Though they do appear. Collier's MS. corrector alters " do" to " did."

Aweary of the world. Cf. *Macb.* v. 5 : " I 'gin to be aweary of the sun." Abbott (Gr. 24) considers the *a-* in *aweary* " a corruption of the A. S. intensive *of.*"

Check'd like a bondman. Cf. *Lear,* ii. 2 : " his master Will check him for't." The noun also is used in the sense of rebuke, reproof. Cf. *Cymb.* iii. 3 : " attending for a check" (that is, dancing attendance only to be paid with reproof) ; *Oth.* iii. 3 : " a fault T' incur a private check," etc.

Dearer than Plutus' mine. The folio has " Deerer then *Pluto*'s Mine," and in *T. and C.* iii. 3, " euery graine of Plutoes gold ;" but in *T. of A.* i. 1 : "*Plutus* the God of Gold."

If that thou beest a Roman. On *that,* see Gr. 287, and on *beest,* Gr. 298.

Dishonour shall be humour. "Any indignity you offer shall be regarded as a mere caprice of the moment" (C.). Both C. and W. suggest that S. may have written " honour."

Yoked with a lamb. Pope read " with a man." As C. remarks, " lamb" can hardly be right.

Have not you love enough, etc. The folio reading. The *Var.* ed. and H. give " Have you not."

For I have seen more years, I'm sure, than ye. Plutarch makes Favonius exclaim, in the words of Nestor (*Iliad,* book i.),

> "'Αλλὰ πίθεσθ'· ἄμφω δὲ νεωτέρω ἐστὸν ἐμεῖο."

For North's translation, see the extract above.

These jigging fools. These rhyming fools. *Jig* used to mean " a metrical composition, as well as a dance" (Malone).

Companion, hence! On this contemptuous use of *companion,* see *Temp.* p. 131, note on *Your fellow.*

How scaped I killing. *Scape* is commonly printed as a contraction of *escape,* but we find it also in prose ; as in Bacon, *Adv. of L.* ii. 14, 9 : " such as had scaped shipwreck," etc. S. uses it much oftener than *escape.* See Wb. s. v.

Upon what sickness? Cf. *M. Ado,* iv. 1 : " When he shall hear she died upon (that is, in consequence of) his words." See Gr. 191. Bacon often uses *upon* in this sense. Cf. *Ess.* 48 : " Factious *Followers* are worse to be liked, which Follow not upon Affection to him, with whom they range Themselves, but upon Discontentment Conceived against some Other ;" *Adv. of L.* ii. 23, 18 : " there are few men so true to themselves and so settled, but that, sometimes upon heat, sometimes upon bravery, sometimes upon kindness, sometimes upon trouble of mind and weakness, they open themselves," etc.

Impatient of my absence, etc. "This speech is throughout a striking exemplification of the tendency of strong emotion to break through the logical forms of grammar, and of how possible it is for language to be perfectly intelligible, sometimes, with the grammar in a more or less chaotic or uncertain state" (C.).

With this she fell distract. See *Introduction*, p. 33. For the form *distract*, see Gr. 342. S. also uses the obsolete *distraught;* as in *R. and J.* i *i.* 3 : "Or, if I wake, shall I not be distraught?"

Her attendants absent, etc. See Gr. 380. Cf. N. (*Life of Brutus*): "And for *Porcia, Brutus* Wife, *Nicolaus* the Philosopher, and *Valerius Maximus* do write, that she determining to kill herself (her Parents and friends carefully looking to her to keep her from it) took hot burning coals and cast them into her mouth, and kept her mouth so close that she choaked herself."

Call in question our necessities. That is, discuss them.

Bending their expedition. Directing their march—"perhaps implying that they were pressing on"(C.).

Myself have letters, etc. The folio reads "My selfe haue Letters of the selfe-same Tenure." *Tenour* and *tenure* have the same derivation. On *myself* as subject, see *Mer.* p. 137, note on *Yourself.*

That by proscription, etc. Cf. N. (*Life of Brutus*): "After that, these three *Octavius Cæsar, Antonius* and *Lepidus* made an agreement between themselves, and by those Articles divided the Provinces belonging to the Empire of ROME among themselves, and did set up Bills of Proscription and Outlawry, condemning two hundred of the noblest men of ROME to suffer death ; and amongst that number, Cicero was one."

Cicero one. Abbott (Gr. 486) makes *one* a dissyllable. Steevens inserted "Ay" before the second "Cicero."

For certain she is dead. On *certain*, see Gr. 1.

With meditating, etc. On *with*, see Gr. 193. Here *once*=some time or other. Cf. *M. W.* iii. 4 : "I pray thee, once to-night Give my sweet Nan this ring." See also *Hen. VIII.* p. 163, note on *Once weak ones.*

I have as much of this in art as you, etc. "*In art* Malone interprets to mean 'in theory.' It rather signifies by acquired knowledge, or learning, as distinguished from natural disposition" (C.).

Well, to our work alive. That is, the work that we the living have to do.

Of force. Of necessity. Cf. Bacon, *Adv. of L.* ii. 5, 2 : "their inquiries must of force have been of a far other kind." Cf. also *perforce*, which is frequent in S., and is still used in poetry.

Come on refresh'd, new-added, etc. The folio reading, retained by St., W., and Camb. ed. "New-aided" was independently suggested by D. and Sr., and is adopted by H. Collier's MS. corrector (followed by C.) has "new-hearted." *New-added*=reinforced.

Omitted. Neglected. See *Temp.* p. 125, and *Hen. VIII.* p. 183.

Our ventures. See *Mer.* p. 128, note on *Had I such venture forth.*

Which we will niggard. C. remarks that this is probably the only passage in the language in which *niggard* is used as a verb. See Gr. 290.

Farewell, good Messala.   C. regards this as a hemistich ; Abbott (Gr. 480) makes it the completion of the line, counting " Farewell" as a trisyllable.   Walker suggested " Fare you well," and Hanmer " Now, farewell."

Poor knave.   That is, poor boy.   See *Mer.* p. 137.   On this passage, see *Introduction*, page 13.

O'erwatch'd.   Worn out with watching.   Cf. *Lear*, ii. 2 : "All weary and o'erwatch'd."   See Gr. 374 (cf. 295).   In *M. N. D.* v. 1, we have it in its active form :

> " I fear we shall outsleep the coming morn
> As much as we this night have overwatch'd."

Some other of my men.   On *other*=others, see *Mer.* p. 128.

Varro and Claudius.   The folio has "*Varrus*, and *Claudio*," and also in the stage-direction that follows.

Canst thou hold up, etc.   The second folio gets the passage "somewhat mixed :"

> " Canst thou hold up thy instrument a straine or two,
> And touch thy heavy eyes a-while."

I know young bloods.   See above (i. 2), on *Noble bloods.*

It was well done.   The *Var.* ed. and H. have " It is well done."

Thy leaden mace.   Cf. Spenser, *F. Q.* i. 4, 44 :

> " But whenas Morpheus had with leaden mace
> Arrested all that courtly company."

In both cases, the mace is the club borne by an officer of justice, not, as Steevens and H. explain it, the *sceptre* of a monarch.   Cf. *C. of E.* iv. 3 : " he (the officer) that sets up his rest (with a play on *rest* and *arrest*) to do more exploits with his mace than a morris-pike."   It means *sceptre* in *Hen. V.* iv. 1 : " The sword, the mace, the crown imperial."

So much wrong to wake thee.   On the ellipsis of *as*, see Gr. 281.

If thou dost nod, thou break'st.   On the tenses, see Gr. 363, 371.

Where I left reading.   Cf. N. (*Life of Brutus*) : "*Brutus* was a careful[*] man, and slept very little, both for that his Diet was moderate, as also because he was continually occupied.   He never slept in the day time, and in the night no longer then the time he was driven to be alone, and when every body else took their rest.   But now whilest he was in War, and his head over-busily occupied to think of his affairs, and what would happen, after he had slumbered a little after supper, he spent all the rest of the night in dispatching of his weightiest Causes ; and after he had taken order for them, if he had any leasure left him, he would read some Book till the third Watch of the night, at what time the Captains, petty Captains and Colonels, did use to come to him.   So, being ready to go into Europe, one night very late (when all the Camp took quiet rest) as he was in his Tent with a little light, thinking of weighty matters, he thought he heard one come in to him, and casting his eye towards the door of his Tent, that he saw a wonderfull strange and monstrous shape of a body coming towards him, and said never a word.   So *Brutus* boldly asked what he was, a God or a man, and what cause brought him thither.   The

---

[*] That is, full of care.   Cf. *C. of E.* v. 1 : " careful hours ;" *Rich. III.* i. 3 :

> " By Him that rais'd me to this careful height
> From that contented hap which I enjoy'd."

Spirit answered him, I am thy evill Spirit, *Brutus :* and thou shalt see me
by the City of PHILIPPES. *Brutus* being no otherwise afraid, replied again
unto it : Well, then I shall see thee again. The Spirit presently vanished
away : and *Brutus* called his men unto him, who told him that they heard
no noise, nor saw any thing at all."

See also the *Life of Cæsar :* "he thought he heard a noise at his Tent
door, and looking towards the light of the Lamp that waxed very dim, he
saw a horrible Vision of a man, of a wonderfull greatness, and dreadfull
look, which at the first made him marvellously afraid. But when he saw
that it did him no hurt, but stood by his bed-side, and said nothing ; at
length he asked him what he was. The Image answered him : I am thy
ill Angell, *Brutus*, and thou shalt see me by the City of PHILIPPES. Then
Brutus replied again, and said, Well, I shall see then. Therewithall, the
Spirit presently vanished from him."

On the introduction of the ghost here, see Ulrici's remarks, quoted
above (p. 20).

And my hair to stare. Cf. *Temp.* i. 2 : "With hair up-staring,—then
like reeds, not hair."

Bid him set on his powers. See above (i. 2), on *Set on*, and (iv. 1) on
Are levying powers.

ACT V.

SCENE I.—*Their battles are at hand.* Their *battalions*, or forces. Cf.
Hen. V. iv. chorus : "Each battle sees the other's umber'd face ; Bacon,
Ess. 58 : "And they were more ignorant in ranging and arraying their
battailes ;" *Adv. of L.* i. 8, 5 : "to see two battles join upon a plain."

To warn us. To summon us. Cf. *Rich. III.* i. 1 : "to warn them to his
royal presence ;" *K. John,* ii. 1 : "warn'd us to the walls," etc.

With fearful bravery. "With a gallant show of courage carrying with
it terror and dismay" (Malone). With "bravery in show or appearance,
which yet is full of real fear or apprehension" (C.). The latter interpretation agrees better with what follows. For *bravery*=bravado, cf. Bacon,
Ess. 57 : "To seek to extinguish anger utterly, is but a bravery of the
Stoicks." For *fearful*=timorous, faint-hearted, see *V. and A.* 677 : "Pur-
sue these fearful creatures o'er the downs"—the creatures being "the
timorous flying hare" (called "the fearful flying hare" in 3 *Hen. VI.* iii. 5),
the fox, and the roe. See also *Judges,* vii. 3 ; *Matthew,* viii. 26, etc.

Their bloody sign of battle. Cf. N. (*Life of Brutus*) : "The next morning
by break of day, the Signall of Battell was set out in *Brutus* and *Cassius*
Camp, which was an arming Scarlet Coat."

In this exigent. That is, this exigency. Cf. *A. and C.* iv. 12 : "when
the exigent should come." In the only other instance in which S. uses
the word (1 *Hen. VI.* ii. 5), it means *end :*

"These eyes, like lamps whose wasting oil is spent,
Grow dim, as drawing to their exigent."

Answer on their charge. Await their onset.

Make forth. "Step forward" (C.).

The posture of your blows are yet unknown. See Gr. 412.

ROMAN SOLDIERS.

The Hybla bees. Hybla in Sicily was famous for its honey. Cf. I *Hen. IV.* i. 2: "the honey of Hybla."

O you flatterers. On the measure, see Gr. 482.

The proof of it. The proof of the arguing; that is, "the arbitrament of the sword, to which it is the prologue or prelude" (C.).

Cæsar's three and thirty wounds. Theo. changed this to "three and twenty," the number given in Plutarch and Suetonius; but this is to deal with poetry in too arithmetical a way.

The sword of traitors. Collier's MS. corrector has "word" for "sword," but Coll., in his second ed., restores the old reading.

The noblest of thy strain. That is, of thy race. Cf. *M. Ado,* ii. 1: "he is of a noble strain;" *Per.* iv. 3: "To think of what a noble strain you are;" Spenser, *F. Q.* iv. 8, 33: "Sprung of the auncient stocke of Princes straine," etc.

More honourable. Thus in the folio, but possibly a misprint for *honourably* (*honourablie*), which W. substitutes.

A peevish schoolboy. "*Peevish* appears to have generally signified, during S.'s days, 'silly, foolish, trifling,' etc., though no doubt the word was for-

merly used, as now, in the sense of 'pettish, perverse,' etc." (D.) Cf.
C. of E. iv. 2 : "How now! a madman! Why, thou peevish sheep, What
ship of Epidamnum stays for me?" 3 *Hen. VI.* v. 6: "Why, what a peevish
fool was that of Crete, That taught his son the office of a fowl !" *Rich. III.*
iv. 4: "And be not peevish-fond in great designs;" *Id.* iv. 2: "When Rich-
mond was a little peevish boy." Trench (*Glossary*, etc.) thinks that the
word meant "self-willed, obstinate," rather than "foolish," but the latter
seems to me the only meaning possible in some of the passages just cited,
and in several others in S. Could we substitute "self-willed" or "obstinate" for "peevish" in the following dialogue from 1 *Hen. VI.* v. 3 ?—

> "*Suffolk.* No loving token to his majesty?
> *Margaret.* Yes, my good lord,—a pure unspotted heart,
> Never yet taint with love, I send the king.
> *Suffolk.* And this withal.   [*Kisses her.*
> *Margaret.* That for thyself :—I will not so presume
> To send such peevish tokens to a king."

As this very day Was Cassius born. See *Temp.* p. 113, note on *As at
that time.*

Be thou my witness. On the change from *thou* to *you* ("You know that
I held," etc.), see Gr. 233.

According to N. (*Life of Brutus*), Cassius said, "*Messala*, I protest unto
thee, and make thee my Witness, that I am compelled against my mind
and will (as *Pompey* the Great was) to jeopard the liberty of our Countrey
to the hazard of a Battell."

Coming from Sardis, etc. On *coming,* see Gr. 379.

Our former ensign. Collier's MS. corrector has "forward," but the
original reading is well enough, and Coll. himself retains it. Cf. N. (*Life
of Brutus*): "When they raised their Camp, there came two Eagles that
flying with a marvellous force, lighted upon two of the foremost Ensigns,
and always followed the Souldiers, which gave them Meat, and fed them,
untill they came near to the City of PHILIPPES ; and there one day onely
before the Battel, they both flew away."

Who to Philippi here consorted us. On *who,* see Gr. 263, 264. On the
transitive use of *consort,* cf. *C. of E.* i. 2: "I'll meet with you upon the
mart, And afterwards consort you till bed-time." Here we have *meet
with* where we should use *meet,* and *consort* for *consort with.* S. also uses
the latter ; as in *R. and J.* iii. 1: "thou consort'st with Romeo," etc.

As we were sickly prey. As *if* we were, etc. Gr. 107.

A canopy most fatal. H. misprints "most faithful."

Lovers in peace. See above (ii. 3), on *Thy lover.*

Rest still incertain. The folio reads "rests still incertaine." See *Mer.*
p. 155, note on *Uncapable.* Gr. 442.

Let's reason with the worst, etc. Cf. N. (*Life of Brutus*): "There Cassius began to speak first, and said : "The gods grant us O *Brutus,* that
this day we may win the Field, and ever after to live all the rest of our
life quietly one with another. But sith the gods have so ordained it, that
the greatest and chiefest things amongst men are most uncertain, and that
if the Battell fall out otherwise to day then we wish or look for, we shall
hardly meet again, what art thou then determined to do, to flie, or die?

M

Brutus answered him, being yet but a young man, and not over greatly experienced in the world, I trust* (I know not how) a certain rule of Philosophy, by the which I did greatly blame and reprove *Cato* for killing himself, as being no lawfull nor godly act, touching the gods : nor concerning men, valiant ; not to give place and yeeld to divine Providence, and not constantly and patiently to take whatsoever it pleaseth him to send us, but to draw back and flie : but being now in the midst of the danger, I am of a contrary mind. For, if it be not the will of God that this Battell fall out fortunate for us, I will look no more for hope, but will rid me of this miserable world, and content me with my fortune."

Even by the rule, etc. The passage stands thus in the folio :

> " Euen by the rule of that Philosophy,
> By which I did blame *Cato*, for the death
> Which he did giue himselfe, I know not how :
> But I do finde it Cowardly, and vile,
> For feare of what might fall, so to preuent
> The time of life, arming my selfe with patience,
> To stay the prouidence of some high Powers,
> That gouerne vs below."

The meaning apparently is, I am determined to *do by* (that is, act in accordance with, govern myself by) the rule of that philosophy, by which I did blame Cato, etc. K., D., and H. make " I know not how . . . the time of life" a parenthesis. Collier and W. put a period after " himself ;" and that pointing, since it gives the same meaning without the long parenthesis, is, on the whole, to be preferred. C. connects " I know not how," etc., with what precedes (" I know not how it is, but I do find it, by the rule of that philosophy, etc., cowardly and vile"), and the Camb. ed. adopts that arrangement.

To prevent The time of life. J. and Steevens take *prevent* in its ordinary meaning ; Malone, D., and H., in its primary sense of *anticipate.* S. uses the word several times in the latter sense, and I prefer that interpretation here. The *time of life* is the full time or natural period of life. Collier's MS. corrector changes " time" to " term," and in the next line " some" to " those ;" and C. adopts both emendations.

To stay the providence. To await it (*not* to hinder or delay it) ; as in 1 *Hen. IV.* i. 3 : " We'll stay your leisure."

Thorough the streets. See *Mer.* p. 144, note on *Throughfares.*

No, Cassius, no, etc. " There has been some controversy about the reasoning of Brutus in this dialogue. Both Steevens and Malone conceive that there is an inconsistency between what he here says and his previous declaration of his determination not to follow the example of Cato. But how did Cato act? He slew himself that he might not witness and outlive the fall of Utica. This was, merely ' for fear of what might fall,' to anticipate the end of life. It did not follow that it would be wrong, in the opinion of Brutus, to commit suicide in order to escape any certain and otherwise inevitable calamity or degradation, such as being led in triumph through the streets of Rome by Octavius and Antony" (C.).

---

* This should obviously be " trusted," but it is " trust" in the edition of 1579, as well as in the later ones.

"Brutus is at first inclined to wait patiently for better times, but is roused by the idea of being 'led in triumph,' to which he will never submit. The loss of the battle would not alone have determined him to kill himself, if he could have lived free" (Ritson).

ROMAN STANDARD-BEARERS.

SCENE II.—On this scene, and the following ones, cf. N. (*Life of Brutus*): "Then *Brutus* prayed *Cassius* he might have the leading of the right Wing, the which men thought was far meeter for *Cassius*, both because he was the elder man, and also for that he had the better experience. But yet *Cassius* gave it him, and willed that *Messala* (who had charge of one of the warlikest Legions they had) should be also in that Wing with *Brutus*. . . . In the mean time *Brutus*, that led the right Wing, sent little Bills to the Colonels and Captains of private Bands, in the which he wrote the word of the Battell."

"First of all he (Cassius) was marvellous angry to see how *Brutus* men ran to give charge upon their Enemies, and tarried not for the word of the Battell, nor commandment to give charge : and it grieved him beside, that after he had overcome them, his men fell straight to spoil, and were not carefull to compass in the rest of the Enemies behind: but with tarrying too long also, more then through the valiantness or foresight of the Captains his Enemies, *Cassius* found himself compassed in with the right wing of his Enemies Army. Whereupon his horsemen brake immediatly, and fled for life towards the Sea. Furthermore, perceiving his Footmen to give ground, he did what he could to keep them from flying, and took an Ensign from one of the Ensign-Bearers that fled, and stuck it fast at his feet: although with much ado he could scant keep his own Guard together. So *Cassius* himself was at length compelled to flie, with a few about him, unto a little Hill, from whence they might easily see what was done in all the plain: howbeit *Cassius* himself saw nothing, for his sight was very bad, saving that he saw (and yet with much ado) how the Enemies spoiled his Camp before his eyes. He saw also a great Troop of Horsemen, whom *Brutus* sent to aid him, and thought that they were his Enemies that followed him: but yet he sent *Titinnius*, one of them that was with him, to go and know what they were. *Brutus* horsemen saw him coming afar off, whom when they knew that he was one of *Cassius* chiefest friends, they shouted out for joy, and they that were familiarly acquainted with him, lighted from their Horses, and went and embraced him. The rest compassed him in round about on horse-back, with Songs of Victory, and great rushing of their Harness, so that they made all the Field ring again for joy. But this marred all. For *Cassius* thinking indeed that *Titinnius* was taken of the Enemies, he then spake these words: Desiring too much to live, I have lived to see one of my best friends taken, for my sake, before my face. After that, he got into a Tent where no body was, and took *Pindarus* with him, one of his Bondmen whom he reserved ever for such a pitch, since the cursed battle of the PARTHIANS where *Crassus*[*] was slain, though he notwithstanding scaped from that overthrow: but then casting his cloak over his head, and holding out his bare neck unto *Pindarus*, he gave him his head to be stricken off. So the head was found severed from the body: but after that time *Pindarus* was never seen more. Whereupon, some took occasion to say that he had slain his master without his commandment. By and by they knew the horsemen that came towards them, and might see *Titinnius* crowned with a Garland of triumph, who came before with great speed unto *Cassius*. But when he perceived, by the cries and tears of his friends which tormented themselves, the misfortune which had chanced to his Captain *Cassius* by mistaking, he drew out his sword, cursing himself a thousand times that he had tarried so long, and slew himself presently in the field. *Brutus* in the mean time came forward still, and understood also that *Cassius* had been overthrown: but he knew nothing of his death, till he came very near to his Camp. So when he was come thither, after he had lamented the death of *Cassius*, calling him the last of all the ROMANS; being unpossible that ROME should ever breed again so noble and valiant a man as he: he caused his body to be buried, and sent it to the city of THASSOS, fearing lest his funerals within the Camp should cause great disorder." . . .

---

[*] Misprinted "*Cassius*" in the ed. of 1676.

"There was the son of *Marcus Cato* slain, valiantly fighting among the lusty youths. For, notwithstanding that he was very weary and over-harried, yet would'he not therefore fly, but manfully fighting and laying about him, telling aloud his name, and also his fathers name, at length he was beaten down among many other dead bodies of his enemies which he had slain round about him. So there were slain in the field, all the chiefest Gentlemen and Nobility that were in his Army, who valiantly ran into any danger to save *Brutus* life: amongst whom there was one of *Brutus* friends called *Lucilius*, who see a troop of barbarous men, making no reckoning of all men else they met in their way, but going altogether right against *Brutus*, he determined to stay them with the hazard of life, and being left behind, told them that he was *Brutus*: and because they should believe him, he prayed them to bring him to *Antonius*, for he said he was afraid of *Cæsar*, and that he did trust *Antonius* better. These barbarous men being very glad of this good hap, and thinking themselves happy men, they carried him in the night, and sent some before unto *Antonius* to tell him of their coming. He was marvellous glad of it, and went out to meet them that brought him. . . . In the meantime *Lucilius* was brought to him, who with a bold countenance said: *Antonius*, I dare assure thee, that no enemy hath taken, or shall take *Marcus Brutus* alive: and I beseech God keep him from that fortune: but wheresoever he be found, alive or dead, he will be found like himself. . . . *Lucilius* words made them all amazed that heard him. *Antonius* on the other side, look-ing upon all them that had brought him, said unto them: My friends, I think ye are sorry you have failed of your purpose, and that you think this man hath done great wrong: but I assure you, you have taken a better booty then that you followed. For, instead of an Enemy, you have brought me a friend: and for my part, if you had brought me *Brutus* alive, truly I cannot tell what I should have done to him. For I had rather have such men as this my friends then my enemies. Then he embraced *Lucilius*, and at that time delivered him to one of his friends in custody; and *Lucilius* ever after served him faithfully, even to his death."

"Furthermore, *Brutus* thought that there was no great number of men slain in battle: and, to know the truth of it, there was one called *Statilius*, that promised to go through his Enemies, for otherwise it was impossible to go see their Camp: and thereupon if all were well, he would lift up a torch-light in the Air, and then return again with speed to him. The torch-light was lift up as he had promised, for *Statilius* went thither: and a good while after *Brutus* seeing that *Statilius* came not again, he said: If *Statilius* be alive he will come again. But his evil fortune was such that, as he came back, he fell into his Enemies hands and was slain. Now the night being far spent, *Brutus* as he sate bowed towards *Clitus* one of his men, and told him somewhat in his ear: the other answered him not, but fell a weeping. Thereupon he proved *Dardanus*, and said somewhat also to him: and at the last he came to *Volumnius* himself, and speaking to him in Greek, prayed him, for the studies sake which brought them ac-quainted together, that he would help him to put his hand to his sword, to thrust it in him to kill him. *Volumnius* denied his request, and so did many others: and amongst the rest, one of them said, there was no tarry-

ing for them there, but they must needs fly.   Then *Brutus* rising up, said,
We must fly indeed, but it must be with our hands, not with our feet.
Then taking every man by the hand, he said these words unto them with
a chearful countenance : It rejoyceth my heart, that none of my friends
hath failed me at my need, and I do not complain of my fortune, but onely
for my countries sake : for as for me, I think my self happier than they
that have overcome, considering that I have a perpetuall fame of vertue
and honesty, the which our Enemies the Conquerors shall never attain
unto by force nor money ; neither can let* their posterity to say, that they
being naughty and unjust men, have slain good men, to usurp tyrannicall
power not pertaining to them.   Having so said, he prayed every man to
shift for himself, and then he went a little aside with two or three onely,
among the which *Strato* was one, with whom he came first acquainted by
the study of Rhetorick.   He came as near to him as he could, and taking
his sword by the hilt with both his hands, and falling down upon the point
of it, ran himself through.   Others say that not he, but *Strato* (at his request) held the sword in his hand, and turned his head aside, and that
Brutus fell down upon it, and so ran himself through, and died presently.
Messala, that had been *Brutus* great friend, reconciled afterwards to be
Octavius Cæsar's friend, and shortly after, *Cæsar* being at good leisure, he
brought *Strato, Brutus* friend unto him, and weeping said : *Cæsar*, behold,
here is he that did the last service to my *Brutus*.   Then *Cæsar* received
him, and afterwards he did as faithfull service in all his affairs, as any
.GRECIAN else he had about him, untill the Battle of ACTIUM."

SCENE III.—*I slew the coward, and did take it from him*.   That is,
took the *ensign* from him.   "Ensign" means either the standard or the
standard-bearer, and here it may be said to be used for both.

Took it too eagerly.   That is, followed up the advantage too eagerly.

Yond troops.   See above (i. 2), on *Yond Cassius*.

Now some light.   W. and H. print "'light," but the word (A. S. *lihtan*)
is not a contraction of *alight*, and is common enough in prose.   See the
description of this scene in N., quoted above ; and cf. *Genesis*, xxiv. 64 ;
2 *Kings*, v. 21, etc.

Saving of thy life.   See Gr. 178.

Take thou the hilts.   Cf. *Rich. III.* i. 4 : "with the hilts of thy sword."
S. uses *hilts* six times, *hilt* three times.

It is but change.   "The battle is only a succession of alternations or
vicissitudes" (C.).

Thou dost sink to night.   K. prints† "to-night ;" but, as C. remarks, "a
far nobler sense is given to the words by taking *sink to night* to be an expression of the same kind with *sink to rest*."   The folio reads "thou doest
sink to night."   The "doest" is of course a misprint, but W. gives "do'st."
S. often has *dost* for *doest* (as in i. 1 : "What dost thou with thy best apparel on ?"), but never, I believe, *doest* for *dost*.

Mistrust of my success.   See above (ii. 2), on *Opinions of success*.   Bacon
(*Adv. of L.* ii. 4, 2) speaks of "the successes and issues of actions."

But hold thee.   See above (i. 3), on *Hold, my hand*.   Gr. 212.

* That is, *hinder*.   † The *second* edition (1867) has "to night."

"Go, Pindarus, get higher on that hill" (v. 3).

Thy Brutus bid me give it thee. S. often uses *bid* for both *bade* and *bidden.* He has *bade* frequently, but *bidden* only once (*M. Ado,* iii. 3). Cf. Gr. 342, 343.

In our own proper entrails. On *in*=into, see Gr. 159. For *proper,* see above (i. 2), on *Proper to myself.*

Look, whe'r. See above (i. 1), note on *Whe'r.*

The last of all the Romans. Rowe conjectured "Thou last;" but N. has the expression (see extract above), and S. probably copied it. Gr. 13.

To Thassos send his body. The folio has "*Tharsus,*" a misprint for the "*Thassos*" of N. Theo. made the correction. The Cambridge ed. gives "Thasos," the classical form of the name.

His funerals. See *Temp.* p. 143, note on *The nuptial.* W. says that "the plural was the commoner form in S.'s day, and is generally used by him." S. uses "funerals" only twice (not counting a third instance, in *M. N. D.* i. 1, where it is a true plural), while he has "funeral" some twenty times. The latter occurs five times (as a noun) in act iii. of the present play.

Labeo and Flavius. The folio has "*Labio* and *Flauio.*" See above (i. 2), on *In Antonius' way.*

SCENE IV.—*What bastard doth not?*   See above (ii. 1), on *A several bastardy.*

Only I yield to die.   For the transposition, see Gr. 420.

There is so much, etc.   So much money, on condition that thou wilt kill me at once.   The meaning seems plain enough, but Warb. mistook it.

I'll tell the news.   The folio has "Ile tell thee newes."   The correction is Theo.'s, and is generally adopted.

Hark thee.   Here *thee* is a corruption for *thou.*   See Gr. 212.

That it runs over.   *So* that, etc.   Gr. 283.

And, this last night, here in Philippi fields.   Cf. N. (*Life of Cæsar*): "The second Battell being at hand, this Spirit appeared again unto him, but spake never a word.   Thereupon *Brutus* knowing that he should die, did put himself to all hazard in Battell, but yet fighting could not be slain." See also *Life of Brutus:* "The ROMANS called the Valley between both Camps, the PHILIPPIAN Fields."   Gr. 22.

· *Have beat us.*   See Gr. 343.

For that our love of old.   See Gr. 13.

Farewell to thee, too, Strato.   The folio reads, "Farewell to thee, to *Strato,* Countrymen;" corrected by Theobald.   For the change from *you* ("Farewell to you," etc.) to *thee,* see Gr. 232.

PHILIPPI.

I found no man but, etc. For *but*, see Gr. 123.

Shall attain unto. See Gr. 457 *a*.

Of a good respect. Cf. i. 2 : "many of the best respect in Rome."

Some smatch of honour. The folio reading. *Smatch* is only another form of *smack*, which S. uses elsewhere, and which W. substitutes here.

I will entertain them. I will take them into my service. Cf. *Lear*, iii. 6 : "You, sir, I entertain for one of my hundred."

Bestow thy time with me. "Give up thy time to me" (C.).

Ay, if Messala will prefer me to thee. "*Prefer* seems to have been the established phrase for *recommending a servant*" (Reed). Cf. Bacon, *Adv. of L.* ii. 21, 1 : "And if it be said, that the cure of men's minds belongeth to sacred divinity, it is most true ; but yet moral philosophy may be preferred unto her as a wise servant and humble handmaid." Here C. thinks it means "to transfer, or hand over," but it seems to me that it merely *implies* the transfer. Messala, of course, could not *recommend* his servant to a new master without giving up his own claim upon him.

This was the noblest Roman, etc. Cf. N. (*Life of Brutus*): "For it was said that *Antonius* spake it openly divers times, that he thought, that of all them that had slain *Cæsar*, there was none but *Brutus* onely that was moved to do it, as thinking the act commendable of it self: but that all the other Conspiratours did conspire his death for some private malice or envy, that they otherwise did bear unto him."

Save only he. See above (iii. 2), on *Save I alone.*

He only, in a general honest thought, etc. The folio reading, retained by all the editors except Collier and C., who adopt the emendation of Collier's MS. corrector :

> "He only in a generous honest thought
> Of common good," etc.

D. prints "general-honest," which Abbott (Gr. 2) is disposed to favour.

His life was gentle, etc. This passage resembles one which appears in the revised edition of Drayton's poem of *The Barons' Wars*, published in 1603, and it has been a matter of dispute among the critics which poet was the borrower. If either, it must have been Drayton, since we know that *Julius Cæsar* was written before 1601 (see *Introduction*, p. 8) ; but there may have been no imitation on either side. "The notion that man was composed of the four elements, earth, air, fire, and water, and that the well-balanced mixture of these produced the perfection of humanity," was then commonly accepted, and often appears in the writers of the period (W.). Cf. B. J., *Cynthia's Revels*, ii. 3 : "A creature of a most perfect and divine temper, one in whom the humours and elements are peaceably met, without emulation of precedency."

The following is the form in which the passage in Drayton appears in the edition of 1603,-and in five subsequent editions published during the next ten years :

> "Such one he was (of him we boldly say)
> In whose rich soul all sovereign powers did suit,
> In whom in peace the elements all lay
> So mixt, as none could sovereignty impute ;
> As all did govern, yet all did obey :
> His lively temper was so absolute,

> That 't seemed, when heaven his model first began,
> In him it showed perfection in a man."

In the edition of 1619 it is recast as follows :

> " He was a man (then boldly dare to say)
> In whose rich soul the virtues well did suit,
> In whom so mixt the elements all lay
> That none to one could sovereignty impute;
> As all did govern, so did all obey:
> He of a temper was so absolute,
> As that it seemed, when nature him began,
> She meant to show all that might be in man."

To part the glories, etc. That is, to share or divide them. See *Hen. VIII.*
p. 199, note on *They had parted.* Cf. *Matthew*, xxvii. 35.

ROMAN TOMB.

INDEX OF WORDS EXPLAINED.

AUGUR'S STAFF.

THE END.

Milton Keynes UK
Ingram Content Group UK Ltd.
UKHW040929180224
437992UK00003B/123